NEMESIS

First Colony - Book Two

KEN LOZITO

Acoustical Books LLC

Published by Acoustical Books, LLC

KenLozito.com

Cover design by Jeff Brown

Editor: Myra Shelley

Proofreader: Tamara Blain

ISBN: 978-1-945223-14-3

CHAPTER ONE

GENERAL CONNOR GATES leaned against the railing on the observation deck of the Montgomery III construction platform and watched the spectacle unfolding before him with flinty eyes. Clutched within the platform's massive robotic arms was the last major section of the *Ark*, the interstellar ship that brought the three hundred thousand colonists living on New Earth to this star system. Bright flashes of light ignited along the partially finished hull of the Colonial Defense Force's first battleship carrier.

"Glaring won't make them work any faster," Reisman said.

Connor arched an eyebrow at Wil Reisman. The man was part of the original Ghost Platoon that Connor had commanded before being "volunteered" into the *Ark* program. At Connor's age, being drugged, stuck in a stasis pod, and then snuck aboard Earth's first interstellar colony ship couldn't exactly be called a kidnapping; "shanghaied" was the nautical term for what happened to Connor and the surviving members of Ghost Platoon. Though it had been seven years since he'd come out of stasis only to learn that he was now part of the colony, it was still sometimes a bitter pill to swallow. But the actions of Admiral Mitch Wilkinson had ultimately been for their benefit. If he hadn't done what he'd done, it was likely that he and his old platoon would have rotted in a military prison—that is, until they perished when all the people back home mysteriously died.

"We're a year behind schedule for this ship," Connor said.

"Priorities," Reisman said. "Titan Space Station came first and is our first line of defense against an attack force."

Connor speared a look at his friend.

"Kasey advised that I was to remind you of the obvious things from time to time," Reisman said.

Connor remembered when Reisman had been just a fresh-faced intelligence officer. His talent for intelligence gathering had made him a valuable asset back then, and now, with the Colonial Defense Force being so small, former Ghosts were nearly irreplaceable. They were among the few who had actual combat experience in the new colony.

A chime sounded from the nearby speakers. "General Gates, please report to the hangar bay for immediate departure," the monotone voice of the computer systems said.

"That's our cue to leave," Connor said.

They left the observation deck and started making their way to the hangar bay, where Connor's shuttle waited for him.

"You wouldn't think it would take a congressional hearing to get resources for the defense of the colony," Connor said.

Reisman shrugged. "Gone are the days of big budgets and a unified effort for a common purpose."

Connor snorted. "Budgets—as if money had anything to do with it."

"Allocation of resources then. There's only so much to go around."

"I guess I should feel lucky that Titan Space Station is at least mostly completed. Now, if we only had enough power stations to operate all the weapons systems at the same time," Connor said dryly.

Reisman pressed his lips together and shrugged, unable to think up a reply.

Connor nodded. "Exactly."

The new governor, Stanton Parish, wasn't their staunchest supporter these days. When they'd first put the CDF together, Connor had the backing of most colonists, but as more people were brought out of stasis over the years, support had begun to wane. Now it was an almost endless debate to get the resources they needed to finish the defense initiatives they'd already begun.

They entered the hangar bay, and Connor shoved the inner doors open. Thinking about meeting with Governor Parish was enough to ruin his mood.

There were fewer than a hundred people stationed on the platform, along with a fleet of robotic workers. Work on the final piece of the *Ark* had only just resumed after the project had been put on hold due to resource constraints.

They crossed the hangar bay to the dull gray shuttle with a golden sunburst painted on the side, the CDF emblem now faded from extensive use. They walked up the loading ramp and entered the transport. Connor's protective detail was waiting for him.

Sean Quinn stuck his head out from the cockpit. "We're cleared to leave."

"Okay, let's get going then," Connor said and sat down near a window. He'd rather be meeting with Tobias Quinn, Sean's father, who had been governor of the colony until the election last year. At least Tobias had given much more than provisional support to the CDF.

One of the perks that came with Connor's rank was that he rarely had to fly himself anywhere. But the thing was, he missed flying. Reisman sat next to him, opened up his PDA, and brought up Connor's schedule.

Connor glanced at the screen. "I'll be right back."

He climbed to his feet and headed for the cockpit, where he opened the door. There were two seats in front of the instrument control panel and an empty seat off to the side.

"Is this seat taken?" Connor asked and sat down.

The copilot's eyes widened.

"All yours, General," Sean said. "Flight check, Lieutenant."

The copilot swung his gaze back to his station. "Cleared for takeoff, sir."

"Acknowledged," Sean said and informed the flight officer that they were ready for launch.

The shuttle lifted off, and the landing gear withdrew into the hull. Connor watched as Sean swung the nose about and took them out of the hangar.

"Let's do a quick flyby," Connor said.

"But, sir, we're already pressed to reach Sierra in time."

Connor looked at the copilot, and his identification appeared on his internal HUD—Lieutenant Anthony Frook, pilot assigned to the protector's division of the Colonial Defense Force.

"They'll wait," Connor said.

Making the congressional committee wait wouldn't increase his chances of getting what he needed, but Connor knew that even if he was on time he was unlikely to get what he needed.

Sean updated their heading and brought the construction site into view. Since they were using part of the *Ark* for the battleship carrier's construction, the interior was already mostly laid out. There were some adjustments to the design that needed to happen to make her a military ship, but it was much quicker than starting from scratch.

"She's coming along. Looks like they've already got some of the heavy cannons installed," Sean said.

Connor glanced up and, indeed, saw the cannons. "Impressive looking but not worth anything without the ammunition tracks to arm the thing or the depot ready to even store the ammunition. I would much rather have had the missile tubes finished than the rail-cannons installed."

Sean didn't reply.

"Alright, take us to Sierra," Connor said.

Sierra was the capital city of the colony on New Earth. Thinking of the colony led Connor to reflect on the humble beginnings of the compound that had been there before. As Sean changed the shuttle's course and started heading toward the planet, the light from the sun illuminated the planetary rings that surrounded New Earth. Connor had long gotten used to seeing them, but they were still a stunningly brilliant display as well as a reminder that no matter what they called this planet, it was a very different place than what they'd left back home.

"Sir, we're being hailed from the *Vigilant*," Sean said.

Connor turned toward the main heads-up display. "Put him through."

Captain Ian Howe appeared on screen. "General, I wanted to let you know that we'll be ready for departure tomorrow. Captain Benson of the cargo ship is waiting for final approval to depart."

"I delayed approval in hopes that there would be some extra things to be added to his manifest," Connor replied.

Howe nodded. "That's what I told him. CDF destroyers *Banshee* and *Wyatt* are on standby for escort duty."

"This is the fun part," Connor said.

Sean glanced at Connor but didn't say anything.

"Since you have the extra time, make sure the *Vigilant* is fully stocked," Connor said.

The sides of Howe's face lifted upward. "Understood, sir. *Vigilant* out."

Connor glanced at Sean. "Yes?"

Sean checked the shuttle's approach to the planet. "Nothing, sir. I was just remembering when I first heard you say those words. The fun part, I mean."

Connor nodded. Sean had been in the first class for Search and Rescue before he transferred to the CDF. He now led his own platoon, which was currently assigned directly to Connor.

"Then I'm sure you can guess what comes next," Connor said.

"Wouldn't be good at my job if I couldn't at least anticipate your orders, sir," Sean said.

Connor left the cockpit and returned to his seat. They were still another forty minutes out. To the casual onlooker, it appeared that Connor was taking a nap, but what he was really doing was using his implants to check that the plans he'd set up were in motion. Since there were so few people in the Colonial Defense Force with actual military experience, Connor went to great lengths to ensure that drills were as realistic as possible. He knew that all the training in the world could only go so far until a soldier was in the thick of it, but he aimed to get their soldiers as ready for action as he could. If that meant an excessive amount of training and mock execution of tactics, then so be it.

CHAPTER TWO

THE SHUTTLE MADE its final approach to the CDF airfield located at Sierra. The sprawling city and expansion projects were enough to keep most of the predators at bay. They didn't live behind electrified fences anymore, thanks to the countermeasures they'd developed to dissuade predators from getting too close. There were also deterrent systems in place that helped defend Sierra's denizens until Field Operations and Security could arrive.

The shuttle landed, and Connor climbed out of his seat. Reisman went ahead of him to make sure ground transportation was ready. The shuttle door opened and a breath of warm, humid air blew inside the cabin. Connor preferred the settlements farther away, where the climate was significantly drier than it was here, but this was the cradle of civilization here on New Earth.

"Sir," Sean called out to him, "there's been another ancient city discovered farther inland. I was wondering if you'd heard about it."

Connor frowned. "Any ryklars in the area?" The last time they'd found a city built by the alien civilization that used to live

on this planet, they'd triggered a silent alarm. The local apex
predators, known as ryklars, had begun hunting humans as a
result. Once they'd disabled the alarm, the ryklars migrated to
another area, and it had been years since any had been seen near
Sierra.

Sean shook his head. "No, and no defense mechanism to call
them in either."

Connor walked down the ramp and saw that there was no
ground transport waiting for them.

"They're requesting that an aerial scan of the alien city be
performed," Sean said and then glanced away to speak to
someone through his comlink.

Connor checked the time.

"Should be here in a few minutes," Reisman said.

Connor started walking and the other men followed. He
glanced at Sean. "Why are you telling me this?"

"I thought you'd be interested," Sean said and looked away
guiltily.

Connor quickened his pace. He knew what Sean was imply-
ing. He hadn't seen Lenora in months.

"And the things the archaeological team discovered
could have—"

"That's enough, Captain," Connor warned. "I don't have
time to placate the people who spend all their time digging in
the dirt—not when there's a colony to defend. If they're in trouble, the request should go through Search and Rescue. If they
want a survey done, that request goes through Field Ops and not
the Colonial Defense Force."

Connor didn't wait for a reply. A ground vehicle that had
been barreling its way toward them came to a stop. Connor
opened the door and climbed inside. "What the hell took you so

long? I hope you can find the congressional building faster than you picked me up."

The driver apologized, and Wil Reisman took the front seat.

Connor opened the window and looked at Sean. "Make sure the shuttle's refueled and ready to leave. I don't plan on being planet-side for long."

The vehicle pulled away, and Reisman turned around with a question on his lips.

Connor held up his index finger. "Don't!"

Reisman frowned and turned back around. Connor was tired of people prying into his personal life. With the safety of New Earth resting squarely on his shoulders, he didn't have much time for relationships, despite the colonial mandate that encouraged procreation among the colonists. Family units in the colony were very different from what they'd been back on Earth. There were children and their immediate parents, but families were also reinforced by extended families and support groups that greatly eased the colonists' burdens of raising children. Education programs were geared toward learning about New Earth, and most things that had comprised Connor's life until seven years ago were referred to as Old Earth history.

While he had a strong connection with Lenora Bishop, she had no interest in having children. She was dedicated to learning all she could about the alien civilization that had thrived here. Most archeologists believed that intelligent life had flourished here from a few hundred to a thousand years before humans arrived. The debate was still ongoing about what had happened to them. But Connor was more concerned with the impact of what that civilization had done to the ecosystem of the planet. Predators like the ryklars and berwolves had been genetically modified, which made them highly intelligent and quite dangerous. The ryklars had abandoned this part of the continent and migrated away once the alien signal that triggered some latent protection protocol within them had been removed. At that point, ryklars had ceased attacking humans. Berwolf hunting packs required more persuasion, but there were some groups living far away from the cities that sought to tame the predators.

The vehicle drove along the paved streets of Sierra. The shimmering, bronze-colored buildings were constructed of a refined alloy they'd discovered among the alien ruins. It was light and strong. The resulting city looked familiar—since the architecture was similar to what they'd had back on Earth—but also alien as well, due in part to the materials used in the construction of the buildings.

They drove toward a large dome-shaped building where the golden sunburst flag draped unmoving in a windless sky. The vehicle pulled to a stop and Connor opened his own door. He and Reisman climbed the stairs and entered the building. Connor sent his credentials along the network, and they quickly passed through the security checkpoint.

A handsome older woman waited for him. She had her arms crossed in front of her chest and her thick brown hair was pulled back.

"Trying to make an entrance by arriving late?" Dr. Ashley Quinn asked and made a show of looking behind Connor. "And you didn't even bring Sean with you."

"No, Mother, I didn't bring him up," Connor replied.

"Mother?" Ashley snorted and arched an eyebrow at him. "I'm certainly not your mother, but I would accept the role of big sister."

Connor leaned in and kissed Ashley on the cheek as she patted his arms. "Well, in that case, I think we're fine then."

Ashley eyed him for a moment. "I know you only need two hours of sleep, but you're looking a bit worse for the wear."

"Why is it that whenever I have to come to one of these things it's you who gets to walk me inside?" Connor asked.

"I figured you'd want to see a friendly face before you get fed to the lions," Ashley said.

They walked through the wide-open atrium, and echoes of conversations gathered above them like a storm.

"At least Tobias believed in the threat we're facing, unlike the current governor," Connor said.

"Parish was the one voted in," Ashley replied.

"By telling people what they wanted to hear," Connor said with a grumble.

They reached the large metallic doors that led to the congressional chambers.

"Well, make them listen, just like you made all of us listen seven years ago," Ashley said.

She entered the chamber first.

"At least you guys were reasonable," Connor called out after her.

She didn't turn around, but Connor knew she'd heard him. His mouth drew downward and he glared at the doorway, waiting for his queue to be allowed inside. Franklin Mallory had insisted that Connor come to this meeting to make the request. Many colonists didn't want to listen to conversation about the proposed danger coming from Earth; they'd prefer to pretend the threat didn't exist. It hadn't always been this way, but the faction that questioned the threat from Earth had gained more and more support over the years.

They called his name. Connor blew out a breath and waited an extra few seconds before going inside.

CHAPTER THREE

CONNOR ENTERED the chamber to the quiet murmurings of those inside. All the seats in the vast chamber were taken, and there were even people standing in the back. Connor squared his shoulders and strode down the center aisle. The far wall showed an image of the *Ark* with the Earth in the background and then changed to the *Ark* with New Earth in the background. New Earth was similar in size and composition to Earth, but where there were several large continents on Earth, New Earth boasted a singular large landmass that occupied nearly a quarter of the planet. Vast oceans covered the rest. The most striking difference between the two planets was the rings that surrounded New Earth. They made for a beautiful sight from any perspective.

Connor walked through the gated threshold and stopped at the central podium, where he looked at the trio of people who led the colony. In the center was a thin man who, though not a particularly imposing person, had managed to convince a majority of the colony to give him the job of governor—Stanton Parish. To his right was the former governor, Tobias Quinn, who was now serving as the head of the judicial committee. To Stanton's left was a dark-skinned woman with long black hair and intense eyes, Selena Brown, who was head of the legislative committee in charge of proposing the laws of the colony.

A woman came through the gates behind Connor and went to stand at another podium nearby. Connor had no idea who she was, and she seemed to regard him as someone she'd rather not have in her presence. Connor thought she must be a Parish loyalist.

Governor Parish started the meeting, and the people in attendance immediately quieted down.

"Thank you for joining us, General Gates," Parish said.

Connor cleared his throat. "I appreciate you taking the time for this request."

"For the sake of this session, can you please touch on the high points of this request for the record," Parish said.

Connor cleared his throat. "Space Station Titan has been completed for over a year and is currently running at half capacity because we haven't been given approval for the resources to bring up the secondary power generator," Connor said.

Governor Parish examined a small holoscreen in front of him. "Yes, I've seen this request come across my desk before. We delayed this in favor of expanding the power grid supplying New Delphia."

Connor mused that this was good for the colonists living in that growing city but bad for the Colonial Defense Force's state of readiness.

"Given the members of this appropriations committee, I didn't think I needed to remind you of the threat we face. Titan Space Station represents our first line of defense," Connor said.

Governor Parish narrowed his beady eyes. "Potential threat, General."

Connor's brows pulled together and he glared at the man.

Parish held up his hand. "I know you don't agree, but, if anything, the last election has proven that not all the people on New Earth agree that the messages received from Earth imply that we're in any danger. They are quite disturbing, I'll grant you that, but there are simply too many unknowns to commit the resources of the entire colony toward efforts that don't best serve the problems we're facing today," Parish said.

Connor leveled his gaze at the governor. "You and I have vastly different opinions on how the colony would be best served, but what you're doing is negligent."

There was a sharp intake of breath by the people nearby.

The woman at the nearby podium looked at him. "We've refuted the standing argument that the offline deep-space buoy network is an indication of an invading force making its way toward this star system."

Connor frowned. "I'm sorry, who are you?"

"Dr. Gabriela Mendoza, astrophysicist."

"Dr. Zabat had a different opinion," Connor said.

"I'm well aware of what my predecessor thought. I'm afraid that the partial message, coupled with the data we've received, influenced his judgment," Dr. Mendoza said.

Connor looked back at the governor. "I thought I was here to address my request for Titan Space Station, not to debate the last message from Earth."

Governor Parish regarded Connor for a moment. "I think it's important to revisit it since what you're requesting represents a significant investment of resources that could be better utilized elsewhere. Dr. Mendoza, please."

"Thank you, Governor. As General Gates has stated, the long-held belief is that because the comms buoys supporting the deep-space network were going offline, it meant that some kind of invasion fleet was making its way to this star system, following a trail of breadcrumbs right to us. However, many astrophysicists agree that the reason for the buoys going offline is simply that they reached the end of their lifecycle," Dr. Mendoza said.

Connor glanced at Tobias, who gave a slight shake of his head.

"So we'll ignore the warning message from Earth and their last act, which was to alter the *Ark's* mission and bring us here instead of the intended destination. I'm sure you're a fine astrophysicist and you could be right about the buoys. They could be failing because they're beyond their life cycle, but even engineers know that the likelihood of these buoys failing sequentially is almost nil," Connor said.

"The only thing we know for sure is that something significant happened to Earth, nothing more than that. A reference to some super virus doesn't mean they're crossing interstellar space to reach us here," Dr. Mendoza said.

"Are you willing to bet your life on that?" Connor asked and swung his gaze toward Parish. "Are you, Governor? Are you willing to bet the lives of the entire colony on that?"

Parish leaned back. "I may be the governor, but this is a decision shared by all colonists."

"You're acting as if your decisions won't have any bearing on whether or not we survive. The decisions you make affect lives. When you have people like Dr. Mendoza spreading doubt about the very real danger we're in, it sends the message that you don't believe the colony is in any danger despite the evidence that supports the claim," Connor said.

"Everyone agrees that the initial message that changed the *Ark's* mission was sent out between ten and twenty years after we left." Dr. Mendoza said. "So, in essence, if there *was* some kind of fleet heading for us, we potentially have thirteen more years before they arrive. That's even if they know exactly where we are in the first place. Even if we err on the side of caution, we still have three years, which leaves a substantial amount of time to address the defense of the colony."

"You're assuming that their speed and method of travel is the same as the *Ark*. You know what the root of the word 'assumption' makes you, right?" Connor asked.

Dr. Mendoza sneered. "I don't have to listen to this."

"General Gates," Parish warned.

"My job is to defend the colony, which means I need the resources to do so without leaving our first line of defense at half capacity. I don't want an invasion. In fact, I hope people like Dr. Mendoza and you, Governor, are right and that we're observing the sequential failure of the deep-space buoy network. But, if you're wrong, wouldn't you sleep a bit better knowing that we're doing everything we can to keep this colony safe?" Connor asked.

Governor Parish leaned forward, and his hands formed a bridge in front of him. "Not every request from the Colonial Defense Force can be pitted against the survival of the colony. Over the past seven years, we've devoted enormous resources to the defense of the colony—from missile-defense platforms to using a large chunk of the *Ark* that went toward the construction of Titan Space Station and the battleship cruiser. So when it comes to our defense capability and the efforts of people like you, General, I sleep *very* well at night."

"So will you approve the request this time?" Connor asked.

"We've approved the creation of the additional supplies you've requested, but in regards to the secondary power system for the space station, that request will be denied. We'll review it again in the next twelve months," Governor Parish said.

Connor pressed his lips together. He wanted to tell them

they were going to become victims of their own shortsightedness and make them all cower in the face of their reckless decisions. Something was coming for them—something that none of them really understood. Connor might have had more doubts if Admiral Wilkinson hadn't been involved. The aged war veteran of the NA Alliance Navy had been nearing the end of his career when he'd snuck Connor and the rest of the Ghosts aboard the *Ark*. Connor wholeheartedly believed that Wilkinson had included his own name in the mission summary brief that changed the *Ark's* destination in order to lend credibility to the content of the brief. It had been a message for Connor, and it was meant as a direct instruction to prepare the colony for invasion.

Connor looked at the governor, and his gaze strayed over to Tobias. He tried to think of something to say that might change their minds but couldn't think of anything that hadn't already been said. Connor didn't want to spread panic across the colony, so he had to work within the current confines, and this wouldn't be the last request he ever made. If anything, the last seven years had taught him that a little bit of tact went a long way.

The session ended, and despite Connor's outwardly calm demeanor, he was seething. He'd thought they'd at least grant the request in a few months' time, and to be put off for an entire year was ridiculous. If only they'd been able to successfully extract more information from the deep-space buoys, but they weren't designed to hold vast amounts of information. They had a specific job to do, which was to relay the data, not store it. After the data had passed through the buoy network, the operating systems expunged it. Connor glanced around the chamber, thinking that there were a few government officials he'd like to expunge.

CHAPTER FOUR

CONNOR THREADED his way out of the congressional chambers. A few people tried to stop him by asking questions, but he put them off, having no interest in glad-handing anyone. He saw Ashley making her way toward him and then getting stopped by a small group of people. Connor used the opportunity to slip away. These requisition-type committees were usually attended by Franklin Mallory, Director of the CDF. Connor couldn't bear attending them, and after getting his request denied again, he had no wish to stand around complaining about it.

Wil Reisman was waiting for him outside the congressional building. Reisman took one look at him and frowned. "Went that well, did it?"

Connor quickly went down the stairs, and Wil walked next to him. "Oh, you know, same old crap. 'This isn't a priority. Come back in a year and perhaps you'll get what you need then.'"

"This administration isn't like the last one," Reisman said.

"At least Tobias listened to reason. Parish flat out refuses to believe there's even a threat to the colony," Connor said.

"What's our next move? Return to the shuttle?"

Connor glanced at the line of electric cars outside the building and couldn't find the one with the CDF designation on the door.

"Yeah, if we can even find the damn car," Connor said.

A high-priority message appeared on his internal heads-up display.

::*Sorry to hear that the request was denied again*,:: F. Mallory said.

::*Maybe the fourth time's the charm*,:: C. Gates replied.

::*I want to meet with you before you leave. I'm working out of Field Ops today*,:: F. Mallory said.

Connor sighed. He just wanted to get going. He had enough to do without spending the afternoon stuck in Field Ops.

::*Do I need to make it an order?*:: F. Mallory asked.

::*On my way*,:: C. Gates replied.

The chat window closed.

"Change of plans," Connor said.

He walked to the nearest car that had the golden sunburst colony emblem. The driver stood outside and glanced at them.

"I need a ride to Field Ops headquarters," Connor said.

The driver frowned at them. "This is Governor Parish's transport."

"Excellent. I'm on official business for the governor, and it's vital that I get to Field Ops as soon as possible," Connor said.

Reisman snorted and had the grace to look away. Connor grabbed the passenger side door handle. The driver glanced up at the congressional building, conflicted.

"Look, it's either you or me driving the car. What's it gonna be?" Connor asked.

"Fine," the driver said and walked around to the other side of the car.

Reisman leaned toward Connor. "He denies your request so you commandeer his ride?"

Connor smirked. "Sometimes it's the little things that get you through the day."

Reisman chuckled and climbed into the back of the car. The driver pulled away, and Connor had him send out the priority signal so they'd move through traffic quickly. Fifteen minutes later they were in front of Field Operations Headquarters. Connor and Reisman climbed out of the car just as a comlink connection came to the driver.

"Hey, wait a minute. You lied to me. The governor is outside the congressional building right now," the driver said.

"Tell him General Gates appreciates the ride," Connor said and walked over to the security checkpoint.

"Couldn't resist rubbing it in his face," Reisman said.

Connor shrugged. He didn't care. The governor had caused him no end of frustration this past year, and he felt a small tinge of satisfaction at taking the man's ride.

The Field Ops security detail snapped a salute toward Connor. "General Gates, Director Mallory said to inform you that he's at his office near command central."

Connor thanked them and headed inside. Field Ops Head-quarters had grown significantly from the prefabricated structure that was there when he'd first arrived. The new building was all angles the color of dark bronze that drank in the sunshine.

His rank granted him priority treatment throughout the building. Before he'd been promoted to general—a rank he'd had no illusions of achieving in the NA Alliance military back on Earth—he'd sometimes found it annoying that the higher-ranked officers received preferential treatment, but as he'd been promoted through the ranks his opinion had changed. With the rank came a significant increase in workload. So, yeah, moving to the head of the line was a perk, but the tradeoff was more work. The Colonial Defense Force wasn't much different from the NA Alliance military in that respect. The one major difference in the two militaries was that the NA Alliance was an actual military force and the CDF was just starting to get its bearings. Connor was a general because there was no one else senior enough in rank who had actual combat experience. More than once he'd experienced fleeting moments when he'd wished there were someone up the chain of command who could take over the defense of the colony. But there wasn't anyone else, so he committed himself to doing the best he could and hoped it would be enough.

The Field Ops Command Center was akin to the mission controls of old. There were several Field Ops centers throughout Sierra and among the smaller settlements on New Earth.

A red-haired man with an almost permanent scowl on his face stuck his head out of an office and waved to Connor. "Why, General Gates, I'm so glad you could come by Field Operations," Damon Mills said.

Connor grinned. "If you keep that up, I'm gonna start calling you Director Mills."

Connor and Damon had gotten off to a rocky start when Connor had first come to the colony, and they'd nearly come to blows on more than one occasion, but all that was ancient history.

"Okay, enough with that nonsense. I'm glad you're here," Mills said and beckoned them to his office. "Franklin is on his way down."

They walked into Mills' office and sat down.

"Why do I get the feeling you're about to ask me to do something for you?" Connor asked.

Mills smiled. "Give and take, and I believe this time *you* owe *me*."

Connor arched an eyebrow. "To be honest, I've lost count."

"Trust me, you do."

"You know I don't trust anyone," Connor said.

Reisman glanced at him.

"Present company excluded, of course," Connor said. "Alright, what is it you need?"

"I have a group of engineers who need a ride to an archaeological dig site past the new frontier boundary," Mills said.

Connor's brows pulled together. "Are you seriously asking me to provide transport for a group of engineers?"

The door to Mills' office opened and Franklin Mallory walked in.

"Good, you're here," Mallory said and looked at Mills. "Did you tell him?"

Mills shook his head. "I was about to."

Connor glanced at Mallory. "The only thing he told me was to ferry a team of engineers to a dig site past the frontier boundary. Are you in on this too?"

Mallory looked confused. "What do you mean?"

"When we landed, Sean kept bringing up Lenora and some find at her new dig site. I assumed—" Connor stopped speaking, suddenly feeling foolish.

"As interesting as you think your personal life is to the rest of us, I can assure you it has no bearing on this request," Mallory said.

Connor looked away and shook his head. Sometimes he walked right into trouble. "Alright, I'm done being an idiot. What's so special about this site?"

"Oh, you mean beyond Dr. Bishop being there? I so wish you guys had stuck together," Mills said, his voice going high.

Reisman snorted, unable to keep it in anymore.

"Look, I have a shuttle waiting for me. Seriously, what's this all about?" Connor asked.

"Lenora may have found another city," Mallory said.

Connor frowned. The last time Lenora had found the ruins of a city, they'd set off some kind of auto-protect protocol that signaled the ryklars to attack them. The ryklars had demonstrated intelligence beyond that of normal predators and many people had died.

"She said this city appears to be larger than what they found seven years ago, but the real find that applies directly to you is an intact power station in the ruins. Lenora knows better than to tinker with what she found. Her team took some preliminary readings, and they look quite promising," Mallory said.

"I still don't see where I figure into all of this," Connor said.

"Oh, it's not you personally; it's just the combat shuttle you're flying around in. It's much faster than our troop transport vehicles. You can drop the engineering team off at the site in half the time it would take one of my carriers," Mills said.

"Well, that's good for you. What's in it for me?" Connor asked.

"How about some gratitude?" Mills said.

"Now who's a pain in the ass?" Connor said.

"Connor," Mallory said. "I want you to take a quick look before you head off to Titan Space Station. Our engineers learned quite a bit from the alloy they found at the last ruined city. They've perfected it since then and we've obviously used it in the construction of Sierra. What if we find something similar in terms of the power station? New fuel for our reactors that has a higher energy output. Can you think of nowhere that would be useful?"

Connor drew in a breath and nodded. "I get it. Definitely worth a look."

"I'm glad you agree," Mallory said.

"I guess I'm the pain in the ass now," Connor said.

"What's this about you stealing the governor's car?" Mallory asked.

Connor's eyes widened. "I didn't steal his car. I had the driver give us a ride here."

Mills palmed his face and shook his head.

"He'd already denied my request for Titan for a year," Connor said.

Mallory's PDA chimed an incoming message. He glanced at it and the edges of his lips pulled upward.

"What is it?" Connor asked.

"Kallie's with the doctor. I'm going to be a father again," Mallory said with a wide grin.

Connor shot out of the chair and shook Franklin's hand, offering congratulations.

"I guess Lars will be an older brother. Where is Lars stationed these days?" Connor asked.

"He's heading up the remote Field Ops centers in the other settlement. He's due to be a father soon, too," Mallory said.

Connor couldn't remember the last time he'd seen Lars Mallory, who was nearly twenty-five years old by now.

"Doing your part for procreation, I see. You're making the rest of us look bad," Mills said.

There was a general colony campaign promoting the importance of having children and how crucial it was to the colony's survival beyond a few generations. Connor felt something cold in the pit of his stomach. He'd left a son behind on Earth. He's always intended to reconnect with his son, but never had the chance.

"I'm sure all three of you will do your part," Mallory said while pointedly looking at each of them.

A wave of fear stole across Reisman's features.

"I'm a bit old—" Mills began.

"Don't talk to me about age. I'm over a hundred years old. Prolong treatments more than double a person's lifespan. There's no excuse for any of you not to start families of your own," Mallory said.

Mills cleared his throat. "About that ride for the engineering team."

"Right, just send them to the shuttle and we'll get them there," Connor said.

Mallory grinned. "You guys are a pair, I tell you."

"I'm happy for you. I really am. But we all know something's coming and the buoys are not just going offline because they're at the end of their lifecycle," Connor said.

Suddenly, the warmth felt like it was being sucked out of the room and the smile fled from Mallory's face.

"I'll leave you to it," Mallory said and left.

Connor made as if to leave but Mills asked him to stay a moment longer. Reisman, sensing the dismissal, left to wait for Connor outside.

"Sometimes you really don't know when to keep that mouth of yours shut. We're all aware of the danger, and we don't need you to keep shoving it in our faces," Mills said.

Connor felt a pang of guilt warm his cheeks, but his iron will choked the life out of it. "I know, but we can't afford to get distracted."

"Distracted! The man just found out he was going to be a father again and you couldn't let him enjoy it for five minutes without bringing up that damn crap from Earth."

Mills was right. Connor *was* being a jerk.

Mills held his hand in front of his chest. "I know you're not doing it to be malicious or cruel, but even you've got to remember that the men and women serving under you have their own personal reasons to fight. Let people like Mallory have his few moments of happiness, even if you won't allow it for yourself."

Connor chewed on the inside of his lip. "You're right. I'll go apologize."

Mills frowned. "Honestly, the best thing you can do right now is just go. Franklin is going to be with Kallie today. In layman's terms, he's taking the day off," Mills said and leaned toward him. "Remember what those were? Now get out of here. And thank you for taking the engineering team."

Connor left Mills' office grim-faced and feeling more foolish than ever. He walked in silence for a few minutes, then glanced at Reisman. "Do you think I drive you guys too hard?"

Reisman's eyes widened in shock and then he laughed almost uncontrollably.

Connor shook his head and quickened his pace. "Forget I asked."

CHAPTER FIVE

A SHORT WHILE LATER, Connor was back at the CDF airfield. He sent a message to Mallory, congratulating him on becoming a father again and apologizing for being such a killjoy. The message would be waiting for Mallory whenever he checked his inbox. After he'd sent it, he pushed all thoughts of Mallory's blossoming family out of his mind.

They entered the CDF hangar, and Connor saw Sean supervising the loading of equipment onto the combat shuttle. Seven passengers were waiting to board, one of whom he immediately recognized.

"Coming out of retirement, Bones?" Connor asked.

A ripcord-thin man with black hair turned around and saluted Connor.

"I'm still with Search and Rescue, sir. Let me introduce you to the team," Joe Ramirez said and presented the team of engineers that was traveling to the archaeological dig site. The engineers seemed friendly enough, but they were quite reserved with him, as if they weren't sure how to act around Connor.

"Those of us with engineering backgrounds also consult on projects," Ramirez said.

Ramirez had been part of the alpha class to go through Connor's first Search and Rescue training program. Some of the graduates of that first class had stayed in Field Ops, while others, like Sean Quinn, joined the Colonial Defense Force as soon as it was ratified.

Connor looked at Sean. "How much longer until we can be under way?"

"This is the last of it, so just a few more minutes, General," Sean said.

The engineering team walked up the loading ramp and checked their equipment containers.

Connor saw Ramirez checking the seats and Connor grinned. "I won't be dumping you out mid-flight this time."

An engineer named Dave Rogers became pale and his gaze darted to Ramirez. "Please tell me that was a joke."

Connor kept walking.

"He only does that to the people under his command," Ramirez said.

"He's the general of the CDF. Doesn't that mean you're still under his command?" Rogers asked.

"That's right," Connor called over his shoulder. "Rarely do I dump people out of my ships twice, but in Ramirez's case I might make an exception."

Never one for riding as a passenger when he didn't have to, he headed up to the cockpit as Ramirez coaxed Rogers back into his seat.

Sean joined him in the cockpit and sat in the copilot's seat.

"Do they really think I'm going to just toss them off the ship?" Connor asked.

Sean pressed his lips together in thought. "Let's just say

you've developed quite a reputation over the years. Go for preflight, sir."

Connor sat in the pilot's seat and set about going through the preflight checklist. Lieutenant Frook entered the cockpit and sat in one of the rear seats. Connor engaged the engines and withdrew the landing gear. He eased the combat shuttle out of the hangar and thrust the stick. The main engine's power output spiked and the shuttle sped forward. He set a heading for the coordinates of the dig site.

Connor opened a comlink to the rear of the shuttle. "Attention, all non-CDF passengers. We'll reach the dig site beyond the frontier border in a little over an hour. Please remain in your seats with your seat belts securely fastened at all times. In the event of a sudden loss of pressure in the shuttle, I will click the eject button and jettison all of you to safety," Connor said and brought up a video feed of the passengers. "Unless you're sitting next to Joe Ramirez. In that case, you might not survive."

Connor grinned as he watched Dave Rogers check his seat belt and then decide to change seats. He heard Ramirez's hearty laughter coming from the rear of the shuttle.

Connor glanced at Sean. "What? I'm just lightening the mood."

"Whose mood would that be?" Sean asked.

Connor opened the comlink again. "Pay no attention to that last bit. This combat shuttle is a Falcon III and survived a two-hundred-year journey through space to get here. She's been flight tested and approved for flight by top Colonial Defense Engineers. Pilot out," Connor said but left the comlink open. "There, see, I took it back. Everything's fine. Oh, did you make sure the power coupling for the mid-tier inertia dampeners was replaced?"

Sean glanced at him, his mouth hanging open. He glanced at the open comlink and smirked. "I submitted the request to the repair technician when we landed. Let me just check their comments . . . hmm, that's strange."

"What's that, Captain?" Connor asked.

They heard Ramirez shouting from the passenger area that they could hear them.

Sean could barely contain himself. "They were replaced, but the diagnostic is showing they're defective. Sir, we're going to have to make an emergency landing or anyone sitting in the middle of the shuttle could fly out of their seats . . . Oh no, sir. That's the master alarm."

"You're right. That inertia dampener is throwing out all kinds of errors in the logs. That's strange. They all have Ramirez's name on them," Connor said.

"It makes for a much more interesting ride," Ramirez shouted.

Connor grinned.

"In all seriousness," Sean said, "the ship is fine. Relax and enjoy the flight."

"Aw crap. I'm showing all kinds of cargo failures now," Connor said. "They could be cut loose at any moment. Do you think that team knows their chief engineer is so incompetent he hardly made it through graduate school? It's no wonder he was kicked out of Search and Rescue. Wait a minute, is that a coolant leak being reported?" Connor said.

Sean closed the comlink and they all burst out laughing, including Lieutenant Frook, who'd never seen his general act this way.

Connor blew out a breath. "God, that was so much fun. I haven't laughed like that in a long time. Remind me to have Reisman tell you what we did to Colonel Douglass after one of our missions."

Connor glanced at the video feed from the back of the

shuttle and saw that Wil Reisman was fast asleep. Typical. That man could sleep anywhere, any time.

Less than an hour later the nav computer displayed an alert that they were nearing their destination. They'd been flying over a large grassland area for the past fifteen minutes. Connor magnified the view and saw the research base up ahead.

"How does Dr. Bishop even find these places?" Sean asked.

Connor peered at the heads-up display. "She hardly sits still for more than a few minutes, for one. Plus, she's really good at her job."

Connor watched as they closed in on the research base, which butted up against a vast dig site.

"Sir, would you like me to land the ship?" Sean asked.

"No, I've got it," Connor said.

There was an area of flattened grassland that looked to be the designated landing area for supply runs. Connor set the combat shuttle down there. He shut down the engines and set the shuttle's computer systems to standby, then climbed out of his seat and left the cockpit. Connor didn't get to fly all that often, but when he did, he always experienced a longing to return to the pilot's seat again. Generals weren't supposed to fly their own ships, but oh how he missed flying sometimes.

Ramirez grinned when he saw Connor.

"That was quite the show," Ramirez said.

Connor gave him a playful slap on the shoulder. "All in good fun. It was really good to see you again, Joe."

Most of the engineering team was much more at ease now that they were on the ground. Dave Rogers gave him a friendly nod.

They lowered the loading ramp and were met by a woman with short brown hair.

"General Gates, I'm Martha Campbell."

Connor shook her hand and stepped off the loading ramp. His internal heads-up display showed that the temperature was a comfortable seventy degrees with ten percent humidity. There wasn't a cloud in the sky. Only the pale rings that surrounded the planet were visible along the southern horizon.

The engineering team began offloading their equipment, and Martha directed them to where they should go. Sean and other members of Connor's protective detail began securing the area.

"At ease, gentlemen. There are no predators around here except for the ones with guns," a familiar voice said.

Connor turned around and saw Lenora, and he felt his lips pull upwards into a smile. Lenora's eyes widened for a moment and she started to smile, but then her eyes narrowed in annoyance. Her long auburn hair hung freely and the soft breeze toyed with the ends.

"It's good to see you, Sean," Lenora said, her gaze softening when she looked over at the young man.

Lenora looked back at Connor. "Do you still have Noah way out on the outskirts of the star system at that space station?"

Connor frowned. "Nice to see you too."

Martha, who'd been standing quietly nearby, gave Lenora a meaningful look.

"I'm sorry," Lenora said. "Thanks for coming out here. Franklin was insistent that you see what we've found."

Lenora gestured for Connor to follow her. He noticed that everyone else seemed to give them some space.

"How did you find a city way out here?" Connor asked.

"Survey flights, and I noticed several structures less than half a mile from where we're standing. Ground-penetrating scans revealed a lot of vast structures under the ground. I assembled a team and we came back out here. We started to survey the area, marking places to dig. That was when we detected the power station," Lenora said.

"Mallory was pretty impressed with your initial report," Connor replied.

Lenora frowned. "That's what I don't get. Why would the CDF be interested in a thousand-year-old power station?"

"Is that how old it is?"

"Tough to say. There's some radiation in the area, which can throw off some of our equipment. And before you ask, the radiation is within acceptable levels," Lenora said, clipping her words as if she were swatting an annoying fly.

"Alright then, why don't you show me what you've found?" Connor said.

"Of course, right this way, General," Lenora said, her voice dripping with sarcasm.

Connor stiffened. She walked ahead of him and he supposed it could have been worse, but not by much. The last time they'd spoken to each other they'd ended up doing more shouting than talking. They hadn't spoken since.

Lenora led them toward a pair of all-terrain vehicles. A large brown ball of fur came from around one of the vehicles and howled. Connor drew his pistol and charged in front of Lenora.

"Don't shoot!" Lenora shouted and ran in front of him.

The berwolf ran gleefully into Lenora's outstretched arms. A large pink tongue lolled out of the blocky head with a mouth full of impressive teeth. The berwolf had a muscular body, but judging by the size, this one was a juvenile. Its black claws could still rend through steel, however. The berwolf nuzzled its head into Lenora's middle and she used both her hands to scratch his thick brown coat.

Lenora glanced up at him. "This is Bull. I found him as a cub."

Connor holstered his weapon and Lenora gestured for him to squat down.

Bull pulled away from Lenora and swung his head toward Connor. The berwolf cub took a few steps toward him but kept his hindquarters leaning against Lenora. Gobs of drool hung from its chops as it peered at Connor.

If this thing charged him, Connor had little chance of deflecting it before getting mauled.

Connor met its gaze and stuck out his hand. "You could have warned me about your new friend," he said.

Lenora grinned. "And miss the look on your face?"

Bull charged. The movement was so sudden that Connor didn't have time to react before the berwolf had him pinned to the ground under two giant paws. The berwolf closed its mouth and lowered its snout to sniff him. Connor heard the shuffling of feet behind him and hoped Sean and the rest of the protective detail didn't do anything stupid to set the creature off.

Connor looked into the berwolf's gaze. "Alright, what now, buddy?"

He reached up and gave the creature a light scratch under its chin. A deep growl rumbled from its massive chest, and Connor slowly moved his hands away.

"I'd like to be friends, but if you don't get off me one of us is going to get hurt," Connor said in a calm voice and started reaching for his sidearm.

Lenora came to Bull's side and nudged him. The berwolf decided to allow Connor to live and pushed himself off. Lenora helped him to his feet.

"Is this how he greets everyone?" Connor asked and dusted himself off.

"He mostly ignores people. That's the first time I've seen him do something like that. Must be your animal magnetism," Lenora said.

"Berwolfs aren't pets," Connor said.

"I don't keep him locked up. He leaves and comes back on his own," Lenora said.

She climbed into one of the ATVs, and Connor got in on the other side. The engineering team, as well as his security forces, divided up and rode in the passenger compartments. Lenora drove away and Connor watched as Bull trotted along beside them, easily keeping up with the ATVs.

"Bull isn't the first berwolf cub to be found. I'm sure he'll wander off when he's ready. I checked with the field biologists' office and they confirmed that since I'd found him so young he'd probably developed an attachment to me," Lenora said.

Not the first male to fall under her spell but definitely the first berwolf ever to do so.

"So, he just follows you to whatever dig site you happen to be on out here?" Connor asked.

"Pretty much. He actually helped us find the power station —the general area at least," Lenora answered.

She drove them toward a series of alien structures. The rounded architecture had twisted metallic pieces on the top. There were ramps that went up the sides of each building. For some strange reason the ancient aliens that built this place hadn't built stairs and instead constructed wide ramps to get to the upper levels.

Lenora stopped the vehicle and they climbed out. Bull came to a stop a few feet outside Connor's door, and he thought about waiting inside the vehicle for the berwolf to move. The creature looked at him as if he was waiting to see what Connor was going to do. Connor opened the door and stepped out of the vehicle. He knew that making eye contact with certain pack animals was the equal of challenging them, so he met the berwolf's gaze and then continued toward Lenora. Hopefully, the berwolf cub wouldn't take it as a sign of submission on Connor's part.

Lenora walked ahead and Bull trotted to her side.

"Looks like you've been replaced," Sean said.

"Seems that way," Connor said.

The path toward the building angled downward, revealing a complex of buildings that had been hidden under the dirt. The parts of the buildings that were exposed all had ramps to the upper levels.

Connor walked over to Lenora, who was directing the engineering team down into the site so they could check the power source.

"Doesn't look like they believed in making stairs," Connor said.

Lenora shook her head. "Just like the other city, though this site seems to predate that one."

Connor frowned. "How can you tell?"

"Well, the other one was built underground and then extended out into the valley. The architectural design was sparse, as if they didn't have time for all the ornamentation we have with these buildings," Lenora said.

Connor glanced around and could see her point. He'd always been fascinated by the things Lenora was able to find.

"Do you want me to take you down inside?" Lenora asked.

"Maybe. I'd like to hear what Ramirez and the others have to say first," Connor replied.

He used his implants to connect to the research base's computer systems and pulled the survey data for the site. The data compiled and an overlay appeared on his internal heads-up display, showing him the vast alien city with only a few buildings aboveground. Connor gasped and took a few steps away from

Lenora as he peeked through a synthetic window to another time. The aliens that lived here had constructed almost everything into a smooth, curved surface without any seams so the appearance was of one continuous piece. Multilevel pathways ran to and fro in an elaborate framework that connected all the buildings in the city.

Lenora peered at him curiously. "You see it, don't you?"

"It's amazing," Connor said in awe.

He almost hated to turn off the overlay on his HUD, but it wasn't something he could have on and safely walk around.

"So Mallory thinks you can use what we learn here as an alternative power source?" Lenora asked.

Connor told Lenora about his request for additional resources being denied for the space station.

"I see their point," Lenora said.

"Don't tell me you doubt the warning now, too," Connor replied.

"Something bad did happen to Earth. I don't doubt that, but why would it come all the way here? What kind of living entity does that?"

Connor shrugged. "Understanding is not a prerequisite for us to take action to defend the colony."

"Yeah, but at what cost? Do we stop building medical facilities in favor of outfitting a space station or whatever war machine the CDF can come up with for a threat that might never manifest? There has to be a balance."

Connor shook his head, not believing what she was saying.

"Look at yourself. I can see it written all over your face. Anyone who doesn't agree with you is dooming the colony and everyone in it," Lenora said.

Connor took a steadying breath. "You don't understand. Whatever this thing is wiped out all the militaries back home.

Wilkinson sent us that warning so we could prepare ourselves to face what's coming."

"And you have. For the past seven years you've worked yourself and everyone around you mercilessly. We have defense platforms, some godawful monstrosity of a space station equipped to fight off an armada, and the last chunk of the *Ark* is devoted to building another ship for the CDF to use. You've never once stopped and thought about what would happen if those things never showed up. What if they don't come for another forty or fifty years? How long can you keep this up?" Lenora asked.

"For as long as I have to until the job is done and you're safe," Connor replied.

Lenora pointed her finger at him like a knife. "Don't you dare say you're doing this for me. I didn't ask you to give up your life in order to work tirelessly for something that might never happen. You're doing this because you love the challenge. It's right up your alley—an intangible obstacle that you have to figure out how to overcome. *That's* why you're doing this."

"So defending the colony isn't a good enough reason?"

"Who are you fighting for?" Lenora shot back, holding her arms out wide. "Who is it? I want to know. You don't have me; you have the soldiers who report to you. So who is it that you fight for? What is it that drives you so hard?"

Connor snarled and turned away from her. Bull twisted his head to the side, looking at him curiously. Lenora came around to his other side so he had to face her.

"The mere thought of this threat not being real scares you more than anything else because it would mean you might have to move forward with your life without a war to fight. We're sixty light years from Earth and the pattern is just the same. You devoted yourself to stopping the Syndicate and you were willing to put everyone else aside, and you're doing the same thing again here," Lenora said.

"No, I'm not," Connor replied.

Lenora drew back in mock surprise. "Is that so? Then give up the Colonial Defense Force. Let someone else take command and stay here and explore these ruins with me. Right here. Right now. Do it."

Connor's heart pounded in his chest. His thoughts couldn't keep up with his emotions. "No one else can—" he began to say.

"Do what? Oversee the armed space station or train soldiers? Yes, they can. Your old platoon was on the *Ark* too, and Kasey Douglass is quite capable, as you've said on more than one occasion," Lenora said.

Her gaze bored mercilessly into his. Connor clenched his hands into fists. "I can't," he said, his voice sounding raw. "I can't sit by and let others fight, knowing there's something I could have done to help."

"You *can* help. You can stay here," Lenora said.

Connor glared at her. "You don't want me here."

"No, I never said that. You walked away from me. Remember?"

Connor swallowed hard and his throat felt thick. "There was too much to do."

"You've done enough. Let it go," Lenora said, and Connor heard the pleading in her tone.

She wasn't one for showing much of her feelings, but he could see it in her eyes. She must have been thinking of these things for a long time.

Connor glanced around and was thankful they were far enough away from other people that they couldn't be overheard. Then he saw Sean, who was pointedly looking away. The security detail assigned to Connor had to stay near him.

Suddenly, there were shouts coming up from inside the dig site, and Ramirez came running over to them.

"Sir, this place is amazing! There's a significant power source here," Ramirez said.

"Is there anything we can take with us?" Connor asked, his voice sounding husky.

Ramirez shook his head. "We need to run some extensive analyses of the systems before we start figuring out how to take it apart. We might be able to use the materials here and convert them as a base for our own power stations, but I'll need more than this small team to figure that out." Ramirez looked at Lenora with excitement. "This is an unbelievable find. My heartiest congratulations to you, Dr. Bishop."

Lenora thanked him.

Ramirez headed back to the research base, saying he needed to send a preliminary report back to Sierra.

Connor stepped closer to Lenora, and she stiffened. "I have to go," he said, hating the words.

Lenora narrowed her gaze. "Go then. Be with your squads, your platoons, your fleets, where you're in charge and can quell any argument anyone makes. Run away, Connor, just like you've always done. Run away from living a life worth remembering," Lenora said and stalked away from him.

Connor watched her go, at a complete loss for words. Bull walked next to her, following her into the dig site. Part of him wanted to lash out at her and scream how she was wrong about everything, especially him, but the words wouldn't come. Deep in the pit of his stomach a gnawing fear uncoiled inside him, whispering that Lenora's words were truer than he was willing to admit.

CHAPTER SIX

CONNOR SAT ALONE, brooding in the back of the combat shuttle. The CDF soldiers occupying the area closer to the cockpit spoke in hushed tones. They'd just left the archaeological dig site. He glared at the blank console in front of him. The harder he tried to push everything Lenora had said from his mind, the more he dwelled on it. He could hear echoes of his arguments with his ex-wife, though Lenora had done a much better job at getting to the point.

Reisman left his seat near the front of the shuttle and walked toward him. The former Ghost eyed him with an arched brow. "So, what'd you do this time?"

Reisman had known him too long to stand on ceremony, and he sat down in the seat next to him.

Connor sighed. "I work too much and I have control issues."

Reisman nodded.

Each of the former members of the Ghosts had experienced varied reactions when they were brought out of stasis aboard the *Ark*, but most of them had reacted much better than Connor.

"Do you ever think about everyone you left behind?" Connor asked.

"Of course, all the time," Reisman said. "Did I ever tell you about what my brother Jamie and I did camping one summer?"

Connor shook his head.

"There were eight of us, but since me and Jamie were so close in age, we stuck together. Strength in numbers. Anyway, one night we kept finding all these frogs roaming around the campground. It was like someone sent out a signal and frogs were everywhere. So we got one of those big five-gallon buckets and started tossing them in. No plan. We just kept catching them and tossing them in the bucket. Eventually, we caught so many frogs we had to drape a towel over the top to keep them from escaping. The bucket became so overloaded we could hardly carry it anymore, so we put it down. Some people walked by, coming from the communal showers. It was nighttime," Reisman said, frowning. "Not sure if I mentioned that or not. Me and Jamie looked up at the bathrooms and then back at our bucket of frogs at the same time." Reisman started laughing. "We knew better than to head directly toward it, so we circled around, using the woods for cover, and ended up on the women's side of the bathroom. We waited until the coast was clear and bolted to the door. We could hear the girls in the stalls and showers, but no one saw us in the doorway. We each took a side of the bucket and heaved it back like a battering ram. My little brother Jamie pulled the towel off at the last second and we must have sent hundreds of frogs into the bathroom," Reisman said, breaking off in fits of laughter, and Connor joined in.

"We hauled ass out of there so fast I think we lost the bucket. Within a minute or two we heard shrieking from the women's bathroom and then the park ranger came driving up to investigate. God, that was so much fun," Reisman said and sighed.

"Did they ever figure out it was you guys?" Connor asked.

Reisman shook his head. "Well, the next morning my dad asked us about the bucket that had gone missing, but before Jamie or I could make something up, he said something about hearing raccoons coming through the campsite the night before. He winked at us and kept whipping up some eggs for breakfast. We got some extra bacon that morning."

Connor snorted.

"So that's what I think of when I think about home," Reisman said, and he became somber. "It beats thinking about that other stuff . . . you know, the virus."

Connor nodded. He'd obsessed over that mysterious message Tobias had shown them all those years ago. They'd hoped that perhaps there were remnant pieces of the detailed data that was alluded to in the message on one of the buoys. They were wrong. Despite their resident tech genius, Noah Barker, and a number of other engineers' valiant attempts to extract data, it turned out to be simply and irrevocably gone.

"What about you? Do you ever think about home?" Reisman asked.

"Sometimes, but as the time goes by it gets harder to remember any of their faces, and it's not like the *Ark* had any of our personal files, since we weren't supposed to be here in the first place," Connor replied.

Not all the Ghosts had adapted well to colony life. Eventually, they'd joined the CDF, and at the time Connor was just happy to have their help. He should have realized that their willingness to devote themselves to this fight went hand in hand with their unwillingness to let go of everything they'd been forced to leave behind. Could he ever walk away from the CDF and leave its fate to someone else?

"General, we're starting our final approach to board the *Vigilant*," Sean's voice said over the speakers.

"Acknowledged," Connor replied, letting his own musings dissipate.

"Time to get back to work," Reisman said. All evidence of former mirth was erased.

"When we get aboard the ship, can you check that the updated targeting protocols for the missile-defense platforms have been pushed out across the system?" Connor asked.

"Yes, sir," Reisman said.

The *Vigilant* was their only heavy cruiser and was orbiting New Earth. Connor had no idea how the NA Alliance military had been convinced to give up a heavy cruiser and two Starwolf-class destroyers for the *Ark's* mission, but he was glad they had or their defense of New Earth would have been primarily near the planet itself.

An immediate sense of familiarity came over Connor as he made his way from the *Vigilant's* main hangar to the bridge. The stark gray battle-steel walls were a reminder of Connor's time in the Alliance military, although the uniforms were different. The colony's selection committee recruitment process did ensure that the people recruited had the skill sets to fly these ships, but they had the bare minimum experience to make them proficient at their jobs. The Colonial Defense Force was an amalgamation of the NA Alliance military branches since their numbers barely scraped above ten thousand soldiers, and even then the actual infantry was only a small portion of the CDF as a whole. They were relying heavily on automated defense platforms and drones. When putting the CDF together, Connor had tried to leverage every asset the colony had available, which made them significantly different than the militaries of old. He hoped it would be enough.

He entered the bridge and the ship's computer announced his presence. Colonel Ian Howe rose from the commander's chair on the raised platform central to the bridge. Like most of the higher-ranked officers in the CDF, he had the rank because he was the most experienced. However, Connor wasn't fooled. No matter how you sliced it, he commanded the most inexperienced military forces in the history of humankind.

"Welcome aboard the *Vigilant*, General," Colonel Howe said.

The colonel was a trim man whose mostly bald head sported close-cropped hair barely beginning to show a color closely matching that of the nearby bulkhead walls.

"Thank you, Colonel. What's the status of the *Banshee* and the *Wyatt*?" Connor asked.

"They're escorting the cargo carrier *Chmiel* to Titan Space Station. They departed ten hours ago," Colonel Howe said.

Connor nodded. "I think we've given them enough of a head start."

"We're ready to depart at your command, sir," Colonel Howe said.

"Make it so," Connor said.

Colonel Howe began issuing orders. The *Vigilant's* fusion reactor core increased its output to the main engines and the ship began moving away from New Earth.

"Comm, send a message to COMCENT that we've gone command blackout and will no longer be sending automated transponder updates for our ship's location," Colonel Howe said and gave Connor a nod once the communication was away.

Connor used his implants to activate a ship-wide broadcast. "Crew of the *Vigilant*, we're about to begin our combat operations drill. Our target will have no advance warning of our intentions and will act accordingly. This is as much a test of Major Corwin and Major Cross's reactions to us as it is to see how well you perform the orders you've been given. Combat drills are nothing new and we will continue to do them long after today. This is our time to prove ourselves and conduct ourselves with the highest orders of excellence. And if that doesn't motivate you, then how about a reminder being given to our two destroyer crews as to why a heavy cruiser is not to be underestimated in this star system."

Connor closed the broadcast and saw the hungry gleam in the eyes of the bridge crew. He looked over at Colonel Howe.

"I've invited senior staff to go over the plan, as well as a few ideas that have cropped up that I thought you might like to hear," Colonel Howe said.

Connor gestured for the colonel to lead the way.

CHAPTER SEVEN

OVER THE NEXT SEVERAL DAYS, Connor observed the crew of the *Vigilant* as they stalked their prey. The Starwolf-class destroyers were restricted to the cargo carrier's best speed. The *Banshee* and the *Wyatt* traded scouting sweeps, patrolling the area ahead of their escort. Their course headings took them near the missile-defense platforms, and Connor noted that they had applied the software updates for the onboard AI cyber warfare suite.

Major Savannah Cross of the destroyer *Banshee* proved to be the more dangerous player in the cat-and-mouse game Connor was executing. Since this was their home system, Major Cross did a fair number of active scans while on scout patrols and had nearly detected the *Vigilant*.

Major Alec Corwin of the destroyer *Wyatt* was a bit more conservative with active scans while on scout patrol and he didn't take his ship as far away from the ship he was escorting as Major Cross had. Both destroyers executed their orders as they saw fit, and there were risks to both of their approaches. Major Corwin liked to stay closer to the cargo carrier and would quickly be able to respond should the carrier run into trouble. Major Cross made wider patrol sweeps and so had more of an insight into the surrounding area but would take longer to respond if the cargo ship got in trouble. Connor preferred Major Cross's approach and noted that in his report. Those reports and analyses would be made available to the destroyer commanders after the training exercise.

Connor also kept an ongoing report on how Colonel Howe and the crew of the *Vigilant* performed. There were times when the colonel had all the subtlety of a blunt instrument. The *Banshee* had almost detected them while Colonel Howe had been on duty and thought that running a scheduled scan of the system was acceptable. Colonel Howe was a good man, but he needed to break free of running his command by adhering to a checklist. Connor glanced over at Reisman, who was sitting across from him, working on his own terminal. They were in a strategy room near the bridge. Connor had taken over the room during his stay on the *Vigilant*.

Reisman was studying a data readout from last night's logs. His green eyes slipped into calculation, and he seemed to reach some sort of conclusion. He noticed Connor watching him. "They can't all be Kasey Douglass," Reisman said.

"No, they can't," Connor replied. "That's the thing I always noticed about ship commanders who've spent too much time on a certain type of vessel. They tend to think only in terms of the vessel's well-established practices and aren't willing to push the limits. Colonel Howe is a good commander. He can get things done, but he lacks a certain finesse when it comes to all this sneaking around."

"Well he does have quite a large ship with great big guns and what not," Reisman said.

Connor glanced over at Sean, who sat at a different terminal. "What do you think?"

Sean twisted his mouth into a thoughtful frown. "He's not a hunter. He commands the ship, firm in the knowledge that he has the tactical weapons advantage in any engagement."

Reisman looked at Connor. "*Colonist.*" He snorted. "You've corrupted this young man."

"Corrupted or not, he's exactly right. The question is what to do about it," Connor said.

"You could shift the ship commanders around, but then you'd need to account for a learning curve. I would suggest taking the straightforward approach—telling him what he's doing wrong," Reisman said.

Connor had already made up his mind but was curious to see what Sean and Reisman would suggest. Sean had great instincts for engagement and had grown into an excellent leader.

"We're due to be on the bridge, sir," Sean said and closed his terminal session.

Reisman did the same and rose from his seat.

"Time to scare the crap out of a few people," Connor said.

They entered the bridge and Connor went over to the command area where Colonel Howe sat. Connor sat in the seat next to him.

"Tactical, confirm the position of the decoys and put it up on the main holoscreen," Colonel Howe said.

The output on the main holoscreen updated to show the current position of the cargo carrier, along with its destroyer escorts. Then fourteen red dots appeared for each of the decoys they'd deployed. When their transponders went active, they would do so with different classes of warship identifications, and the decoys could also generate the drive signature of vessels both large and small.

Connor used his implants to check a few data feeds and saw something that gave him pause. "Tactical, don't activate the decoys yet. We just need them to check in on the passive channels. It will take longer because of the distance, but it won't give away their position just yet."

The tactical officer paled. "Yes, General. I'm sorry. I was just looking to get the quickest response possible."

Colonel Howe glanced at Connor. "Pre-mission jitters."

"We're playing poker, and once this thing begins we'll see how well Corwin and Cross can play," Connor said.

CHAPTER EIGHT

MAJOR ALEC CORWIN slouched in the commander's chair on the bridge of the *Wyatt*. They'd been at this combat patrol for nearly a week and it was extremely tedious work. However, the work seemed to suit Savannah Cross just fine; she loved this stuff. Corwin would have preferred to see a bit more action. Weapons training on nearby asteroids was more fulfilling than running escort duty. It was thrilling to fire the rail-guns and missiles, giving the destroyer's weapons system a chance to clear its throat.

There was nothing out here that hadn't been placed here by the CDF. He glanced at his terminal, and it was the same as before. All the weapons platforms in the system were active and their onboard diagnostics indicated that they were functioning normally. Perhaps on one of the next scouting missions he'd push the engines a little more as a way to break up the monotony. The crew always appreciated that. There was only so much a person could learn running training drills anyway.

"Major, I've detected an anomaly with the last passive scan," Lieutenant Green said.

"On screen," Corwin ordered.

The main screen showed the scan data from the most recent passive scan. There were two anomalous detections, and Corwin glanced at his tactical officer.

"The second one was just detected, Major. The computer matches the drive signature to that of a Raptor-class cruiser," Lieutenant Green said.

"Comms, are we being hailed?" Corwin asked.

"No, Major," Lieutenant Kordek replied.

Corwin pressed his lips together in a thoughtful frown. "Can you confirm these are actual ships and not decoys?"

"Running diagnostics on the system. It checks out," Lieutenant Green replied.

"Run an active scan of the area," Corwin said.

"Major," Kordek said, "Captain Benson of the *Chmiel* is asking for a status update. He says that the two ships are appearing on his sensors as well."

Corwin sat up in his chair. If those ships were being detected on a cargo carrier's sensors, they must be closer than initially thought.

"Comms, open a channel back to COMCENT," Corwin said.

"Sir, the time lapse is over an hour," Lieutenant Kordek said.

"Okay, never mind that—"

"Sir, one of the ships is on an intercept course," Lieutenant Green said. "Make that both of them."

Corwin sat in the command chair with an ugly twisting feeling churning in his gut. If those ships weren't decoys, could they be part of the alien fleet that had rampaged Earth? Could they have made it here already? And how would they have gotten this far into the system without being detected? Surely the automated defenses for the turrets and missile-defense platforms would have detected them.

"They're heading right for us, Major," Lieutenant Green said. "What are your orders?"

Corwin's mouth became dry and he couldn't tear his eyes off the main screen.

"Three more ships detected, sir."

"Orders, Major."

Corwin sat in the chair, unable to move or think. This couldn't be happening. This must be some kind of drill, but what if it wasn't? He was out here with just one other destroyer. There was no way they could stand against Raptor-class cruisers. The armament differential was too great, and they already knew the *Wyatt* was here.

"What are your orders, Major?" Lieutenant Green's voice went up an octave.

The breath caught in Corwin's throat as he tried to think of something they could do.

"Any response to our hails?" Major Savannah Cross asked.

"No, Major," Lieutenant Daniels said.

"Okay, they had their chance. Action stations, set Condition One," Major Cross said. "Helm, move us ahead of the *Chmiel*. Operations, I want the anomalies designated by groups, beginning with alpha. Tactical, I want firing solutions ready to go, both long and short range, if any of them decide to close in."

Her orders were confirmed and carried out. Savannah peered at the main screen, which showed that the *Wyatt* hadn't changed course.

"Comms, link up the ship's systems to any defense platforms in the area. Tactical, I want you to account for missile platforms' capabilities in your firing solution. If these really are hostiles, I want to be able to return fire as soon as possible," Savannah said.

"Yes, Major," Lieutenant Daniels said.

Captain John Elder, who sat next to her, leaned over. "Major, with so many potential hostiles in the area, should we necessarily wait for them to fire their weapons first before we engage?"

Savannah eyed him for a moment. "You know the rules of engagement. We're away from COMCENT, and until they make their intentions known, I don't want to be the one to fire first. We'll tag them so they know we mean business but won't fire our weapons just yet."

Captain Elder nodded, but he still looked pale. Savannah understood his concern. With five potential hostiles, three of them cruiser-class or above, they might not survive the first salvo.

"Comms, any word from the *Wyatt*?" Savannah asked and was unable to keep a tinge of annoyance from her voice.

"No, Major. I've tried to reach them multiple times, but they won't respond," Lieutenant Daniels replied.

"Open a comlink to the *Chmiel*," Savannah said.

A successful connection to the cargo carrier registered on the main screen.

"Captain Benson, I need you to update your course to the space station with the one we're sending you now," Savannah said.

"Course received," Captain Benson said, his voice sounding relieved. "We tried to reach Major Corwin but haven't had a reply."

"They could be having an issue with their communications array," Savannah said.

John Elder glanced at her, making his opinion of Major Corwin known with just a passing look.

Savannah shrugged.

"Use best speed available and we'll cover you," Savannah said.

"Understood, Major, and thank you," Benson replied.

The comlink was severed and she looked at her comms officer.

"Still no reply from the *Wyatt*, Major."

Savannah nodded. She hoped he was having a communications issue and just couldn't respond. "Computer, record the following," she said, and the status on the main holoscreen showed that the computer was ready. "Major Corwin, I've sent the *Chmiel* an updated navigation course for Titan Space Station. Our current firing solution will cover their escape for a time. We've been unsuccessful in opening a comlink to the *Wyatt*. If you're receiving this, can you go on an intercept course to the cargo carrier to protect them in the event that these anomalies do prove to be hostiles? End recording. Send message."

"Message sent, Major," Lieutenant Daniels said.

"Contact!" Lieutenant Brennan said. "Incoming missiles detected."

Savannah swung her gaze to the main screen. The missiles were almost on top of them. They shouldn't have been able to get this close and avoid detection. "Launch countermeasures. Evasive maneuvers," Savannah said.

Since they were already at battle stations, the bridge crew was strapped to their chairs.

"Tactical, launch firing solutions alpha, bravo, and charlie groups," Savannah said.

Savannah noted the time and waited for the confirmation that their weapons had successfully fired. She watched as the main screen showed missiles closing in on the *Banshee*. They each had an unknown designation, so she didn't even know who the hell was firing on them. There had been no communication from the hostile ships.

"Still waiting on that confirmation, tactical," Savannah snapped.

"I'm sorry, Major. I authorized the firing solutions as you ordered. The system won't respond," Lieutenant Brennan said.

"Major, we're being hailed by General Gates on the *Vigilant*. Transponder codes and authorization clearance are a match," Lieutenant Daniels said.

Savannah's brows pulled together and she narrowed her gaze. "On screen," she said.

General Gates' face appeared on the main screen. "Major Cross, stand down. This is a training exercise designed to test your actions against a surprise attack force."

Savannah clenched her teeth. General Gates had a reputation for being opportunistic with his training exercises. She felt her racing heartbeat slow down but only slightly. "Acknowledged, General. *Banshee* will stand down."

General Gates' hard gaze softened for a moment. "Major Cross, please congratulate your crew on their exemplary performance. They did well, but there's a lot of room for improvement, as I'm sure you're aware. I want you to review the data from this encounter and in the next twenty-four hours I want you to present to me ten alternative actions you could have taken. *Vigilant* out."

General Gates' face disappeared as the comlink was severed. Savannah blew out a breath and John Elder did the same.

"Alright, you heard the general. This was a training exercise. Set action stations to condition three. I want the entire dataset from this encounter, beginning with the first onset of the anomaly detection, put up in the simulators so we can start running combat scenarios against them," Savannah said.

"How does he already know that we could have done better, Major?" John asked.

"Because General Gates designed this whole encounter. Do you think he didn't already have more than a few tactical solutions on how best to deal with this scenario ready to go?" Savannah asked.

"I see your point, Major," John replied.

She got up from her seat and walked over to Lieutenant Brennan. Her tactical officer's hands shook as he tried to work through the menu options on his terminal.

"You didn't do anything wrong. You followed my orders, which is exactly what you were supposed to do," Savannah said.

Lieutenant Brennan sucked in a deep breath and glanced up at her. "It all happened so fast. I don't know what I could have done differently, Major."

"That's the whole point of this exercise. The secrecy of its execution was the best way to test us. I know once we all calm down and put our heads together we'll improve our performance. Let's get to work, shall we?" Savannah said.

"Yes, Major, and thank you," Brennan replied.

Savannah went back to her command chair.

"What the hell happened to the *Wyatt*?" John asked.

Savannah nodded. "An excellent question and one I'm keen to know the answer to myself," she said and pressed her lips together. "One of the first scenarios I'd like to run is a coordinated response that includes the *Wyatt*."

"But they weren't available during the encounter," John said.

"Doesn't matter. We know the capabilities of our own ship, and that's a resource we have available. The fact of the matter is that if this had been a true encounter, we would have died. Don't get me wrong, we would have bloodied the enemy, but we would have died or come close to it. We need to devise a way to respond to that scenario where we don't lose our capacity to fight, and we only have twenty-four hours to do it," Savannah said.

"Understood, Major."

Savannah nodded. "Call in your reserves to the bridge. We'll need all hands working on this for the time being. I want ideas and solutions for the current engagement, and don't be afraid to stretch the encounter with a couple of 'what if'-type scenarios."

The call went out and Savannah sent her orders to the rest of the crew, bringing them up to speed. She knew there was a better way to respond to the threat they'd just faced. Now she needed to set her mind to finding the best solution so the next time General Gates wanted to test them, the *Banshee*, at least, would be ready for the encounter.

CHAPTER NINE

CONNOR COULD SCARCELY KEEP the scowl from his face. The comlink to the destroyer *Wyatt* had just been closed. Throughout his military career he'd seen all manner of people who'd frozen up at the first real sign of danger, but this was the first time he'd seen the commander of a damn destroyer do so. Had this been the NA Alliance military, Major Alec Corwin would have been relieved of duty and replaced with a more capable commander.

He sat in the officers' conference room near the bridge with Reisman and Sean across from him, and they were joined by Colonel Howe and Major Nathan Hayes.

"The shit hit the fan," Connor said. "I can't have a destroyer commander freezing up like that. By all accounts, it was Corwin who failed to even execute a rudimentary response to the hostile forces in this exercise. Where was his XO?"

"She was performing an inspection in Engineering when the attack occurred," Major Nathan Hayes, XO of the *Vigilant*, answered.

Colonel Howe leaned forward. "Captain Mattison hightailed

it to the bridge shortly after the attack began, but by then the damage had already been done. That crew has suffered a major blow to their morale that I'm not sure they can recover from."

"So that's one for replacing Alec Corwin as the commanding officer of the *Wyatt*," Connor said and looked at Major Hayes.

"There's a pool of candidates we can draw from if we go that route, and I agree with the colonel. Major Corwin should be relieved of command," Major Hayes said.

"General, meaning no disrespect to anyone here, but I disagree," Sean said.

Connor glanced at him, considering. "Care to elaborate, Captain?"

"The training drills are designed to expose weaknesses so they can be addressed. Simply yanking Corwin off that ship won't help us in the long run," Sean said.

Connor narrowed his eyes thoughtfully. "There are some things you don't get a second chance on. The lives of the hundred and fifty crewmembers aboard the *Wyatt* depend on their chain of command not faltering at the first sign of danger. I'd initially thought his approach to escort duty was on the conservative side, but now I'm thinking Major Corwin was just being lazy."

Reisman brought up some data on his personal holoscreen. "General, there's nothing in his performance history that indicates a dereliction of duty. If you're taking votes, sir, mine is to allow the major to complete the escort duty and return to New Earth. Then we can decide what to do with him."

Connor sighed and looked at all of them. "Two of you think I should yank him out of the chair and two of you think I should give him another shot. You guys are no help."

Reisman chuckled. "One other thing to consider is the amount of time that went into training Major Corwin. I know

Captain Mattison. She's a topnotch officer, and I'm sure things would have been different had she actually been on the bridge."

"That's not good enough," Connor said.

Colonel Howe cleared his throat and drummed his fingers on the table. "I may have been hasty with my recommendation. I'd like to see what Major Corwin and his crew can come up with in terms of solutions to the combat drill. To me, that will be very telling as to whether he should be left in command."

Connor nodded. "I agree. Okay, let's move on to the *Banshee*. Wil, put the simulation up on the main screen."

Reisman tapped a few commands into his personal terminal and the main holoscreen came on.

Connor leaned back in his chair and watched the simulation play out. This gave an accurate representation of how Major Savannah Cross had handled the combat drill.

"She's a scrapper," Connor said. "She tried to hail the unknowns, and when they didn't respond she had her tactical team formulate multiple firing solutions. Those firing solutions provided the maximum coverage for the cargo carrier, and she even sent an updated course to Captain Benson of the *Chmiel*, which was accounted for in her plans. Pause the simulation," Connor said. "She followed the rules of engagement and even tried to leverage use of the missile-defense platforms nearby. If I had another heavy cruiser, I'd give it to her right now. Alright, resume the simulation and let's see how this plays out."

The combat simulation sped forward, and the destroyer was able to extract a heavy toll from the enemy forces, but there was still a ninety percent certainty that the *Banshee* would have been destroyed.

"Look at that. The computer shows an eighty percent estimate that the *Chmiel* would have escaped the encounter unscathed," Sean said.

"That's right. So now, a test for *you* guys. What could Major Cross have done differently that would have allowed her ship to survive the encounter?" Connor said and looked squarely at Colonel Howe.

"I see this is for me," Colonel Howe said and narrowed his gaze thoughtfully. "Assuming the raiders or enemy forces were only after the cargo carrier, she could have leveraged that to her advantage, using them as bait to draw them farther inside the envelope of the missile-defense platforms. That would have given her more cover and provided protection for the cargo carrier."

"That's not bad. Wil, can you input Ian's changes into the simulation and see how that plays out?" Connor said.

Reisman nodded and began updating the parameters for the simulation. "Okay, playing back at one-half speed."

They watched as the simulation played out. The *Banshee* did survive the encounter but still sustained significant damage.

"I think that, given the situation, drawing the enemy forces toward the missile-defense envelope is a good way to go. The one thing that's missing is the other destroyer," Connor said, and Colonel Howe's eyes lit up in understanding. "If Corwin and Cross had coordinated their efforts, they would not only have survived the attack but inflicted significant damage on the enemy. This represents one of my primary concerns." Connor glanced at the *Vigilant's* commander and XO. "We're too siloed in our approach to enemy engagement. I take partial responsibility for that. We need to come up with some combat drills of our own that necessitate the coordinated use of our resources."

Colonel Howe nodded. "I see what you're saying. I don't think I would have seen it if it hadn't been thrown in my face."

"That's why we train. I want you to have a private word with Major Corwin and lay it out for him. His job is on the line if he can't convince me that he deserves to be in the commander's chair. I also want Major Cross informed that she's promoted to squadron commander," Connor said.

"Yes, General," Colonel Howe said.

"I know you have a ship to run, Colonel, but I want the tactical officers rotated through here to undergo these simulations and propose changes of their own. The best ones become the standard for the CDF Fleet."

CHAPTER TEN

MAJOR SAVANNAH CROSS splashed cold water on her face and then patted her cheeks and neck down with a towel. The commanding officer's room had its own private bathroom. She would have loved to have a shower, but short on time, she'd elected to get some chow instead. If she were being particularly wishful, a swim in one of the lakes near Sierra would have drained the tension right out of her. She wondered if she could convince the engineers who designed the next class of starships to include a lap pool.

She deposited the towel into the reclamation canister that would separate the water from the towel for recycling, then ran a brush through her short blonde hair and put on a fresh uniform. She and her crew had been working for twelve hours straight, poring over the recorded events from the last combat drill. They'd come up with some clever alternative actions that she was sure would meet General Gates' criteria for success. While the various teams worked in shifts, Savannah and John Elder had taken turns working with them all to come up with acceptable alternatives that would change the outcome of the combat training exercise. Between that and the fact that she'd already been awake for a long time before the "attack," she hadn't slept for almost thirty hours, but she'd managed to get four hours' rack time and was preparing to meet with her XO to finalize their simulations on alternative ways they could have handled General Gates' surprise training exercise.

Her personal terminal alerted an incoming call, voice only.

"Yes," Savannah said.

"Major, I have a comlink from Major Corwin, who'd like to speak with you privately, ma'am," Lieutenant Kordek said.

Savannah frowned. Had the shift changed already? She glanced at the ship's clock.

"Alright, put him through," Savannah said.

Major Corwin's thin face appeared on her terminal. He looked haggard, as if he hadn't slept much. He was speaking to her from his own quarters on the *Wyatt*.

"What can I do for you, Alec?" Savannah asked.

"Thank you for speaking with me," Major Corwin said.

Savannah nodded. "I'm due to meet with my team in a few minutes."

"That's what I wanted to speak with you about—the presentation to General Gates."

Savannah watched as Corwin's brown eyes slipped into calculation while he considered what he was going to say.

"Savannah, I messed up big time," Corwin said and sighed.

Savannah felt the skin around her eyes tighten for a moment and then she sat down. "What happened to you?"

Corwin shook his head. "I froze. When those ships started to appear, I panicked. I knew what I was supposed to do, the ROE and protocols we were to follow. I even remembered all the training drills we'd done as a crew, but when it came down to it, I just couldn't . . ."

Savannah leaned toward the holoscreen. "You screwed up. You can't change that, but the fact that they haven't taken your command away means you're getting a chance to convince them you belong in the commander's chair."

Corwin nodded and swallowed hard. "I know, it's just . . . I saw how you responded to them. How'd you even do that? You were ready to lay it all on the line."

"I hit back, but there were things we could have done much better. As for how I knew what to do," Savannah said and speared a look at the floundering destroyer commander, "we're here to protect the colony against any threat that comes our way. I stuck to our mission parameters—protect the cargo carrier. If you think you can't do that, it's your responsibility to take yourself out of that chair and let your XO finish the mission. The way I see it, you can try to pull the pieces together and learn from your mistakes because General Gates is never going to let up. He's relentless in the training of the CDF because he believes there's a threat coming for all of us from Earth. It's what drives him, and it's what drives me. Why are you here?" Savannah asked.

Corwin's eyebrows pulled together. "Same as you. To protect the colony."

"Well then, get back to work instead of talking to me," Savannah said.

Corwin regarded her for a moment and nodded. "Thank you, Major Cross."

The holoscreen went blank as the call ended, and Savannah shook her head. She hoped Corwin could pull himself together both for himself and the sake of his crew. He wasn't a bad person, but he lacked motivation. Had Corwin been under her command, she'd have ridden him until he either broke or rose up and confirmed his right to wear the uniform. The *Banshee's* crew was no stranger to her no-nonsense attitude.

She rose from the chair and left her quarters. They had a few hours until their meeting with General Gates, and she aimed to squeeze every ounce of productivity from her crew during the time they had left.

She headed to the bridge, and the ship's computer announced her presence as she approached the commander's chair, currently occupied by Captain Elder.

"What have you got?" Savannah asked.

Elder's face lit up and he glanced over at Lieutenant Green, who worked at his tactical station. "I think you're going to be impressed with what we've come up with."

"We'll see about that. Dazzle me," Savannah said.

The crew of the *Banshee* had come together during this exercise and Savannah felt her chest swell with pride for her crew. She knew Alec Corwin had a much harder road to travel to get the same from his crew and hoped he rose to the task. If not, she might have to replace her XO because he was a prime candidate to take command of the *Wyatt*.

CHAPTER ELEVEN

GENERAL GATES TO INFIRMARY TWO.

The announcement resonated along the corridor Connor was in since the ship's computer would only send the message to his location. He'd been speaking with the *Vigilant's* lead engineer, who had an idea about updating the cooling systems for the rail-cannons.

"Increasing the rail-cannons' rate of fire is extremely important. Run the numbers for your proposal, and if they check out, we can try it," Connor said.

"Will do, General," Major James Hatly said.

They left the forward aft gunnery area, where Connor had been making good on his promise to personally visit different sections of the ship.

He glanced at Reisman. "Where's Howe?" Connor asked.

The *Vigilant's* commanding officer was overdue to meet with them.

"According to his locator, he's already at the infirmary," Reisman said.

Connor frowned and pulled up the ship's layout on his internal heads-up display. The *Vigilant* had two medical bays on the ship, each located mid-ship toward either the bow or the stern. They made their way through the ship, soldiers giving way to Connor. As they closed in on the medical bay, there was a line of pale-looking soldiers waiting to be seen.

Connor quickened his pace and walked into the bay. There were beds along the far wall, and all of them were occupied. Doctors and nurses were rushing around, all of them with face masks on to block contagions. Connor glanced to the side where a desk clerk sat. Multiple people surrounded the desk, all asking questions at once. There was a clear plastic container that had more face masks, and Connor reached in and grabbed two of them. He tossed one to Reisman and put the other one on.

The desk clerk glanced at him, noting the gold collars of his uniform.

"Dr. Allen is down over there, sir," the clerk said.

Connor thanked her and headed in the direction the clerk had gestured. They came to an area of the medical bay that was sealed off from everyone else, and he saw several medical personnel surrounding two beds that were just beyond the barrier. Connor peered inside and his eyes widened. Lying on the bed closest to him was Colonel Ian Howe, and right next to him was his XO, Major Nathan Hayes. They were both intubated.

"This doesn't look good," Reisman said.

"No, it doesn't," Connor replied grimly.

Connor pressed the button on the comlink for the quarantine area. "Is Dr. Allen in there?"

One of the doctors leaned away from the others, who were still huddled around the two patients. Dr. Allen waved to Connor and then quickly spoke to his colleagues before going through the airlock separating the two areas. The medical officer waited in the airlock, going through decontamination protocols, and then came out.

"General, thank you for coming so quickly," Dr. Allen said.

"What's going on, doctor?" Connor asked.

"The colonel and major are experiencing symptoms of an acute allergic reaction and we're trying to identify the source," Dr. Allen said.

Connor glanced over at Ian Howe. "That looks like more than an allergic reaction to something."

"We intubated them to force the airway to stay clear and induced a medical coma," Dr. Allen said.

"You have them quarantined. What's the risk to the rest of the crew?" Connor asked.

Epidemics on a ship could be catastrophic if the crew couldn't perform their jobs.

"Only a precaution in case we've missed something," Dr. Allen said.

"We saw a line of soldiers waiting to get in here. Has this thing already spread?"

"Too soon to tell. What I know so far is that the colonel and the major ate at the same mess hall, and there have been several allergic reactions experienced by other soldiers who ate there—anything from upset stomach to severe vomiting. In extreme cases, the soldiers in question have reported problems breathing," Dr. Allen said.

Connor pulled off his face mask. "So if it's something they ingested, I don't need to wear this mask."

"Correct, General. As the ranking officer on this ship, I must inform you that you are now the commanding officer of the *Vigilant.* I will send you status updates every hour unless something changes, but I expect you'll be wanting to go to the bridge," Dr. Allen said.

Connor took another look at the bedridden colonel and major. He pulled up each of their files on his internal heads-up display, and neither of them had any known allergies.

"Very well. If you need anything to get them back on their feet, you let me know," Connor said.

"Yes, of course, General," Dr. Allen said.

Connor and Reisman left the medical bay. He opened a comlink to the bridge.

"Who has the con?" Connor asked.

"I do, General. Lieutenant Vladimir LaCroix."

"I want three security teams to make a sweep of the mess halls, looking for any signs of tampering or spoilage, and I want it done with the cooperation of the officer in charge," Connor said.

"Do you suspect foul play, General?" Lieutenant LaCroix asked.

"I'm not sure, Sergeant. I'm on my way to the bridge," Connor said and switched off the comlink.

"It's a good question," Reisman said.

"I don't think anyone deliberately sabotaged our food storage, but we need to rule it out. I *am* concerned that the senior officers were more affected than the others so far," Connor said.

"I guess it was luck that we're here," Reisman said.

"If we were lucky, no one would be getting sick. The question is: what changed? The *Vigilant* has made multiple trips to the Titan Space Station," Connor said and pressed his lips together. He opened a comlink to Sean Quinn. "Listen, I need you and your team to review the change logs for critical ship systems, particularly things like food and water, but expand it to filtration systems and our air supply. And we need a list of soldiers who've accessed those systems within the last forty-eight hours."

"At once, General," Sean answered.

Once the comlink went dark, Reisman cleared his throat. "Your protégé is coming along nicely."

Connor arched a brow. "Sean is quite capable."

"Yes, he is, and he goes to great lengths to serve at your side," Reisman said.

Connor shrugged. "I'll admit I do like him. He gets things done and has good instincts. Remind me to tell you how he came to be under my command."

Reisman grinned. "Diaz already told me about that. The kid stored himself in a high-impact storage crate you promptly dumped out of the troop carrier for a low-altitude drop-off at that first training camp. Kid's lucky to be alive."

"You can say that again. Fortunate for him, he stored himself with some delicate equipment so there was adequate padding. Sean has proven to be quite a soldier. If we were back home, I'd have recruited him to be part of the Ghosts," Connor said.

Reisman's eyes widened. "Now that *is* high praise. Too bad Diaz prefers to stay planet-side these days he would have made a good addition to the Ghosts as well."

Connor nodded. Juan Diaz was part of the Colonial Defense Force but was on leave now for the birth of his second child. Diaz had requested a post that allowed him to train infantry troops, which would keep him planet-side and much closer to home. Diaz was his first friend in the colony, and Connor made a mental note to check in on him when he returned to New Earth.

They entered the bridge and Lieutenant LaCroix surrendered the commander's chair to him.

Connor sat in the chair and opened a broadcast channel to the entire ship. "Crew of the *Vigilant*, this is General Gates. A short while ago I was informed that both Colonel Howe and

Major Hayes are in the medical bay due to a severe allergic reaction and are being carefully watched over by the chief medical officer, Major Richard Allen. Therefore, I'm assuming command of this ship. We will continue with our mission, which is to escort the cargo vessel *Chmiel* to Titan Space Station, as well as make our own delivery of supplies. Stay focused on your assignments and continue to execute your duties with the absolute excellence I've come to expect from this crew. Gates out."

Reisman sat in the XO's chair next to his.

"Comms," Connor said, "there will be a medical briefing circulated throughout the ship. I want to be informed the moment it's sent out."

"Yes, General," Sergeant Boers said. "Oh, General, I have Major Cross and Major Corwin standing by."

Connor glanced over at Reisman.

"We're scheduled to review their proposed solutions for the combat drill," Reisman reminded him.

"Ah yes. Lost track of time. Put them through," Connor said.

A few seconds later both Major Cross and Major Corwin appeared on the main screen.

"I apologize for the delay," Connor said and told the two destroyer commanders what had happened. "Major Cross, as squad commander for the destroyer group, you'll present first, but before you begin I have a few things I'd like to say to you both."

Savannah Cross gave him a firm nod and Alec Corwin looked as if he expected to be yelled at.

"No doubt you and your crews have spent the last twenty-four hours going over the combat scenario that was part of the drill. You were tasked with providing multiple solutions to the engagement, and given the circumstances, I expect there to be some overlap in your approach, so don't be alarmed if that happens. Is that understood?" Connor asked.

Both of them said yes.

Connor swung his gaze toward Major Corwin. "Let's get the elephant out of the room, shall we, Major?"

Corwin looked startled to be spoken to and Connor felt his temper rising.

"Major Corwin, I expect nothing but complete professionalism for the duration of this meeting," Connor said.

Corwin directed his gaze into the camera. "Yes, General."

Connor glanced over at Major Cross. "I think we're ready to begin."

Over the next few hours, both majors presented their solutions to the combat drill engagement. As Connor expected, Major Savannah Cross had done her homework and improved on even his own plans for how the combat scenario should have been addressed. Alec Corwin did come up with acceptable solutions to the combat drill, but there was still a lingering doubt in Connor's mind as to whether Corwin should remain in command of that ship.

"I think everyone here has learned a great deal. Savannah, I particularly enjoyed the solution whereby you used the *Chmiel* as bait to entice the enemy forces to come within the missile-defense platform's envelope. It was a bold move, and I concur with the line of thinking that the cargo ship was already at risk and could, therefore, be leveraged as an asset while not increasing the risk to it," Connor said.

"Thank you, General," Major Cross said.

Connor gave her an approving smile. "We'll use some of these solutions as the training standard."

Connor swung his gaze to Major Corwin and pressed his lips together.

"Major Corwin," Connor said sternly.

"Yes, General."

"Is Captain Mattison with you?" Connor asked.

Major Corwin frowned for a moment. "No, sir . . . I . . . she's on the bridge."

Connor glanced over at Sergeant Boers at the comms station. "Open a comlink to the *Wyatt's* bridge."

A third window opened, showing a young dark-skinned woman. She was standing near the command chair and gave Connor a determined look.

"Captain Delta Mattison, I'm ordering you to assume command of the destroyer *Wyatt* as the ranking officer on the ship," Connor said and looked over at Major Corwin. "Major, you are hereby relieved of duty as commander of the *Wyatt*. You are confined to your quarters until we reach Titan Space Station, and arrangements will be made to take you back to New Earth. Your performance in command of the *Wyatt* was reprehensible, and no amount of pathetic looks is going to convince me to give you a second chance. The soldiers serving aboard that ship would not get a second chance if they all died because you froze up at the first sign of battle. This next part is for all of you," Connor said and glanced at the rest of them. "I know it's become a popular notion to question whether there really is an attack force heading to this star system. Our job in the Colonial Defense Force isn't to agree one way or another, but I think you know what I believe. Regardless, every one of us has to be prepared for the unexpected. We don't have a fleet of ships at our disposal. We're all we've got for the time being. It will be years before we build enough ships to defend the colony. Major Corwin, I want you to think long and hard about your performance and the road that led you to where you are today. You're not commanding officer material, but perhaps there's some other way you can contribute to the CDF. As commanding officers, we set the standard, and it would be outright negligence on my part to leave you in command of that ship."

Major Corwin's shoulders slumped and a flush swept across his face. A moment later he stood up straight and gave a salute. "Yes, sir," Corwin said, and the video feed cut out.

Connor softened his gaze and looked over at Delta Mattison. "Captain, are you equipped to carry out the orders I've given you?"

Captain Mattison stood ramrod straight. "Yes, sir."

Connor bobbed his head. "Okay then. I'll need a list of candidates who can serve as your XO, at least until we return to New Earth."

"Yes, General," Captain Mattison said.

Connor looked at Reisman. "Send the data burst to them now."

Reisman opened a menu on his terminal and, after a few moments, said, "Encrypted orders sent, sir."

Connor turned back to the main screen. "Alright, ladies, time for the real fun to begin. What Colonel Reisman has sent over is an updated mission plan for Titan Space Station. At the *Chmiel's* best speed, we're still several days out from Titan Space Station. However, we can and will go much faster than that. I expect you to review the plans with your crew. If you have any suggestions, I want to hear about it."

"General, may I ask a question?" Major Cross asked.

"Yes, Major."

"Colonel Douglass is in command of the Space Station. Won't he expect something like this?"

"I know I've developed something of a reputation for springing training missions when you least expect them, and I'd hate to disappoint Colonel Douglass. He and I have served together for a long time. If anything, these surprise drills teach us how we will react in tough situations," Connor said.

"Grace under pressure, sir," Major Cross said.

"Yes, and if we succeed, you have my permission to lord it over Colonel Douglass whenever you see him," Connor said.

"I'll do my best, General," Major Cross said.

Connor dismissed the two of them so they would have time to review the details of his planned assault on the space station.

"She's right. Kasey is expecting something like this," Reisman said.

"He better be or I'll bust him down to private," Connor said.

"I have a question, if you don't mind," Reisman said.

"Go ahead, Wil."

"Major Corwin. Had you already decided to relieve him of command, or did you decide during the presentation?" Reisman asked.

"I meant everything I said before. If I wasn't convinced he should be in command, then he was done. The thing I'm debating now is whether to send you over to the *Wyatt* to take command," Connor said.

"Wouldn't be my first tour of duty on a destroyer. If you give the order, I'll go over there and whip that ship into shape, but you might miss me," Reisman said with a wry grin.

"Watch it or you'll draw that short straw to be the pregnant woman this time," Connor said.

Reisman's eyes lit up. "Samson Denton! God, he hated when that happened to him. Too bad we don't have any of those Ghost combat suits here. I could have a lot of fun with that."

Connor laughed. "Let's go over our assault plan with the rest of this crew. I really want to catch Kasey off guard."

"If you really want to catch him off guard, you should send

Sean in with a small team to temporarily disable some key systems," Reisman said.

Connor's eyebrows rose. "That's not a bad idea. Too bad we don't have any stealth combat shuttles."

"Therein lies the fun," Reisman said.

Connor shook his head. "We're not modifying our shuttles. The heat stabilizers are there for a reason and I won't risk a shuttle for the sake of a training mission."

"Fine," Reisman said, feigning disappointment. "I'll come up with another way."

"I'm sure you will," Connor said and glanced at the main holoscreen, which now showed a star map and their trajectory to the space station.

Connor studied the area beyond the space station and sighed. For everything they'd accomplished in the past seven years, they still didn't know what was beyond the nearest buoy. Noah Barker had thrown himself at the problem, trying a multitude of ways to glean more intelligence from them. They'd even debated sending a deep-space probe out there as an early warning device. At least then they'd have some confirmation that an attack force was coming for them. But this was around the time Stanton Parish had been voted into office, and the proposal was denied. So Connor had devoted time and resources to Titan Space Station instead. The station was their first line of defense and he hoped it was enough. He'd much rather be the fool who was wrong than be right and have everyone else pay the price if the CDF failed.

CHAPTER TWELVE

NOAH RAN his fingers through his short-cropped hair as he waited for the latest diagnostic to finish for the modified HADES IV missile system. He'd ditched his long hair years ago when he joined the Colonial Defense Force. Sometimes he missed it, though having long hair wasn't the most practical of things to maintain. In truth, he liked not having to deal with it when he got up in the morning.

He was in a cramped engineering work area on Titan Space Station and had been for eight months, which was longer than he'd originally been assigned, but the work he was doing here was important. The bulk of Titan Space Station's infrastructure had been taken from the original *Ark*. On more than one occasion Noah'd had trouble imagining that the space station was once part of the massive colony ship that ferried over three hundred thousand humans to this star system. The original intention for the *Ark* had been to be broken up and taken to the surface of New Earth to be used by the colony. Those goals had changed.

The colony needed this outpost to monitor and scan for any threats that meant the colony harm. Titan Space Station was the first line of defense for the entire star system. They maintained their position relative to the nearest deep-space buoy. Over the years, Noah had come to appreciate the engineering marvel of the deep-space buoy network that was put in place as a means to bolster communication signals from Earth. He was also well aware of their shortcomings. For years he'd worked on trying to glean any piece of data off of the deep-space buoys that would give them some insight into what catastrophe had befallen Earth and whether there was an invasion force coming for the colony. He'd failed on both counts.

The powered door to the Engineering lab hissed open and Noah glanced behind him.

Kara walked in, carrying two cups of glorious, steaming coffee.

Noah perked up in his seat. "You're a saint. Thank you."

The edges of Kara's lips curved upward into a smile that exposed an adorable dimple on the side of her cheek. She handed him his coffee and set hers down.

"Where we at?" Kara asked.

Noah took a sip of his coffee and relished the taste of the creamy brew. "Oh, attempt number eight hundred and thirty-six . . . maybe thirty-seven," he said, bringing up the simulation iterance number and frowning.

"Only slightly off there, genius. You're at eight hundred and forty-seven. What did you change this time?" Kara asked.

She rested her hand on his shoulder and peered at the holo-screen in front of them.

Noah turned toward her and caught the sweet scent of the lavender shampoo she'd used.

Kara glanced at him and smiled, then gave him a quick peck on the lips and sat down.

"When I stopped thinking of these things as missiles and thought of them as small spacecraft, I had the idea of adding additional systems. Primarily I added a secondary targeting array and had the shielding for it pop off during its flight. I even added a third, which will enable the guidance system to stay on target and not get blinded by other detonations or point defense systems," Noah said.

Kara frowned and had the computer highlight the systems that were modified. "I can see that it's longer, but show me—" She stopped speaking and took control of the interface. The simulation showed that the HADES IV long-range missile had reconfigured itself during its flight toward its intended target. "I can see why Colonel Douglass was so excited by this."

"He just said that no matter what I changed, the missile still had to fit in the tube. But once it leaves the ship it doesn't need to retain its shape, which gives us some flexibility. It's not like there's any aerodynamics in the near vacuum of space," Noah said.

Kara frowned. "Yeah, but there *is* always a cost. The engines still need to push the added weight along. See, the range is cut down by twenty percent."

"Yeah, but it's more accurate. What's more important—that we hit our target or how far away we can miss them?" Noah asked. He'd known the additional equipment would impact the range, but he'd rather stand a better chance of hitting his mark.

"Depends, and it's not up to us, regardless," Kara said.

"The range of the missile isn't fixed, so couldn't we modify that to get the twenty percent back?" Noah asked.

"We could. It just depends on how far away the targets are

and it also depends on the warhead on it. Let's run a few more simulations and then take it to the colonel," Kara said.

Noah nodded and took another sip of his coffee. Kara was the lead engineer when it came to the defense systems of Titan Space Station. Noah had learned that with any weapons of war it was a game of give and take. Higher accuracy required more sophisticated systems, which impacted other things like weight and yield. There was always a price to pay.

"I'm not saying the colonel won't like the idea, but we need to be upfront about the system's limitations. However, given that we're constantly being expected to accomplish more with less leads me to believe he'll approve these changes," Kara said.

Noah nodded and stood up. He stretched his arms overhead and worked out some of the stiffness in his shoulders.

"He'll probably want to know how many HADES IVs we can modify," Noah said.

Kara grinned and shook her head. "You're learning, but it won't be you and me modifying all these missiles. We'll need to come up with a process so we can task my team with it."

Noah pressed his lips together. "I'm not sure—"

"You just worry about the technical steps and I'll worry about how to get it done once I make sure you won't blow us up," Kara said. "I was kidding," she followed up quickly.

"That was a long time ago," Noah said, getting a bit defensive.

He'd made a quick update of the power relay systems when he'd first arrived and nearly destroyed one of the subsections of the space station. He'd only been trying to help, but he'd thought Colonel Douglass was going to ship him back to New Earth before the cargo carrier left. Noah hadn't been particularly enthused to be assigned to the space station, but Connor insisted that they could use his help. It was only supposed to be for one six-month rotation, but he'd requested to stay when his six months were up, which was in no small part due to the work being done and meeting Kara. He'd even sent a vid to Lenora telling her about Titan's lead engineer. Though they weren't related, Lenora Bishop was like a big sister to him and she was as close to family as he had here on the colony. He looked forward to introducing Kara to Lenora one day.

Noah spent the next few hours finalizing the process required to modify the HADES IV missiles. The best thing about his proposed process was that it required very little in the way of fabrication. They could feasibly get away with the supplies they had on hand. When it came to work, Kara Roberts was all business, and just because she happened to be in a relationship with Noah didn't mean she took it easy on him in the slightest. She went over his proposed process with a fine-toothed comb and refined the areas where it was lacking.

"This should be good enough to present to Colonel Douglass, but we'll likely adjust it more as we have more people analyze it," Kara said.

"Only if they want to break what I've done," Noah replied.

He'd had some engineer jockeys go through his work for other projects and try to improve on them, only to break the system entirely. If they'd just followed his process, things would've worked out fine.

"We'll see," Kara said and climbed out of her chair.

She arched her back, and Noah couldn't help it as his gaze took in the sight of her.

"Eyes up. We don't have time for that now," Kara said.

As Noah complied and turned toward the door, he felt Kara's hand squeeze his shoulder and her breath tickle his neck.

"Perhaps tonight, if you're lucky," she said in a breathy tone.

Oh god. If she kept that up, he'd have trouble walking down

the hallway. Kara darted ahead of him and Noah had to run to catch up to her. One thing he definitely didn't like about the space station was that the corridors were so small.

He wondered if he could convince Kara to come back to New Earth with him, not that he'd have much time on the planet. He had a feeling that Connor would send him to help work on the battleship carrier being constructed with the last section of the *Ark*, but he should be able to make a decent argument that his next assignment be planet-side instead of in space. He missed the good old days when he was simply dispatched to different parts of the colony to set up systems and fix things. Once Connor Gates showed up, that all changed. The CDF founder and general had snatched him up and would only share him with Lenora, at least for a time. Lenora and Connor hardly spoke to each other anymore, which was a shame because he liked them both and thought they were a good pair.

They waited for the elevator that would take them up to the Command Center level. He checked the elevator's location and noted its steady descent. A cluster of CDF personnel approached and waited to get on the same elevator. Suddenly, the lighting in the area went out and the emergency lighting came on.

The station's AI chimed and then spoke: "Power consumption exceeds the usage designated for this area of Titan Space Station. Mandatory power rationing is in effect."

Noah looked at Kara and rolled his eyes.

"Apologies, folks on E deck. We're testing the failover system for the power relay between the upper and lower decks. The power should be restored momentarily," a man's voice said over the nearby speaker.

Noah glanced at Kara. "Next, we'll hear Butters screwed up the assembly again and what should be a five-minute fix turns into a five-day nightmare for the rest of us."

"You really don't like that guy," Kara said.

"I'm sure he's a great guy who works awfully hard to make stupid mistakes. Makes me wonder if he was sent out here as some kind of punishment," Noah replied.

Kara grabbed his arm and guided him toward the ladder shafts they could use to climb to the upper levels. She started climbing first and Noah followed.

"Too bad they didn't put in stairs," Noah said as he climbed.

"Wouldn't work well here," Kara answered.

"Why not? Certainly would be easier than climbing a ladder," Noah said.

"Stairs are fine when there's gravity, but when there isn't, you'd be glad for the ladder instead of the stairs, trust me," Kara replied.

"Great. Maybe they can get Butters to work on the artificial gravity fields next," Noah said.

Kara didn't reply and they continued to climb. Noah glanced down and wished he hadn't. Beneath him was a dizzying view of a ladder shaft that was eight decks long. He swung his gaze in front of him and squeezed his eyes shut for a moment. He should have waited for the elevator.

They got out of the ladder shaft a few levels above and took the elevator the rest of the way. The Command Center for Titan Space Station was a large open space with many workstations that rivaled the bridge of most ships. Titan was more of a space port than merely a station, given the size of the place. Most of it had been converted and retrofitted with missile tubes and various types of heavy cannons. There were plans for another hangar bay to be added to support a squadron or two of small attack spacecraft.

Command Center had a large observation area with a clear view into the great expanse of space. Noah glanced over and, even from this distance, still saw an ocean of stars beyond the station. He often took some time to go and take in the view from the observation decks on the station. They weren't constructed specifically for the station but had, in fact, been repurposed from the *Ark*. The view was spectacular and humbling at the same time.

They found Colonel Kasey Douglass standing amidst a throng of CDF personnel. He was speaking to them and gave Noah and Kara an acknowledging nod as they closed in. Then the colonel dismissed the people around them.

"Good, I was wondering if you two were going to make it on time. Walk with me," Colonel Douglass said.

The colonel was a tall man, trim and extremely professional. Kasey Douglass had been part of Connor's infamous Ghosts special ops team that had been shanghaied onto the *Ark* by Admiral Mitch Wilkinson. The soldiers of the Colonial Defense Force had their roots in the NA Alliance military and aspired to the same level of professionalism that people like Connor and Kasey exuded. Once given an objective or committed to an objective, they worked toward it, leveraging all the resources at their disposal. Noah had found it interesting that the old Ghost Platoon still supported Connor in his belief that an extinction-level event had happened in Earth's solar system. Noah still believed as well and didn't care for the wavering loyalty that the current political climate fostered in Sierra.

"I think we've got it, Colonel," Noah said.

"You've increased the accuracy of the HADES IV?" Colonel Douglass asked.

"Yes, with modifications to the existing missiles we were able to increase their accuracy substantially," Noah said.

"But," Kara interjected, "there's a potential impact to the range of up to twenty percent, Colonel."

Colonel Douglass's gaze darted back to Noah.

"That's right, but based on the simulation variables for an engagement, you get a fifty percent gain in accuracy over what you had before," Noah said.

Colonel Douglass pressed his lips together in thought. "How do these changes affect the field envelope for potential targets? Is the fifty percent gain persistent regardless of the distance, or does it waver the farther out we go?"

Noah took a moment to think about it. "It really depends, and I know you hate that answer, so please bear with me for a second."

They headed to Titan's Central Command cradle, which was the heart of all the space station's activities.

"It's better if I show you," Noah said and went over to a vacant terminal. He powered it on and expanded a blank canvas so he could draw freestyle. "Let's say that this circle here is us and these guys way over here are the enemy," Noah said and pointed to his rough drawing of a ship. "Right now, we launch our missiles and update their targeting systems while the missile is traveling at near relativistic speeds. If the enemy detects the incoming missile, they'll launch countermeasures and decoys that can effectively blind our missile so it will most likely miss its intended target. This is why a barrage of missiles is sent—in the hopes that at least one of them will detonate its warhead in proximity to the intended target." Noah drew multiple lines from the space station to the enemy fleet.

Colonel Douglass arched an eyebrow. "Get to the point. Tell me how you increased the accuracy."

Noah swiped his hands to the side, clearing what he'd just drawn. "What I did was modify the missiles with secondary and tertiary targeting systems that are shielded respectively. The missiles are launched in groups and are networked together so they can receive a signal from us, as well as communicate with each other. As each sensor array is blinded by countermeasures, the secondary systems are engaged and so forth for the entire group. So, if we sent twenty missiles to target a battleship cruiser, or anything really, the missiles would get new eyes on the target and adjust their trajectory accordingly and then communicate the most up-to-date information within the group; thus, giving you a higher chance of hitting your target," Noah said and finished his drawing with the decimation of the enemy fleet. He added a smiley face for good measure.

Colonel Douglass rubbed his chin in thought and then glanced at Kara. "What are your thoughts on this, Major?"

"We've run the numbers and all the simulations support it, Colonel," Kara replied.

"How long would it take to modify the HADES IV missiles for proof of concept and"—Colonel Douglass elevated his tone before Noah could quickly answer—"will this work on smaller, mid-range missiles like the HORNET IIs?"

"We could work on that," Noah answered. "My first thought for the smaller missiles is to only have a secondary targeting system and lose the tertiary. That way, even if our sensors were blinded for some reason, they could still target an enemy ship."

Colonel Douglass nodded. "Okay, you're cleared for the second phase of this project. Since you're using existing technology, the test bed can be larger than we normally would try. How long would it take you to modify a hundred HADES IVs?"

Noah's eyes widened and he glanced over at Kara.

"If I assign a few teams to it, it should only take about six hours for the group. We have a process written out. We just need to go over it with the teams; otherwise, the timeline would be much shorter," Kara said.

Colonel Douglass smiled. "Excellent work, you two. I'm

really quite impressed, or I will be if it works as well as you say it will. So, I guess I'm hopeful."

Noah swallowed hard. "Thank you, sir."

"Colonel, has there been any word from New Earth regarding the additional power generator?" Kara asked.

The lines of Colonel Douglass's face became grim. "Our request was denied for a further twelve months."

Noah's mouth hung open. "Twelve months!"

"I can assure you that General Gates had quite a few more colorful metaphors to describe what he thought of that decision," Colonel Douglass said.

"I bet, knowing Connor," Noah said.

"Oh, that reminds me," Colonel Douglass said, looking at Noah. "You're being recalled back to New Earth. You'll be shipping out in a few days."

Noah felt Kara stiffen at his side. "Back to New Earth? Did they say why?"

Colonel Douglass speared him a look. "Yes, of course, every bit of the general's thinking was explained to me in detail. No! You go where you're ordered to go."

Noah straightened his shoulders. "I'm sorry, Colonel, I just thought I'd be here for another six months."

Colonel Douglass's face softened. "I certainly don't want to lose you and I doubt others are ecstatic with the decision, but that's the way it is."

Noah nodded. While he didn't exactly love life on the space station, he had reasons for wanting to stay. He glanced at Kara and her face might have been carved from stone for all the information it yielded to him.

Colonel Douglass dismissed them and they left the Command Center, hardly uttering a word to each other. Kara walked behind him and Noah resisted the urge to turn around since the corridor was hardly the appropriate place for what he wanted to say. CDF personnel were walking to and from the Command Center in a steady stream. Noah felt as if someone had punched him in the stomach. They reached a set of elevators that for once weren't crowded with people waiting for them, and he pressed the button to summon the car with only a slight shake in his hands. He risked a glance at Kara. Her honey-brown eyes were staring at a fixed point in front of her and her normally full lips formed a thin line.

Noah glared at the progress indicator that showed the elevator taking about two hundred years to reach them. Eventually the speaker above the elevator doors chimed and they opened. Noah stepped inside and he allowed his shoulders to slump. Kara stood next to him and glared out the open doors. There were a couple of CDF personnel who approached the elevator doors, but upon seeing Kara's expression they decided to wait for the next elevator.

The doors closed and Noah felt the elevator begin its slow descent.

"So, I guess I have to leave in a few days," Noah said while staring at the floor.

He glanced at Kara and saw that her shoulders were drawn up near her ears. He reached out and placed a hand on her shoulder and she winced. She turned toward him, her eyes intense.

"Shut up," Kara said and grabbed his shirt, pushing him against the wall and proceeding to kiss him until he forgot he was in an elevator.

A few minutes later they reached the engineering level and the elevator doors opened. Kara pulled away from him. "This isn't over, Barker," she said and stormed out.

Noah stepped away from the wall and saw more than a few

people grinning at him from outside the elevator. He left them behind and had to run to catch up to Kara. If he'd had any doubts about whether she wanted to return to New Earth with him, they were now gone. All that stood in their way was whether she'd be allowed to come with him.

CHAPTER THIRTEEN

THE NEXT SEVEN hours were packed with so much work that Noah had hardly any time to see Kara. The engineering deck was flooded with teams tasked with learning the process to modify the HADES IV missiles. The actual modifications only occurred after the engineering teams went through and provided their input on Noah's process. A few of them made some good points, which Noah had to concede. He even got a head start with the modification proposal for the HORNET II missiles, which was going pretty much as he suspected. Due to the size and sophistication of the missile, he was limited in what he could get away with. He could add only one additional sensor array and targeting computer core for the missile. It would help, but they wouldn't see the improvements they expected to see with the HADES IV.

Noah was on his way back to the Command Center. They were going to test five HADES IV missiles for a live proof-of-concept test. The high-yield payloads were removed so they wouldn't be wasted. The purpose of the test was to prove that the

modified missiles could retarget an objective after standard countermeasures and point defense protocols were used. Noah knew
all eyes would be on him since he'd boldly made the claim that it
was not only possible to improve the accuracy of long-range
missiles but that he could have it done in a matter of a few
weeks. This fed the reputation he had of being a loudmouth and
a show-off, but if this worked, it would shut a few of those
doubters up.

Noah sucked in a deep breath as he strode toward the
Command Center doors. They seemed larger than they'd been
before. He should have gotten something to drink before
coming up here. Had they applied the guidance software patch
before loading the missile into the tubes? He needed to
check that.

Noah glanced around. He was supposed to meet Kara. She'd
been supervising the teams doing the modifications, so they
hadn't had much of a chance to talk. He stood right outside the
Command Center doors. It was quiet here, and he knew once
those doors opened there would be no turning back. He'd either
prove that he was worth the reputation he'd earned over the past
seven years, or he'd be a laughing stock who was amusing to
those in power for a time.

The metal doors split open as someone left the Command
Center, and the peaceful quietness of the corridor vanished.
Noah walked inside with a determined stride and saw that the
Command Center was fully staffed, with all teams being brought
on deck for this test.

Noah went straight toward the cradle. Colonel Douglass was
pacing with his hands clasped behind him. The colonel gave him
a grim nod as he approached.

"Still confident this will work?" Colonel Douglass asked.

No.

Noah met the colonel's gaze. "Yes, sir. Get ready to be wowed."

Colonel Douglass blinked a few times. "Connor warned me you were a bit unorthodox. Alright, take that workstation right over there and let's see if you're as good as you think you are."

Noah went over to the work area nearest the colonel and collapsed into the chair, although he preferred to stand while he was working. He used his implants to authenticate to the workstation and the holoscreen came on.

"Colonel, we're go for Icarus test at your command," Noah said.

"Acknowledged," Colonel Douglass said. "Tactical, is our target in place?"

"Yes, Colonel. The broadcast beacon has been checking in for the last half hour."

Noah looked over to see who was working the tactical workstation and saw Caleb Thorne.

Noah glanced back at the colonel.

"Go ahead, Captain."

"Yes, sir," Noah said. "Tactical, I'm showing HADES IV-B missiles are in tubes one through five. Can you confirm?"

"Confirmed. Ready for launch," Thorne said.

"You're go for launch," Colonel Douglass said.

"Yes, sir, HADES away," Thorne said.

Noah watched the data output as the five missiles successfully launched from the tubes—not surprising because all they'd done was add a few more systems on top of the existing missile structure.

"Targeting package has been beamed to the missile group alpha. Target reference is zeta," Thorne said.

Noah waited for the status update to be sent back from the missiles. "Showing that all five missiles have good connections."

Confirming the successful network connections between the missiles was the first step. The real test would come after the first waves of countermeasures were launched.

"Missiles locked on target, Colonel," Thorne said.

Colonel Douglass stood next to Noah, watching the holo-screen. "Deploy countermeasure package bravo and have zeta move to coordinates beta."

Thorne confirmed the command and executed. There was nothing for them to see other than the data on screen, but Noah tried to imagine the missiles barreling toward their target and the bright flashes of countermeasures being fired to thwart their targeting systems. This, of course, was completely inaccurate as to what was truly taking place. Standard ship countermeasures were for blinding sensor arrays, with broad-stream lasers designed to sweep the area the missiles were coming in from.

"Missiles still on target," Thorne said.

"Launch second set of countermeasures and have zeta move to the next series of coordinates. Proceed on automation, initial time interval fifteen seconds," Colonel Douglass said.

Noah watched as the missiles continued to close in on zeta, but after the third set of countermeasures, they failed to update their trajectory to align with zeta's new position.

"Confirm the secondary targeting computer has been brought online," Noah said.

The missiles were moving at a fraction of the speed that was possible, which made it possible for them to manually execute the test and monitor the engagement. Otherwise, the engagement would be over in only a few seconds or less at this distance.

Noah hardly dared to breathe. This was a crucial step in the test and would happen almost simultaneously. The missile track showed a change in course toward zeta, but Noah knew the countermeasures would be fired more frequently, attempting to blind the missile systems. The duration between updates became shorter, and those in the cradle watched the mock battle unfold on the large main holoscreen.

Noah pressed his fist to his lips as he watched. The targeting updates showed the zeta darting to a predetermined set of coordinates and the missiles course-correcting as they closed in. The blips seemed to spontaneously move about the screen until the zeta ceased to report its position, followed by the confirmed detonation signal sent from the missiles.

Noah felt a wide smile spread. There were cheers from those CDF personnel working in the cradle, and Noah turned toward Colonel Douglass.

"I see the general's confidence in you is not misplaced in the slightest. Amazing thing you've done," Colonel Douglass said and looked at Lieutenant Colonel Donnelly. "I want all the HADES IV missiles modified as soon as possible."

"I'll put four teams on it, sir," Lieutenant Colonel Donnelly said.

Colonel Douglass turned back toward Noah. "I don't think you fully realize what you've accomplished."

"But the impact to range. There's got to be a way to maximize that deficit," Noah said.

"Oh I'm sure there is, and I know Major Roberts is more than up to the task. I'm sorry to see you go," Colonel Douglass said.

Noah felt a mix of pride and a growing lump in his throat. He wanted to request that Kara return to New Earth with him, but he knew that not only was it not appropriate for him to make the request but when Kara found out she'd be livid with him. Noah believed she wanted to come with him, but her sense of duty would win over and she'd remain here on the station.

Noah glanced around, trying to find Kara, but she was

nowhere to be seen. More than a few people came over to congratulate him. Noah returned to Caleb Thorne, who had his hand pressed against his ear so he could hear someone else on his comlink.

Caleb glanced over at him and jutted his chin up in greeting.

"I think you owe me a beer, or three of them," Noah said.

"You're the man of the hour. In thirty minutes, I'm buying," Caleb replied and then frowned as he looked away from Noah. "Seriously. I'll put it on screen."

Caleb made a quick swiping gesture toward the holoscreen and all the data was swept away. Noah watched as a live feed from the PRADIS console came on. The console showed multiple groups of unknown ship signatures.

"Multiple contacts, Colonel," Thorne announced.

Colonel Douglass turned from the conversation he was having and glanced at the screen. A hush swept over the CDF personnel in the cradle.

"Action stations. Set Condition One throughout the station," Colonel said.

Months of training drills kicked into gear. Noah went back to his workstation and waited for orders. Klaxon alarms sounded in the Command Center and Noah knew they could be heard throughout the station. CDF personnel ran to their posts.

"Colonel, we have multiple contacts showing in delta quadrant. At this range they could be fleet groups bunched together to hide their true numbers," Thorne said.

Noah brought up a PRADIS feed on his own console. At least the unknown contacts weren't coming from gamma quadrant, which was the direction of the deep-space buoy network.

"Ops, run a diagnostic on PRADIS. I want to know if the system is malfunctioning," Colonel Douglass said. "Comms, prepare to beam open hails on my command."

Lieutenant Colonel Donnelly came over to Noah's side. Not sure what else he should do, Noah started to surrender his workstation.

"You're fine right where you are, Captain," Lieutenant Colonel Donnelly said.

"Colonel, PRADIS is functioning normally. Signals are good," Lieutenant Gabriel said from the Ops work area.

"Acknowledged. Start recording the engagement," Colonel Douglass responded. "Comms, send our standard hails to them in the open channels. See if we can get a response."

Noah swallowed hard. He kept watching PRADIS, hoping that there was some kind of glitch in the system and those ships . . . contacts . . . would disappear. Contacts didn't become ships until they were confirmed.

"Comms, what's the status of our hails?" Colonel Douglass asked.

"No response, Colonel," Lieutenant Foster said.

Colonel Douglass rubbed his chin in thought and glanced at Lieutenant Colonel Donnelly.

"Wrong quadrant," Lieutenant Colonel Donnelly said.

Colonel Douglass nodded. "Comms, authorize first-contact communications package."

Noah's mouth hung open. First-contact protocols were only used if they suspected they were encountering an alien species— something that had never occurred on Earth, but they had nonetheless established a standard protocol for the situation.

"Colonel, they're still heading right for us," Thorne said.

"Acknowledged," Colonel Douglass said. "Comms, still waiting on that first-contact communications package."

Noah watched as Lieutenant Colonel Donnelly walked over to Lieutenant Foster's workstation. The frazzled lieutenant was having trouble finding what she was looking for and Lieutenant Colonel Donnelly leaned down to help her find it.

"First-contact communications package has been sent, Colonel," Lieutenant Foster said.

"Now, we wait," Colonel Douglass said.

Noah's heart thumped in his chest. He didn't know how the colonel could be so focused. Who or what was heading for them? What did they want? Did they know they were here?

"Colonel," Lieutenant Foster said, "judging by the distance, the unknown contacts should have received our first-contact communications package."

"Acknowledged," Colonel Douglass said. "Tactical, I want firing solutions on unknown contacts ready to go."

"Colonel, do you want to give them a warning shot or an all-out assault?" Thorne asked.

"I want solutions for both, Captain. Authorize HADES IV in available tubes. I want half of those tubes loaded with the HADES IV-Bs," Colonel Douglass said.

"Yes, sir. I'll have firing solutions for you in sixty seconds," Captain Thorne said.

Noah glanced back at the colonel.

"We might get to do more than test the modified missiles," Colonel Douglass said.

Not knowing how to respond, Noah merely nodded and his mouth went dry.

"Computer, open a broadcast channel to the entire station," Colonel Douglass said. "Titan Space Station, we have unknown contacts showing up on PRADIS. We've attempted to communicate with them using open hails and I've authorized the use of first-contact protocols. If we don't get a reply, we'll fire our weapons at them. Our mandate for this station is quite clear. We're the first line of defense for the colony. If these are hostiles, they'll know we're not an easy target. If we're wrong and this is an unknown alien species coming to make first contact, the responsibility is mine. Given the status of the deep-space buoy network and the fact that there was a catastrophic event on Earth, I'm not inclined to let any species just waltz their way here unopposed. Douglass, out."

Colonel Douglass closed the broadcast channel. "Comms, send a data burst back to New Earth with our current status."

Noah glanced at the PRADIS console. The unknown contacts were now well within their long-range missiles.

Colonel Douglass looked at the main holoscreen.

"HADES IV and HADES IV-Bs loaded in all available missile tubes, Colonel," Captain Thorne said.

Noah couldn't believe this was happening. Just a short while ago they'd been running a proof-of-concept test and now they were about to open fire on an unknown enemy.

"Fire alpha salvo, and I want bravo ready to go," Colonel Douglass said.

Silence dragged throughout the normally lively Command Center for Titan Space Station.

"Confirm missile launch, Captain," Colonel Douglass said.

Noah swung his gaze toward Caleb Thorne, who was frowning at his output. "Colonel, I don't understand. I submitted the command as you ordered, but the system won't take it."

The edges of Colonel Douglass's lips pulled upward. "Stand down, Captain. Comms, open a channel on CDF-encrypted ship channels." The colonel waited a few moments for the channel to connect. "General Gates, did we pass your test?"

There were a few moments of silence.

"With flying colors, Colonel Douglass. Please extend my congratulations to the CDF personnel on Titan Space Station."

"As you wish, General."

"Did I get you worried even a little bit?"

"You had us worried there for a few minutes, and then we were going to unleash holy hell on you," Colonel Douglass said.

"I can see that. What are HADES IV-B missiles?"

"I'll tell you about it when you come aboard, General," Colonel Douglass said.

Noah blew out the breath he'd been holding.

"Understood," Connor replied. "For the record, Wil wanted me to authorize a covert ops team to take the Command Center."

Colonel Douglass chuckled. "You tell that slippery little twerp that any time he wants to receive a good ass-kicking he should go ahead and try to sneak aboard my station."

Noah heard muffled laughter on the comlink. The unknown ships on PRADIS disappeared and were replaced by CDF transponder codes along with the cargo carrier.

"Colonel, I have the cargo carrier *Chmiel* requesting to dock with the station," Lieutenant Foster said.

"Permission granted," Colonel Douglass said.

Noah felt the tension leave his shoulders. He could use a hot shower and something to eat. He wondered where Kara was since she hadn't shown up for the missile test. He thought about reaching out to her through his comlink, but she likely just wanted some space, so he resisted the urge. Noah logged off the console and stepped away from the workstation. A comlink wouldn't do for what he wanted to ask Kara anyway. Knowing Connor Gates, he wouldn't be at Titan Station for very long before returning to New Earth, which meant that Noah had twelve hours max to find Kara and personally ask her to come back to New Earth with him. She might say no. She could be stubborn at times . . . well, most times. He smiled. He just knew that asking her to change her life for him was better handled in person than on a comlink.

Noah was about to leave the cradle when he heard Caleb Thorne call out to Colonel Douglass again.

"Colonel, I have multiple unknown contacts again, this time on the fringes of PRADIS," Thorne said.

Noah looked at the PRADIS output, which was still on the main holoscreen. This grouping was in a different quadrant than before. Noah's gaze slid down to the quadrant's designation, and his brows pulled together as he read.

"It's gamma quadrant, Colonel," Thorne said.

Noah went cold and then pressed his lips together. "Is this another drill?" He'd voiced his question aloud without thinking about it.

"Open a comlink to the *Vigilant*," Colonel Douglass ordered.

"Comlink ready, Colonel," Lieutenant Foster said.

"*Vigilant*, this is Titan Space Station. PRADIS is showing us multiple unknown contact groups at the edge of its range coming from the gamma quadrant. Can you confirm the drill is over?" Colonel Douglass asked.

Noah hardly moved while they waited for a response.

"The drill is over. Those contacts are real," Connor replied.

Colonel Douglass frowned. "Shit," he said.

"You got that right," Connor said.

A grim silence took hold of the CDF crew at the Command Center. The drill had been gut-wrenching, and it hadn't even been real. Noah felt something cold seize his stomach. The contacts were real, and they were heading right for them.

CHAPTER FOURTEEN

CONNOR STOOD on the bridge of the *Vigilant*. Several bridge officers turned in his direction, awaiting his orders. He had no more training drills planned and they all knew that whatever was being detected on PRADIS was a true anomaly.

"Tactical, can you confirm anomalous detection on PRADIS?" Connor asked.

"Negative, General. They were there and now whatever it was is gone," Lieutenant LaCroix said.

Connor pressed his lips together in a tight frown. He activated the comlink to Titan Space Station. "Titan, the anomaly has disappeared from our PRADIS. Can you confirm whether it still appears on yours?"

"Confirm, the anomaly is gone from our PRADIS. We're running a diagnostic on the PRADIS system," Kasey said.

Connor gave Vladimir LaCroix a meaningful look and the tactical officer began running diagnostics on the *Vigilant's* PRADIS system. After a few moments, he looked over at Connor and shook his head.

"Go to a private channel, Colonel," Connor said.

He used his implants to authorize a separate encrypted communications link with Titan Space Station.

"Ain't this a pickle," Kasey said.

"I don't like this at all," Connor said.

"Agreed, and I don't believe this is just some system glitch," Kasey replied.

"Suggestions?" Connor asked.

"Monitor and see if it shows up again. At that range, it could be nothing," Kasey replied.

Connor muted the line. "Nav, I want a course plotted to put us in better range of the anomaly so we can get a better PRADIS detection. Just send the plot to my terminal."

Connor walked over to his terminal and unmuted the line to Kasey. "I was going to come aboard and pay you a visit, but I think I'll stay right where I am."

"I could send a shuttle out to get you," Kasey offered.

"It's not that. We've got a bit of a situation here on the *Vigilant*," Connor said and told Kasey about Colonel Howe and Major Hayes.

"Are they the only ones who got sick?" Kasey asked.

"No, there are some others. So I need to stay because I don't want to run the risk of spreading whatever this is to the space station," Connor said and rubbed the tips of his fingers together. If he had an actual fleet of ships, he'd send a taskforce to investigate. "Let's continue to monitor and alert me if you detect anything. I'll have the crew of the *Vigilant* do the same."

"I do have an update for you that you're going to like," Kasey said.

"I'm always ready for some good news," Connor said.

Kasey told him about Noah's upgrade procedure for the

HADES IV missile and how it vastly increased the missile's targeting systems.

"I told you that kid was something. That's why I snatched him up when I first got here," Connor said.

"There's no shortage of bright spots in the colony, but I'll admit Noah is brighter than most, just a bit rough around the edges on some things. Speaking of which, he didn't seem particularly keen on leaving here," Kasey replied.

Connor felt his eyebrows rise. "He wasn't excited to go to Titan either."

"I'm sure it has nothing to do with Major Kara Roberts, a lead engineer here," Kasey said.

"What is it with these guys? Someone turns their head and suddenly they won't do what we need them to do," Connor replied.

"They've been very professional. Honestly, situations like this in the CDF are becoming more frequent. It's not like the Alliance," Kasey said.

Connor shook his head. "No, that it's not," he agreed. "Don't tell me you're another one."

He heard Kasey snort.

"No way. If we live another ten years, then maybe," Kasey said.

A message from Dr. Allen appeared on Connor's terminal.

::*General, Colonel Howe's condition has taken a turn for the worse. I've had him moved to the main medical bay. Please come at your earliest convenience,*:: Dr. R. Allen said.

::*Understood. I'll be there shortly,*:: Gen. C. Gates said.

Connor closed the chat window.

"Kasey, I need to report to the medical bay. I'll follow up with you later. Also, send over the upgrade procedure you have for the HADES IV. We don't have nearly as many of them as you do, but that advantage is too good to pass up," Connor said.

"Yes, sir, I'll see to it that a data burst gets sent to the *Vigilant* in a few minutes. One more thing, though. The odds of a commanding officer and his XO getting sick at the same time are minuscule," Kasey said.

Connor rubbed his eyes. "Yeah, I know. So far nothing has turned up."

He closed the comlink and rose from his seat. "Colonel, you have the con. Titan Space Station is going to be sending an upgrade procedure for the HADES IV missiles. I want them immediately sent down to Engineering to be worked on as their top priority."

"Yes, General," Reisman said.

"If you need me, I'll be down at the main medical bay with Dr. Allen," Connor said.

Reisman went to the command chair. "I'll inform you if that anomaly returns."

Connor left the bridge. Just outside, he saw Sean speaking with a few members of his CDF Squad. Upon seeing Connor they stopped what they were doing and saluted him.

Connor looked at Sean. "Walk with me."

Sean walked next to Connor while the rest of his squad followed them at a distance.

"What did you find?" Connor asked.

"We've looked into all the change logs since we left New Earth. I even cross-referenced them with the lead officers responsible for the specific ship systems. Everything checks out. The security team that checked all the equipment in the mess hall didn't find any signs of tampering," Sean said.

"Did you check?" Connor asked.

Sean frowned. "No, sir, I didn't. There's nothing suspicious going on that I could find. I can make a sweep of the mess hall now if you'd like me to, but it's been put back into operation."

Connor shook his head. "That won't be necessary."

"You still believe there's foul play involved?" Sean asked.

Connor regarded the young man for a moment. He was extremely intelligent in most respects and still young enough to be naive in others. "You used to be a sniper. A hunter. If you had a target you needed to hit and you couldn't use your firearm, how would you do it?"

Sean's gaze narrowed and he glanced around to be sure they weren't being overheard by anyone. "You think this was an assassination attempt?"

"I can't afford to rule anything out at this point," Connor said.

Sean pressed his lips together and then blew out a breath, shaking his head. "I can't imagine anyone in the colony, let alone the CDF, doing something like this."

"I'm heading to see Dr. Allen and I want you to come with me," Connor said.

"Of course. What do you need me to do?" Sean asked.

"Keep a lookout for anything that doesn't seem right," Connor replied.

"You can count on me, sir," Sean said.

They reached the *Vigilant's* main medical bay a few minutes later. The door opened and Connor walked through. The medical bay was quiet and not at all like the infirmary he and Reisman had been to a few days ago.

Dr. Allen walked over to them. "Thank you for coming so quickly, General."

"What's Ian's status?" Connor asked.

Dr. Allen's expression became grim. "His organs are shutting down."

"What!" Connor exclaimed. "I thought this was just an allergic reaction."

Dr. Allen nodded. "That's what I thought too. Those were his symptoms. I had him brought here so I could get him into a medical capsule."

Dr. Allen led them over to the quarantined area of the medical bay. "We'll need to go into decontamination one at a time and then I'll show you."

One by one they each went through the decontamination and entered the chamber where the *Vigilant's* commanding officer and his executive officer clung to life. Connor approached the medical capsule and looked at Colonel Ian Howe. He was deathly pale, and if not for the steady rise and fall of his chest because of the breathing tube, Connor would have believed the man was already dead.

Connor glanced over at Nathan Hayes. The *Vigilant's* XO rested in a bed, and though he was also intubated, he didn't look anywhere near as sick as Howe.

Dr. Allen went over to the control panel for the medical capsule.

"I need to know what happened, doctor," Connor said.

Dr. Allen looked up from the control console. "This isn't a contagion. His organs are shutting down. I looked up his symptoms in the medical database on the ship and the artificial intelligence keeps coming up with the same answer."

Connor glanced at Howe again and then looked back at Dr. Allen.

"He's suffering from acute radiation poisoning," Dr. Allen said.

Connor's brows pulled together tightly. "Radiation poisoning? There were no leaks reported. How could he be suffering from that?"

"I know. I checked with Engineering to see if there were any leaks or anything else that could have done this. There was nothing," Dr. Allen said.

"Then how could he be dying of radiation poisoning?" Sean asked.

Dr. Allen swallowed hard and looked worried. "I found lethal levels of Polonium-210. I haven't filed the report yet because I thought you'd want to hear this first, but the colonel was poisoned."

"Hold on a minute," Connor said. "We were in the aft gunnery area of the ship and Ian was at the munitions station. There could have been a containment leak there but on a small enough scale that it wasn't detected by onboard systems."

Dr. Allen shook his head. "I researched Polonium-210's usage and we haven't used it in any great capacity in over a hundred and fifty years."

Connor shook his head. "This is rich. You're telling me that Ian is dying of radiation sickness from some kind of element we don't even use anymore. How the hell did he get exposed to it then?"

"He was in the mess hall, so he must have ingested it somehow," Dr. Allen said.

Connor sighed heavily. "Still doesn't explain where it came from," he said, rubbing his chin and then glancing over at Hayes. "Was he exposed?"

"Yes, but he'll make a full recovery. His exposure must have been much less than Colonel Howe's," Dr. Allen said.

"And the rest of the people at the infirmary?" Connor asked.

"Mixed. Some had allergic reactions and others had various other symptoms," Dr. Allen said.

"I need them tested to see if they were exposed, too," Connor said and looked at Sean. "I want you and your team to go to the munitions center and look for trace detections of any radioactive material. If anyone asks, you're doing a spot inspection at my request."

"Yes, sir," Sean said and left.

Connor looked at Dr. Allen. "You said Major Hayes is going to make a full recovery. When is he going to wake up?"

"It won't be for a few more hours. The treatment is helping his cells rebuild and it's working so far," Dr. Allen said.

"Okay, I want to be informed the moment he's awake," Connor said.

"Understood, General," Dr. Allen said.

"I'm going to assign a security detail to the medical bay," Connor said and looked over at Ian Howe inside the medical capsule. "Can you wake him up? There might be something he could tell us."

"I could, but I won't do that to him," Dr. Allen said.

"Why not?" Connor asked in a hard tone.

"If I were to wake him up, he'd be in so much pain that I doubt he'd be coherent. I wouldn't put anyone in that kind of pain. The only thing we can do now is make him as comfortable as possible," Dr. Allen said.

"You're wrong, Doctor. That's not the only thing we can do for him," Connor said and walked toward the door. "We can find the son of a bitch who did this. I'll have that security detail here soon and I want you to file your report under DSP protocol."

Dr. Allen frowned. "I'm not familiar with DSP protocol."

"Enter it in the type field for your report and the interface will handle all the rest. Basically it'll seal the records so only you and I can review the contents," Connor replied.

"What if something happens to either of us?" Dr. Allen asked.

"I'll authorize a few others, including Captain Quinn, who you just met, and Colonel Reisman. That's it. In the event that we all die—unlikely, I know—but in that event, only senior bridge officers or COMCENT can open those records. You're part of this investigation now. If you think of anything else, I want you to contact either myself, Captain Quinn, or Colonel Reisman."

"Understood, General," Dr. Allen said.

Connor paused at the door. "One more thing. Keep them in here. I don't want the guilty parties to know we're onto them yet."

Dr. Allen bobbed his head once.

Connor left the medical bay and stormed down the corridor. There was a potentially hostile force on the edge of PRADIS and now a murder on his hands. One of these things he was better prepared to face and the other just made him sick. Why would anyone want to murder Ian Howe? His mind refused to come up with any reason that made sense. His brows pushed forward and Connor clenched his teeth. Attempting to kill the leader of the CDF, however...That would make sense. There were no murders at the colony and now there was an assassination attempt? Nothing was ever easy.

A few hours later Connor was still on the bridge. The bridge crew had changed shifts and he was reviewing the latest progress reports on his terminal at the command chair when he noticed someone walking toward him. The man was tall and thickly muscled. He came to a stop near Connor and snapped a salute.

"May I have a word with you in private, General?" the man asked, and Connor looked up to meet intense dark eyes.

Connor glanced at the PRADIS status screen, which was still empty. Whatever the anomaly had been, it hadn't returned.

"And you are?" Connor asked.

"Captain Toro, Head of Security, sir."

Connor knew that Sean was making steady progress with his investigation, so Connor should have expected a visit like this. He stood up. "LaCroix, you have the con."

"Yes, sir," Lieutenant LaCroix responded.

"Right this way, Captain," Connor said.

They left the bridge and entered the nearby ready room. It was sparsely furnished with a curved desk that had wooden accents along the edges. A wallscreen activated when he walked in and showed a view of the stars. Next to the desk was a cylindrical aquarium with an impressive coral reef growing through the middle. Several species of fish swam in the churning water. The interior lights of the aquarium sent small bands of reflected light onto the walls. It was soothing. Connor hadn't realized that Colonel Howe had created such a space on his ship and he was left to wonder how much he really knew about the people who were serving under him.

He went over to the cubby and selected the option for black coffee. He asked Captain Toro if he wanted some, but the captain refused.

Connor sat down on the cushioned chair behind the desk and gestured for Captain Toro to have a seat on either of the padded chairs on the other side of the desk.

The captain took a moment to appreciate the aquarium and then swung his gaze toward Connor.

"General, I'd like to know if I'm suspected of a crime," Captain Toro said.

"No, you're not, Captain," Connor answered.

"Then why is there an investigation being conducted without my knowledge? I'm the head of security on this ship and those issues should have been raised through my department, sir," Captain Toro said.

"Why don't you tell me what you know, Captain," Connor said.

"Just that Captain Quinn is performing spot inspections near the munitions centers, which may fool the average officer but not me. I'd wager a guess that he's looking for something dangerous, something radioactive. The question is why," Captain Toro said.

Connor nodded. "We have reason to suspect that Colonel Howe was poisoned."

Captain Toro's eyes widened and he frowned.

"Dr. Allen informed me that Howe was exposed to lethal levels of a radioactive substance," Connor said.

Captain Toro's brows furrowed and his lips twisted into a partial sneer. "This doesn't make any sense. You said lethal levels. Are you saying Ian is going to die?"

"Yes," Connor confirmed.

Captain Toro looked away.

"How well do you know Colonel Howe?" Connor asked.

"He's godfather to my daughter, sir."

Connor drew in a deep breath.

"Put me to work, sir. Tell me what you know and I can find out who did this," Captain Toro said.

Connor pressed his lips together. "I'm not sure that's such a good idea."

"Not good enough. I can't sit by while this is happening. The safety of the *Vigilant's* crew is my responsibility, so if you don't suspect me, I should be involved in this investigation. There were more than a few people sick and we thought there was some kind of new virus spreading, but when no one else got sick I decided to do some checking of my own," Captain Toro said.

"Captain Quinn is already investigating this," Connor said.

"Yes, but he doesn't know this ship like I do," Captain Toro said.

Connor bridged his fingers in front of his chest.

"Please, sir."

"Alright, I'll inform Captain Quinn that you're now part of this investigation, but I want to make this perfectly clear to you. Quinn is on point and you will take your direction from him. The sophistication and nature of this crime means there are a limited number of people with the skills capable of pulling it off," Connor said. He glanced at his coffee, trying to decide if he still wanted it.

"Thank you, sir. I'll report to Captain Quinn immediately and offer my services," Captain Toro said.

Connor rose from his seat and came around the desk. "We'll find who did this, I promise," he said.

Captain Toro came to his feet as well. A chime came from the speaker near the door.

"General, I have Colonel Douglass on a comlink to speak with you. Shall I patch it to your ready room, sir?" Sergeant Boers asked.

"No, I'm returning to the bridge," Connor said and headed for the door.

"Sir," Captain Toro said.

Connor turned back toward him.

"Your coffee," Captain Toro said and handed him the mug.

Connor took it and thanked him. Toro headed away from the bridge. The big man's foot stomps could be heard as he left.

Connor entered the bridge and glanced down at the coffee,

deciding he didn't want it after all. The corporal at the door glanced at him.

"Sir, I can take care of that for you if you want," the corporal said.

"Thanks," Connor said and handed him the mug.

Connor headed toward the command chair and sat down. "Comms, put Colonel Douglass on screen."

The main holoscreen flickered as the comlink was connected and Kasey Douglass's bearded face came on.

"After multiple diagnostics on our PRADIS and connected systems, my engineers assure me that the systems are functioning properly," Kasey said.

Connor had expected as much. "Same here. I don't like leaving this to chance. That's why I'm ordering the *Vigilant*, along with the *Banshee* and the *Wyatt*, to make a scouting run to see if we can find this anomaly if we extend PRADIS's range."

Kasey nodded. "I suspected you would, which is why I must advise against it, sir."

"Noted, Colonel," Connor replied.

"Sir, I'm not disputing the need to investigate. What I'm protesting is whether you should be the one doing the investigating," Kasey said.

Connor considered what Kasey said and he was right. This was something he *should* delegate. "Ordinarily you'd be correct, but with the possibility of an unknown virus on this ship, I can't risk the exposure to Titan," he lied.

Kasey narrowed his gaze. Connor knew there was no argument Kasey could make that wouldn't bring more suspicion to what was really happening on the *Vigilant*.

"Understood, sir. We'll relay your preliminary reports back to New Earth," Kasey said as a soft reminder that Connor needed to keep the government of the colony informed.

"Thank you. We'll get underway and I'll be in touch. In the meantime, keep a ready status," Connor said.

"Yes, General," Kasey replied.

Connor severed the comlink. "Nav, plot us a course into gamma quadrant. Let's see if anything's lurking in the void that we should know about."

CHAPTER FIFTEEN

CONNOR SAT in the ready room just off from the bridge. It was one of the few places he could be alone to get his head straight. It had been thirty-six hours since they'd left Titan Space Station behind. There were regular check-ins with Major Cross of the *Banshee* and acting commander, Captain Mattison, of the *Wyatt*. Connor had considered leaving the *Wyatt* at the space station, but if there was trouble brewing out beyond the fringes of known space, he needed firepower. This was a scouting mission, but if they found something, it could just as easily become a first-strike mission.

The chime sounded at his door.

"Come in," Connor said.

The door opened and Major Hayes hovered in the doorway. He was back in CDF-standard blues with the golden sunburst displaying proudly on his shoulder.

"Nathan, come inside," Connor said, rising from his seat. "I was glad to hear about your recovery."

Major Hayes stepped inside. He still looked a bit pale, like he could use several healthy meals and more sleep.

"Sir, I'm no good to you lying in bed," Major Hayes said.

Connor glanced at the man's hands. They were sometimes fidgety and then sometimes clenched.

"You've been through a lot," Connor said.

"I got to walk away. I'm ready to resume my duties as XO, sir," Major Hayes said.

"Alright, I'll bring you up to speed, but there's something I need to know first," Connor said.

"I told Dr. Allen everything I could remember. Colonel Howe and I were just finishing up our meal and he collapsed to the floor," Major Hayes said.

"I'm aware of that, but what I want to know is if you know of anyone who has voiced an opinion that makes you question whether they should be on this ship," Connor said.

Major Hayes looked away, taking a second to think about it. "Nothing comes to mind. Some people become frustrated from time to time, but there've been no red flags that indicate anyone is unfit for duty, sir."

Connor nodded. "I keep hearing the same thing from other officers, but I wanted to confirm with you."

"The *Vigilant* has a good crew. How's the investigation going?" Major Hayes asked.

"Ongoing, I'm afraid. We've started questioning crewmen about their whereabouts on that day and we've been scanning the interior of the ship for trace amounts of radioactive material," Connor said.

"And this scouting mission? Is there anything I need to know about that, sir?"

Connor told Major Hayes about the anomaly that had been detected by the PRADIS system on Titan Space Station and how they'd confirmed it on their own system, but the anomaly hadn't shown up again.

"So that's why we're traveling at such a slow speed," Major Hayes said.

"I just want to take a look," Connor replied.

"And when will we reach the end of the envelope for this scouting mission?"

"In eight hours. At that time, if nothing's been detected, we'll turn around and head back to Titan Space Station," Connor said.

Major Hayes traced the stubble of his mustache and beard. "I saw in the logs that you've ordered engineering crews to modify the HADES IV missiles."

"Yes, but we can only modify twenty percent of our arsenal. Engineer Hatly came up with an alternative. It's not as good as the actual upgrades, but it helps," Connor said.

He brought up a holoscreen and opened a high-level schematic of the HADES IV. "See, the proposed upgrades add systems to the existing missiles. What we're doing with the missiles we can't upgrade is updating the command-and-control software so it will accept updates to targeting from the HADES IV-B missiles," Connor said.

Major Hayes read the information on screen. "This is really something. You're making the unmodified HADES IVs slaves to the HADES IV-Bs. Too bad we can't increase the range of PRADIS. Don't you think we should have detected something by now?"

"I expected us to detect something several hours away from Titan, but that wasn't the case," Connor said and rubbed his eyes. He didn't need much sleep but he couldn't remember the last time he'd had some rack time.

"So in eight hours we turn around and go back home," Major Hayes said.

"That's correct. We know that PRADIS is less accurate at extreme distances," Connor said.

"I understand now, sir."

Connor powered off the holoscreen and stood up. "I'm due to relieve Colonel Reisman for the next watch."

Major Hayes came to his feet. "Do you mind if I take this watch, sir?"

Connor glanced at the major for a moment. "Are you sure you're feeling up to it?"

"Yes, sir."

"Alright, you take this shift. I'll be along in a few hours to take over," Connor said.

"Understood, sir," Major Hayes said and headed for the bridge.

Connor stood up and thought about going to his quarters. "Dim the lights," he said.

He sat on the long couch and then lay down. After setting an alarm to wake him in two hours' time, Connor closed his eyes and went to sleep.

THE ALARM gently pulled Connor from a deep sleep, but years of training kicked in and he was fully awake in moments. He swung his legs off the couch and stood up, walked to the head, and waved his hand in front of the faucet to activate it. He splashed cool water on his face and rinsed his mouth out.

Connor used his implants to reconnect to the *Vigilant's* computer systems and narrowed his gaze at the ship's status. He quickly dried his hands and face and left the ready room. He strode onto the bridge and saw Major Hayes speaking with Lieutenant LaCroix.

"Sir, I'm not following. PRADIS should already be able to detect what you're asking me to do," Lieutenant LaCroix said.

Major Hayes glanced over at Connor for a moment and then looked back at LaCroix. "Just get it ready, Lieutenant," Major Hayes said.

"Yes, sir," LaCroix said and went back to the tactical workstation.

Connor approached the command area. "Why are we stopping?"

"Playing a hunch. If you'll allow it, I can explain," Major Hayes said.

Connor's brows pulled together angrily. He had very little patience for his orders being countermanded. "This had better be some hunch," Connor warned.

The door to the bridge opened and Wil Reisman raced in.

"General," Colonel Reisman said, "Major Hayes checked with me before making any changes."

Connor smoothed his features and nodded at Major Hayes. "Alright, give it to me straight."

"Prior to this mission, Colonel Howe and I were working on fine-tuning the PRADIS detection system. We were actually talking about it when . . . we got sick. This anomaly disappeared once we detected it on our PRADIS systems. We know that the accuracy of PRADIS is significantly reduced when hitting the fringes of its range. It got me thinking: what if the anomaly we first detected is able to cloak itself somehow and become invisible to PRADIS?" Major Hayes said.

"You can't cloak a fleet of ships. The NA Alliance military spent stupendous amounts of resources trying to achieve what you're saying and failed to do so," Connor replied.

"You're right, we can't, but perhaps someone else could," Major Hayes said.

Connor felt his stomach clench at the thought. "You've got my attention, Major."

Major Hayes nodded, clearly relieved that Connor was going to hear him out. "You had us moving at a slower speed already as a precautionary measure. What I ordered our taskforce to do was to slow us down even further so we're now moving at a fraction of our former speed. You see, our forward motion can interfere with PRADIS detections."

"This is the first I'm hearing of this," Connor said.

Colonel Reisman raised his hands in front of his chest. "Give him a chance to explain."

Connor nodded for Hayes to continue.

"PRADIS looks for a hard return in order to register a contact; then our cyber warfare suite attempts to catalog the detection with known vessels. This didn't work before and we didn't get enough of a signature to be of any use. So, instead of using PRADIS to scan for active contacts, I have LaCroix updating the parameters to look for evidence of ship wakes instead," Major Hayes said.

Connor frowned as he thought about it. "So you think that if there *is* a fleet of enemy ships out there that can avoid contact with PRADIS, they'll be unable to mask the effects of their ships flying through space?"

"Precisely," Major Hayes said.

Connor glanced at Reisman, who gave him an I-told-you-so look. "Alright, let's see what we've got."

He wasn't going to start congratulating anyone just yet, but Connor had to admit that it seemed like a clever tactic.

"Tactical, what's the status of PRADIS?" Major Hayes asked.

"The PRADIS system has accepted the updated parameters, sir," LaCroix answered.

"Put the output on the main wallscreen," Major Hayes said.

The PRADIS output showed a three-dimensional field out away from the *Vigilant*. Nothing showed up in the scanning field. Connor and the rest of the bridge crew watched for a few minutes. He glanced at Reisman and arched an eyebrow, but then there was an audible chime. Connor's gaze snapped toward the main holoscreen, which showed the first contact. Another contact quickly followed, until the chimes for additional contacts detected became almost one continuous stream. Each chime was like a shot to the gut, describing what could only be the wake of a massive fleet coming right toward them.

The PRADIS output continued to show the wake fields of starship engines. Connor darted his gaze to the data output on the PRADIS system.

"They're not going very fast," Colonel Reisman said.

Connor went to the command chair. "They don't need to if they think we can't see them," he said and brought up the ship command interface. "Action stations, action stations. Set Condition One throughout the ship. This is not a drill."

Connor heard Sergeant Boers repeat the ship alert as she transmitted to the battle group.

"Tactical, I want a firing solution for that group nearest us and the main group," Connor said.

"Sir, it's going to take a few minutes because PRADIS is just finding the engine wakes and not the actual ships themselves," Lieutenant LaCroix said.

"Understood, Lieutenant. I need those solutions as soon as you have them. Major Hayes, please double-check the firing solutions once they're ready," Connor said.

"General, may I have a word?" Colonel Reisman asked.

Connor gestured for him to come closer. "Comms, I need our targeting data sent to both the *Banshee* and the *Wyatt*."

"Yes, sir," Sergeant Boers said.

Reisman leaned in and spoke softly. "Sir, should we spend more time learning about the potential hostiles?"

Connor frowned. "Potential hostiles," he repeated. "The fact that they're trying to sneak up on us pretty much states their intent."

"Understood, sir, but we're not exactly sure what we're dealing with. I'm just trying to say that we should take a few moments and see if we can learn more about them," Colonel Reisman said.

Connor pursed his lips in thought. "We have an opportunity here. If we start sending probes to take a closer look, we'll give away the fact that we know their positions. I'd much rather send a stronger message."

Connor watched as his long-time friend tried to come up with another argument for delaying the inevitable.

"I know what you're saying, Wil, but the criteria for engagement have been met. Hails have already been sent from Titan Space Station, and if this force intended to answer, they would have done so by now," Connor said.

Reisman swallowed hard. "Yes, General."

"Tactical, I need that firing solution," Connor said.

Connor watched as Major Hayes and Lieutenant LaCroix worked. After a few moments Major Hayes looked over at Connor. "We have a solution, sir, but it's not pretty."

"Let's have it," Connor said.

"We send the first wave of HORNETs into the area we expect the enemy ships are and hold the HADES IVs in reserve until we can confirm targeting," Major Hayes said.

Connor brought up LaCroix's console on his own screen.

"Negative, Major, lead with the HORNETs, then hit them immediately after with the HADES IVs. No delay. Relay the firing solution to the rest of the battle group."

"Yes, sir," Major Hayes said.

Less than a minute later, he heard, "Weapons systems ready, sir."

"Fire," Connor said.

The Panther-class heavy cruisers were similar in construction to most of the other warships humans fielded. The hull was roughly cigar shaped, though flattened to provide a narrower side profile and a wider top and bottom upon which to mount the super structure and the mag-cannon turrets. Between the turrets were the missile tubes, which at this moment were launching the first salvo of HORNETs. The mid-range missiles were being used to paint the targets.

Connor watched the countdown for the HADES IVs.

"Targeting profile uploaded to the HADES IVs to track the HORNETs, sir," Lieutenant LaCroix said.

"Very well," Connor said.

The timer chewed down to zero and then the HADES IV missiles launched. Connor looked at the statuses for the two destroyers. They were ready to fire but were waiting.

"Helm, plot a course back to Titan Space Station," Connor said and looked back at the plot as the missiles fully engaged their engines. Missile systems were delayed from main engine burst to make it harder for the enemy to determine where they'd been fired from.

"Comms, send a data burst back to Titan Space Station with our current status," Connor said.

"Yes, sir, sending now," Sergeant Boers said.

Connor looked at Reisman. "Now, we wait."

"You don't want the *Banshee* and the *Wyatt* to fire their missiles?" Colonel Reisman asked.

Connor shook his head. "No, I want them to fire theirs on the second wave after the enemy has given away their position."

Connor noted the time after the missiles began their initial burn. "Ops, begin visual scans of the enemy force with the high-power optics."

"Sir, I'm not able to get confirmation that Titan Space Station has received our data burst," Sergeant Boers said.

Connor peered at the main screen. "Request current status of the *Banshee* and the *Wyatt*."

Connor watched as Sergeant Boers did as he asked. She looked back at him helplessly.

"Sir, it's the same thing. We're sending the data, but we're unable to get confirmation."

Connor glanced at Reisman and saw the same grim acknowledgment on his face that he was feeling.

"Sir, the *Banshee* has just gone offline—make that the *Wyatt,* too. Both destroyers are no longer reporting," Sergeant Boers said with rising panic in her voice.

"We're being jammed," Connor said.

Reisman's eyes widened.

"Helm, all ahead one half. Go evasive," Connor said.

"Confirmed, all ahead one half, evasive," Sergeant Edwards said.

"Contact!" Lieutenant LaCroix said.

Connor's eyes darted to the main screen. For an instant, the screen showed a looming, irregularly shaped mass that Connor thought could be an asteroid or other natural formation.

"Sir, target is maneuvering," Lieutenant LaCroix reported.

"Engage point defense systems. Target that ship," Connor ordered.

"Sir, the target is appearing on PRADIS now," Lieutenant LaCroix said.

"They must have realized we can see them. What's the status of our missiles?" Connor asked.

"No confirmed status sent back to us," Ops reported.

"Sergeant Boers, prepare a comms drone for quick launch back to Titan Space Station. We need to inform COMCENT that we've encountered a new enemy," Connor said.

"Yes, sir," the normally unflappable Sela Boers said in a trembling voice. "Drone is ready."

"Launch it. Now!" Connor said.

The drone launch registered on the main screen and then the alert immediately minimized.

"Sir, I have sensors back," LaCroix said.

"Reload the tubes and target that ship," Connor said.

"Sir, I have confirmed detonation of missiles," Ops reported.

"Put it on screen," Connor said.

The main screen showed multiple detonations along the front of the main enemy forces. They must have moved beyond the enemy ship's jamming signal or they wouldn't be seeing anything. The PRADIS contact was intermittent, so it was clear they were trying to get another lock on them.

More missiles appeared on the main screen, fired from the *Banshee* and the *Wyatt*. Connor watched the seemingly pathetically slow tracks creep across the main display as the computer opened another window to show the *Vigilant* in relation to the enemy ships.

"Ops, do we have another visual?" Connor asked.

"Negative, sir. With the detonation of our missiles, it's going to take some time to filter it out," Ops replied.

"Multiple targets are on the move. They're tracking toward us," LaCroix said.

"They're moving pretty fast. Are the missiles updating their targeting profile?"

"Yes, sir," Tactical reported. "Tubes one through eight are reloaded."

"Target the ship tracking us," Connor said.

"Missiles away, sir," LaCroix said.

The enemy ship didn't try and dodge or intercept the missiles bearing down on it. The hardened nose cones of the HADES IVs slammed into the organic-looking hull of the target. The engines would fire one more time to maximize penetration before detonating the warhead. A bright flash swamped the main screen as multiple missiles bombarded the target. Once the flash cleared, the *Vigilant's* optical sensors showed the enemy ship's hull peeled back where the missiles had hit it.

"Sir, I'm getting intermittent transmissions from the *Wyatt*," Sergeant Boers said with a hand held to her earpiece and her brows pulled together in concentration. "It's messy, sir. Something about . . . repelling boarders."

Connor's gaze darted to Reisman. "That's why they haven't returned fire yet."

"Maybe, or they could just be seeing what we throw at them," Colonel Reisman said.

"Sir, the *Wyatt* is offline," Ops reported.

"Could they be jamming us again?" Colonel Reisman asked.

"Negative, sir. The signal is clear. One moment they were there and now only the enemy ship is there," Tactical said.

"Helm, can you plot an intercept course?" Connor asked.

"Negative, sir, not with that enemy behemoth bearing down on us," Edwards replied.

Connor clenched his teeth. "What about the *Banshee*? Do we have their location?"

While he suspected the answer wouldn't be what he wanted

to hear, he needed to ask anyway.

"Negative, sir. The last transmission from them was confirmation that they fired their weapons," Tactical said.

"Helm, push our nose to port by six degrees and punch it," Connor said. "All ahead full."

"Ahead full. Yes, sir," the helmsman reported.

The ship began to shake as the engines came to full power and the *Vigilant* surged toward their target.

"Sir, our window of engagement just narrowed with the velocity change," Tactical warned.

"Then don't miss," Connor said. "Nav, once we pass the target I need a course best speed to Titan Space Station."

"We're running away?" Reisman asked.

"We're collecting invaluable data," Connor replied. "Slugging it out with a fleet we hardly know won't help anyone. We make this pass and see what damage we can deliver."

"If we survive the pass," Reisman said.

"Right, if we survive," Connor agreed.

The bridge crew of the *Vigilant* watched the main holoscreen tensely as the nearest ship resolved in greater detail. The high-resolution optics showed the asymmetrical hull, the profile of which tugged at the back of Connor's memory, but he couldn't make sense of it.

"Point defense engaged. Firing proton beams!" Lieutenant LaCroix called out, startling anyone who hadn't been watching the range countdown. Several nonessential systems dropped out so the power draw for the proton beams could be met. Connor watched as the projectors heated up under the continuous fire, but he saw parts of the damaged enemy hull get sloughed away by the powerful beams.

"We've got a thermal buildup along the target's starboard side," Lieutenant LaCroix said.

"Let's get a—" Connor's command was cut off as a brilliant flash lanced out from the enemy ship and slammed into the *Vigilant* full on the nose of the ship. The main display winked out and all other sensor feeds were cut in an instant. Klaxon alarms were blaring on the bridge and the terminals that were still working were scrolling a seemingly endless list of warnings.

"Some sort of high energy thermal blast. Most of the sensors are out!" Colonel Reisman said.

"Switch to backups," Connor said and tried to access his own terminal, but it was down. "Get damage control teams to the affected areas and get me a casualty report."

Secondary sensor systems came online as the armored hatches opened along the forward edge of the *Vigilant's* hull. Soon the main holodisplay popped back up. The enemy ship was venting a substance into space but didn't show any signs of slowing down.

"Helm, once we're on course, cut the engines. Tactical, go to passive scans," Connor said.

Reisman frowned at him. "We're not leaving?"

Connor shook his head. "No. We still have more we can do here."

"Sir, we can't make a stand against so many. We don't have the firepower for that. You've seen how many there are," Reisman said.

"I know that, Colonel!" Connor shouted and clenched his teeth for a moment. "Listen up, and this goes for the rest of the crew. Nothing we're about to do is going to follow the established procedures for facing an enemy force. Those procedures would have us either tuck tail and run or stand our ground and die, neither of which appeals to me. We still have more damage we can do to the enemy so there'll be that many fewer Titan Space Station has to face. We know they're out there. The fact that they now show up on PRADIS means Titan Space Station knows as well. We're not going anywhere. The *Banshee* is still out there and likely went silent to avoid enemy detection."

Reisman arched a brow and nodded. "The *Wyatt's* last transmission had to do with repelling boarders. Whoever they are might be seeking to capture us rather than destroy us."

"Let's work the problem. Tactical, bring up the last known position of enemy ships," Connor said.

The holoscreen flicked on and showed a populated tactical readout of the engagement.

"There it is. This is what we couldn't see before. They sent out a smaller group for this engagement," Connor said.

Major Hayes stood near the tactical workstation. "Why are we able to see this now, sir?"

"The cyber warfare AI is still going through the captured tactical data and is now filling in some of the gaps we couldn't see before," Connor said.

"Then there's still more of the enemy in the area and we can't use active scans or we'll give away our position," Reisman said.

Connor nodded. "Major Hayes, you are to be commended. If it hadn't been for your actions, we wouldn't have known the enemy fleet was there until it was much too late."

Major Hayes looked uncomfortable for a moment. "Thank you, sir."

Connor looked over at Reisman, who was working on something on his own terminal. "We hit their main fleet," Reisman said.

"How can you tell?" Major Hayes asked.

"We can't track where the HADES IVs detonated. We can only see the aftermath from the fission warheads. It's likely their main fleet is as blinded as we are right now," Reisman said.

Major Hayes glanced at Connor. "Who are they?"

Connor noticed that most of the crew on the bridge craned their necks in his direction. They knew who it was but needed to hear it from him. They needed their commanding officer to confirm it for them.

"You all know who they are. These are the forces we were warned about over seven years ago. A last warning from Earth," Connor said.

"But these aren't Earth ships, and their firepower is beyond anything I've ever seen before," Major Hayes said.

Connor glanced around at all the CDF crew on the bridge. Most looked pale, as if they were walking over their own graves. "The question of whether a malevolent attack force is coming to New Earth has been answered. Humanity's enemy is right out there. They've traveled across the void to get here, to get to you and your families. This is why we formed the Colonial Defense Force. We don't cave in to fear. Only the best of us came onto the *Ark* all those years ago.

"Now, there are a lot of unanswered questions and we have our work cut out for us getting those answers. Accept that there is nowhere we can run or hide. They wouldn't have come as they did if they sought an alliance with us. We need to settle down and focus on our jobs. We have a lot of data to go through and we need to keep a sharp eye out because they're hunting for us. They have the advantage both in numbers and in knowing the capabilities of our ships. What they haven't counted on is us, people like Major Hayes, who had the insight to configure PRADIS to scan for ship wakes through space. This is where we pull together and face our enemy."

Determination burned from the eyes of the bridge crew and they went back to their assigned tasks with renewed vigor. Connor gestured for Reisman and Hayes to come closer so they could speak.

Reisman gave him a hungry look. "It's been a long time since we've been in the thick of it. What's our next move?"

Major Hayes frowned. "I sometimes forget that you two served together before becoming part of the colony."

Connor felt the edges of his lips curve just a tad. "You're doing fine. I want you on damage assessment. You've spent more time on this ship than either Wil or me. I need to know what systems were damaged and what we have in terms of weapons capability."

"Sir, I have to admit . . . when I heard you order us to make a head-on pass, I froze up," Major Hayes said.

"So did I, for a moment," Connor said. "We do the best we can with the information we have."

"You'll get used to it, Major. I've learned to trust the general's instincts over the years." Reisman shrugged.

"We haven't used the mag-cannons yet. I could have the engineering team check the accelerator rails in each gun and recalibrate the turret actuators to be sure they're fully operational," Major Hayes said.

Connor shared a look with Reisman. "Good thinking. Feel free to share any more gems like that."

"I'll get to it," Major Hayes said and left the bridge.

Connor turned toward the main holoscreen. Nothing on the passive scans indicated a change in any of the known enemy contacts.

"This isn't going to last long," Reisman said.

"I know. We need to come up with a plan now that we have more of an idea of what we're dealing with," Connor said and brought up the first visual they had of the enemy ship. The image had been refined and compiled against the closer scans from their engagement.

"That hull looks like it's carved out of an asteroid," Reisman said.

Connor rubbed his chin and squinted. "There's something familiar about its shape. Computer, can you put a spectral analysis on the ship's interior?"

An error message appeared on the screen, indicating insufficient data.

"Not like an asteroid," Reisman said and zoomed in on a smooth section that curved as if it were blanketed over something else. "That kind of shape doesn't occur naturally."

Like lightning, a thought blazed across his mind. "I've got it!" Connor said. He opened another window on the main holoscreen and brought up a schematic diagram of a Barracuda-class battleship carrier. "Computer, scale the schematic diagram so it's of the same dimensions as the enemy vessel."

The image resized to the parameters Connor had given. "Overlay schematics on top of the enemy ship. Angle the plane so it matches the approach vector."

The two images came together and Connor blew out a breath.

Reisman's eyes widened and he stepped closer to the image. "I don't believe it," he said.

"Can't be a coincidence," Connor replied. "Computer, run an analysis of the dynamic planes and their alignment relative to the enemy ship."

Ninety percent match.

Connor's mouth went dry. They'd just traded blows with a ship that out-massed them by more than twenty times their tonnage.

"What the hell happened to the ship?" Reisman asked.

"The substructure is that of a Barracuda-class battleship

carrier. I have no idea what that hull is made of, but you can be damn sure it's not an asteroid," Connor said.

He glanced at Reisman, who seemed to have had a thought and then shook his head.

"Spit it out, Wil. I'll take anything at this point," Connor said.

"It's like someone put an exoskeleton over the existing ship. Like a clam that grows its own shell one layer at a time," Reisman said.

Connor pinched his lips together. "In space?"

Reisman shrugged. "It's the first thing I thought of. I didn't say it made any sense."

"Let's see if we have images of the damage we caused. Maybe there's a clue in there that will indicate what it is," Connor said.

"If these are old alliance military ships encased in some kind of living exoskeleton, that could be the reason they're so hard to detect on PRADIS," Reisman said.

Connor sighed. "I hope the mag-cannons are operational."

Reisman frowned. "Why is that?"

"Because proton beams and perhaps even the HADES IVs aren't going to be enough to penetrate the armored hull, whatever that material is. Maybe a good old-fashioned slug shot can cause more damage and pave the way for a more powerful warhead," Connor said.

Reisman grunted.

"Let's get this organized. Piecemeal out the analysis," Connor said.

"And just hope they don't detect us before we can detect them," Reisman replied.

Connor didn't respond. He didn't have to. They were on borrowed time. Hopefully the intelligence they gleaned from their encounter would pay dividends going forward.

CHAPTER SIXTEEN

NOAH GLANCED at the time in the upper right corner of his terminal session's display. It was oh three hundred hours and he'd slept only a handful of hours since the battle group had left to investigate the anomaly that appeared on PRADIS. Since then, Colonel Douglass had set the status for Titan Space Station at Condition Two for the existence of a probable threat that wasn't present yet. Noah had worked almost around the clock to upgrade the HADES IV missiles. And it wasn't just him. Colonel Douglass had ordered every able-bodied person to help with that effort, as well as getting additional weapons systems online.

A message appeared on his holoscreen.

::*Report to the Command Center a.s.a.p,*:: Col. K. Douglass said.

Noah acknowledged the message and closed down his session. He was alone in the Engineering lab, where he'd been checking the calibrations for the subsystems of the HADES IV-B. If he'd had more time, he might have worked out a way to add some kind of point defense systems to the highly accurate missiles, but he couldn't make it work and fit them into the launch tubes they had available.

Noah glanced around at the Engineering lab. He'd hoped to see Kara before he was due to leave but that had been all but impossible with what was happening. She could have been avoiding him, but he wasn't sure of that. He couldn't be sure of anything given how tired he was.

Noah double-timed it to the Command Center and headed right toward the cradle, where he knew Colonel Douglass would be. The heart of the Command Center was fully staffed, with each workstation occupied by CDF personnel.

Noah glanced at the PRADIS screen that showed the CDF attack group. They were nearing the predetermined range where they'd turn around and head back to the station.

"Comms, open a link to the *Chmiel* and find out why Captain Benson is sticking around. He was cleared to disembark hours ago," Colonel Douglass said.

"Sir, you requested to see me," Noah said and stood at attention just outside the cradle.

Colonel Douglass glanced at him.

"Colonel, Captain Benson is requesting to speak to you," Lieutenant Jason Lew said.

Colonel Douglass raised his finger for Noah to wait. "Put him through," Douglass said. "This is Titan actual."

"Colonel, I thought I'd stick around in case you needed further assistance," Captain Benson said.

"I appreciate the gesture, Captain, but the best thing you can do is disembark and head directly back to New Earth," Colonel Douglass said.

"I'd be happy to extend an invitation to any noncombatants you need off the station," Captain Benson said.

The cargo ship captain wasn't part of the Colonial Defense Forces and wasn't required to stick around to offer assistance.

"Thank you, Captain. All personnel on Titan Space Station are essential to its operation," Colonel Douglass replied.

"Understood, Colonel. The *Chmiel* will shove off within the hour. Captain Benson out."

The cargo ship captain sounded disappointed that he couldn't help in some way.

Colonel Douglass turned toward Noah. "Just the engineer I wanted to see."

"I'm at your disposal, sir," Noah replied.

"We received a partial data burst from the *Vigilant* and I'd like you to take a look. We've tried the known reassembly protocols, but they're not working, and I know you have extensive experience with this type of work," Colonel Douglass said.

Noah had spent years trying to get data from the deep-space buoy network in order to glean more information about what had happened to Earth and why the buoy network was failing. Despite all his efforts, he'd only been able to get precious little information from the colony's only link to Earth, but he had developed a talent for deciphering partial data dumps.

"Absolutely, sir," Noah said.

"Excellent. Take over the aux work area over there and report to me when you have something," Colonel Douglass said.

The aux work area was at the edge of the cradle. Noah went over to it, sat down, opened up a terminal session, and went to work. The signal appeared to be intermittent, as if part of the burst had been cut out at different intervals. Noah quickly coded an algorithm to isolate the data burst into individual chunks that the system could interpret. That should make the comms system cooperate and become useful rather than throwing up errors.

Noah then started reviewing the data, and in an instant, his exhaustion evaporated in a rush of adrenaline. He stood up.

"Multiple PRADIS contacts!" Captain Thorne said.

Noah glanced up at PRADIS and frowned. The *Vigilant* disappeared from PRADIS, only to reappear a few moments later. The same went for the *Banshee* and the *Wyatt*.

"Keep tracking," Colonel Douglass said and glanced over at him. "What have you got?"

"I broke down the data burst. They modified how PRADIS scans and had it focus on ship wakes through space," Noah said.

Colonel Douglass became somber. "Put what you found on the main screen."

Noah used his fingers to snatch the image on his terminal, and he flicked it toward the main screen. A PRADIS output showed a massive force that was almost atop the scout force.

A hush came over the Command Center at the image on display. Noah glanced at Colonel Douglass, who was studying the display intently.

"Tactical, configure our PRADIS to alternate scanning intervals for active contacts and ship wakes," Colonel Douglass said.

"Sir, I'm not sure—" Captain Thorne began.

"I can help him, sir," Noah said and darted over to Caleb's workstation.

He showed Caleb where the settings were hidden amongst the options.

"Comms, set Condition One," Colonel Douglass said.

Throughout Titan Space Station for the second time in its history, they readied for imminent attack.

Noah stepped away from Caleb's workstation once it was clear that it was ready. An updated PRADIS feed showed on the main screen.

"Multiple warhead detonations detected," Captain Thorne reported.

Noah searched through the crowded PRADIS screen. "Where's the *Vigilant*?"

"Connor is likely masking the ship's presence from the enemy," Colonel Douglass said.

Noah's face twisted into a confused frown, but he remained quiet.

"Tactical, I want a firing solution on the main attack group," Colonel Douglass said.

"Sir, the intermittent returns on PRADIS will make precise targeting a problem," Captain Thorne replied.

"Understood. Ready the HADES IV-Bs. I want them in the tubes, ready to go," Colonel Douglass said.

Since Noah wasn't assigned to a particular workstation, he went to the colonel's side.

"Sir, if we launch the missiles, isn't there a chance we'll hit the CDF scout force?" Noah asked.

Colonel Douglass regarded Noah for a moment and he had the distinct impression he'd overstepped his bounds.

"I'm sorry, sir," Noah said quickly.

"Listen up," Colonel Douglass bellowed. "There are very few of you who've actually fought in a war. This is the day where that all changes. The CDF scout group has engaged the enemy fleets. From here on out, that is how we will refer to them. General Gates is commanding the *Vigilant*. We'll work like hell not to hurt one of our own, but it may not be helped. War is messy. Our job is to defend the colony from attack. We suspected that this enemy fleet from whatever damn hell they crawled out of was coming for us. The colony is depending on us to do our jobs, and we will."

The CDF soldiers in the Command Center went back to

work. Noah looked at Colonel Douglass. "What do you need me to do?"

"Help me figure out how to stop that fleet. Is there anything else in the data burst?" Colonel Douglass asked.

"Just the PRADIS configuration update to detect ship wakes and that they were engaging the enemy. The rest doesn't make much sense. If we get more information, I can try and parse it into what we already have," Noah replied.

"Understood. I want you to stick around. Sit with Captain Thorne at the Tactical work area and lend assistance as needed," Colonel Douglass said.

"Yes, sir," Noah replied.

Noah walked over and sat down in the seat next to Caleb. "The colonel wants me to give you a hand," Noah said.

"Thanks for the assist earlier. I didn't know PRADIS could be configured to scan like that," Caleb replied.

"How do you decide what to target?" Noah asked.

Caleb pinched his lips together. "It's all about establishing priority targets. We have some time because they're still pretty far out."

"How much time do we really have? Couldn't they have already fired their weapons . . . you know, missiles of their own?" Noah asked.

"They could, but we would have detected them," Caleb said.

Noah frowned at the tactical display. "Why haven't they fired on us yet?"

"I have no idea. What I have here is a long-range firing solution. It's pretty run of the mill, designed to strike at the heart of this main attack force. Since we're targeting ship wakes, we have to guess where the ships actually are," Caleb replied.

"If you launched the missiles in groups, wouldn't the targeting systems update?" Noah asked.

"Yes, but that's assuming a strong PRADIS contact. What we have is essentially a passive scan," Caleb said.

"Tactical, still waiting on that firing solution," Colonel Douglass said.

"Alpha, bravo, and charlie packages uploaded and awaiting your approval, sir," Caleb said.

Noah glanced over at Colonel Douglass, wondering what the man was thinking. Noah didn't know what he would do if he were in the colonel's shoes. At this range, even if they launched their missiles, it would still be hours before they reached their targets.

"Approved. Launch the first salvo now," Colonel Douglass said.

Noah watched as Caleb authorized the launch. Armored hatches opened as the HADES IV-B missiles launched from their tubes. The automated loaders were already loading more missiles.

"This is the first of many salvos," Caleb said.

Noah nodded. What would they do after all their birds were in the air? Noah wondered if he should say a prayer. He wanted to know why the enemy fleet hadn't attacked them yet. He looked at the PRADIS screen and hoped his friends serving aboard the *Vigilant* were okay.

CHAPTER SEVENTEEN

CONNOR SAT in the command chair on the *Vigilant's* bridge. Several hours had passed since their initial encounter with the enemy fleet. Major Hayes had just reported in.

"That's four of the main projectors that are simply gone," Reisman said.

"Could have been a lot worse. A few degrees lower and the entire bulkhead for that section might have been gone," Connor replied.

Reisman's brow furrowed as he read through the damage report.

"Excuse me, sir," Sergeant Boers said, standing at attention outside the command area.

Connor waved her over. "Yes, what is it, Sergeant?"

"I've been going back through the recorded signals during the encounter and I was able to make something out. I've isolated some transmissions from the *Wyatt* and I thought you'd like to hear it," Sergeant Boers said.

"Sure thing. Anything we can learn about them will help," Connor said.

Sergeant Boers held up her tablet computer and replayed the signal she'd recorded.

The sounds stemmed from a partial transmission from the *Wyatt*.

". . . They're right on top of us. . . prepare to repel boarders. They're coming through the hangar bay . . ." The person speaking faded away to static. Then another voice spoke in a deep rasp. "Vemus . . ."

The recorded signal finished and Sergeant Boers closed the tablet interface.

"Vemus? Is that all there is?" Connor asked.

"I've heard that word spoken a few other times, but it always sounds the same. Shortly after this recording was when the *Wyatt* went offline. I cross-referenced it in our systems and came up empty," Sergeant Boers said.

"Thank you, Sergeant," Connor said.

The comms officer returned to her workstation and Reisman came over. "We should consider posting security teams at the hangar bay and the airlocks," Reisman said.

"Agreed. I wish I knew why they would try to board a ship in the first place. They clearly have ample firepower," Connor said.

"Vemus. Not sure what that even means," Reisman said.

"Could be a war cry of some sort. The fact that we can't find any remains of the *Wyatt* means they might have been captured instead of destroyed. Two hundred CDF soldiers unaccounted for," Connor said.

"We haven't heard from the *Banshee* either. Do you think they've been captured as well?" Reisman asked.

Connor shook his head. "No. Our scans show there were no enemy ships near them. I suspect Savannah went comms silent to protect their position and she's waiting for our cue on how to proceed. Her greatest weapon is the fact that she's able to sneak around."

Reisman tilted his head, considering. "That's a hell of a gamble."

"And one we'll need to account for in our plans," Connor said.

Reisman blew out a breath. "Good, so you have a plan," he said with mock severity.

Connor was momentarily taken aback and then snorted. "You'd think after all these years I'd be expecting that kind of crap."

The doors to the bridge opened and Sean walked in, leading two other men from his team. He turned back and gave them some orders, and they began using handheld scanners to make a sweep of the bridge.

Connor had received a message from Dr. Allen that Colonel Ian Howe had died a short while ago. The body had been preserved. He needed the perpetrators found, but this was a distraction he couldn't afford right now.

Sean came over. "Sir, we're making a sweep of the bridge."

"Do you really expect to find traces of radioactivity here?" Connor asked.

"Leave no stone unturned, sir," Captain Quinn replied. "We've narrowed it down to a specific type of radiation and have found trace amounts of it in the mess hall and in common areas of the ship. We searched through crewman quarters, but that didn't yield anything."

Connor glanced over at the two CDF soldiers scanning the bridge. They earned themselves more than one annoyed glance from the busy bridge crew.

"We've questioned soldiers who had access to equipment that

would extract the substance used to poison Colonel Howe, but they all check out. They all had alibis and a reputation for being loyal to Howe," Sean said.

The soldiers waited just outside the command area, and Connor gestured for them to come do what they needed to do. The soldiers hastened inside.

"Has Captain Toro turned up anything?" Connor asked.

"He's chasing down a few leads but nothing so far. We've been widening our search beyond the most direct places. Engineer Hatly has been helpful in showing the bare minimum we would need to extract polonium. Unfortunately, a crude setup can be hidden almost anywhere," Sean said and glanced over at the soldiers who were scanning the area. They'd stopped around the command chair.

"Do you have something, Lieutenant?" Sean asked.

The soldier nodded. "I have trace readings on the arms of the chair and on the terminal interface."

Connor walked over and looked at the data on the scanner. There was just enough to show that someone who'd been in the command chair had come into contact with the polonium.

"Trace readings though, so not an immediate danger," Reisman said.

The soldier with the scanner pointed it at Reisman and then at Connor. "You're fine," the lieutenant said.

"This narrows things down," Connor said, glancing at his hands.

Throughout his career as a soldier, people had tried to kill him, but it had always been more direct, such as with a gun in hand.

"Sir, I need your authorization for the command logs to the bridge, as well as your personal quarters and anywhere else you've been for the past week," Sean said.

Reisman's brows pulled together in surprise and he looked at Connor. "You're the target?"

Connor clenched his teeth for a moment. "You can have whatever you need. Catch the bastard."

"Sir, in light of this recent development, I need to assign you a security detail for your own protection. They'll be with you at all times until this is resolved," Sean said.

Connor shook his head in disgust. They needed to focus their attention on the enemy, not be suspicious of one another. "Comms, give me a ship-wide broadcast channel," he said and waited for Sergeant Boers to open the channel. Connor stepped toward the railing that separated the command area from the rest of the bridge. With teeth clenched, he grabbed the metallic bar and squeezed as if he could choke the life from it. "Crew of the *Vigilant*, this is General Gates," Connor said, his voice sounding harsh. "I have disturbing news to share with you beyond the enemies nipping at our heels. Colonel Ian Howe has died. He's been murdered. I realize this comes as a shock to most of you. By all reports, Colonel Howe was highly respected by his crew, and he will be deeply missed. The fact that he was murdered by a despicable act of cowardice leaves little doubt in my mind that we have a traitor in our midst. Colonel Howe was poisoned, and the guilty parties are still at large. Dr. Allen informed me that Colonel Howe succumbed to radiation poisoning. Though Dr. Allen made him as comfortable as possible, it was not gentle. He died in pain and he suffered. Crew of the *Vigilant*, rest assured that I will do everything in my power to find the people responsible for this and they will be dealt with decisively." Connor paused with a sneer and glared upwards. "And to the people responsible for this, I know you're out there, listening on this ship-wide broadcast, wondering what you're going to do next. Don't bother. I'm going to find your traitorous ass and I'm going to nail it to the wall. You may be hiding now, scurrying in the shadows, but there is nowhere you can hide from me!"

Connor cut the broadcast. Of all the things they should be focusing on right now, a traitor among them wasn't at the top of his list. That slippery son of a bitch was going to pay. The one thing above all others that couldn't be tolerated in any military was a betrayal of one's own.

Connor swung his gaze toward Sean. "Find who did this."

Sean leveled his gaze in return. "You have my word, sir. I will find them."

Connor nodded and turned his gaze back to the main holo-screen. Sean left the bridge and sent in two security officers, posting them just outside the command area.

Reisman came to stand beside him. "You think your speech will smoke out our assassin?"

"I hope so. I have a very short list of people I absolutely trust. You and Sean are on the top of that list," Connor said.

"It's going to take more than two of us to survive this," Reisman said.

"Now we have more than two of us. Howe was loved by his crew. It was a cruel twist of fate that he got caught in the cross-fire, but this also proves something else," Connor said.

"What's that?"

"This would-be assassin didn't act alone. Someone told him to do this," Connor said.

Reisman frowned while he thought about it. "Governor Parish?"

Connor shrugged. "Or one of his supporters. He's been the most vocal about his thoughts on the CDF. Even if he didn't give the actual order, someone in his administration did. If we live through what we're doing out here, I hope we find out who."

"I'll make sure the next comms drone we send back has an extra package for Frank Mallory," Reisman said.

Connor smiled grimly. "Time to move forward with the plan," he said.

Connor scowled at the command chair. He couldn't use it until it had been decontaminated. He stood in the middle of the command area with his hands clasped behind him. "Ops, I want a scanner drone deployed. Use only CDF encrypted channels. I want anything remotely related to the old NA Alliance protocols isolated from the system. Lock out those options unless I give my express permission."

"Yes, sir, initiating lockout of Alliance protocols from the system," Sergeant Browning said.

"Tactical, can you isolate the enemy ship that took the *Wyatt*?" Connor asked.

"I have its position at the time of the engagement. We've been drawing steadily toward Titan Space Station," Lieutenant LaCroix said.

"Sir, scanner drone has been deployed. Configured to go active on your command," Sergeant Browning said.

"Acknowledged," Connor responded.

"Once we activate that drone, they'll know we're scanning the area," Reisman said.

"I'm counting on it. We'll need to move quickly once we get targeting data," Connor said.

"What about using the *Banshee*? I think I have a way to send specific instructions to Major Cross," Reisman said.

"Now that we know the enemy fleet is made up of NA Alliance military ships, we do have an insight into their capabilities. You find a way to reach the *Banshee*, and if you succeed, I want her to send her missiles at the main fleet while continuing on toward Titan Space Station," Connor said.

"We should be within long-range missiles. Kasey will likely have already launched them," Reisman said.

"Yup, which means our window to find which of these ships has the *Wyatt* is closing. I'll leave you to it. I need to speak to LaCroix," Connor said.

He walked over to the Tactical response work area of the bridge. "Lieutenant, I need you to do a couple of things for me. Some of them will seem unorthodox," Connor said.

Lieutenant Vladimir LaCroix looked up at Connor. "Ready when you are, sir."

"First, I want you to bring up the schematics of a Barracuda-class battleship carrier. Mark all the enemy ships identified as having that ship design and give them the designation Vemus," Connor said.

Lieutenant LaCroix updated the output on the main holo-screen. There were over a hundred ships of the Vemus fleet that had that designation, but there were still many ships that didn't meet that criteria, and Connor wasn't sure what they were.

"We'll need to do this with the known ship types and try to align them with Vemus ships. Allow for a ten percent tolerance to account for that additional exoskeleton the ships seem to have," Connor said.

"Understood, sir. I have a suggestion," LaCroix said.

"Go ahead," Connor replied.

"We do have the ability to deploy mines using a cold launch so they won't be detected. I'm thinking that littering the battle-field with them and just setting an old-fashioned timer to deto-nate when the bulk of the enemy fleet is on them would have some lasting results," LaCroix said.

"That could work and does get around the fact that they can block our communications. I'm just not sure how effective they'll be," Connor said.

"Just something to consider, sir," LaCroix said.

"We'll hold off on it for now. Once we activate the scanner drone, I'll need firing solutions fairly rapidly," Connor said.

"What's the targeting priority, sir?"

"The way their fleet is deployed makes me think they expect to take their hits at the very front—the line of battle, if you will. I want to bypass them and have our birds hit them in the middle. The HADES IV-B should be able to handle that. How the ships on the line react will reveal which one of them has the *Wyatt*. They likely latched onto the ship somehow, which would make that ship oddly shaped, unless they try to fit it in the middle hangar. It would be a tight fit, and I expect that ship would be the least likely to react," Connor said.

"That's the one you want me to isolate when the scanners go live?" LaCroix asked.

"Yes, and I'll need a solution for disabling that ship," Connor said.

"What's this about disabling a ship?" Reisman asked as he walked over.

Connor glanced over at the colonel. "We'll need a boarding party of our own, unless we get confirmation that the *Wyatt* has been destroyed and all her crew lost. Otherwise we go get them back and try to learn more about the enemy," Connor said.

Reisman's mouth hung open. "That's likely to be a one-way trip."

Connor leveled a look at him. "With as many ships as we've snuck aboard, is this any different?"

"Very much so. We don't even know who's flying those ships," Reisman said.

"Exactly. We need more intelligence," Connor said.

"Let me guess. You want to lead the team over there," Reisman said.

Connor frowned and leaned back.

"It's not appropriate for a general to be on the away team," Reisman said.

"Fine, I'll promote you to general and demote myself. Either way it's gonna happen. There's no one more qualified to lead a team for that," Connor replied.

"We'll see about that," Reisman said.

Lieutenant LaCroix glanced at both of them, looking extremely uncomfortable. "I don't want to get in the middle of this," he muttered.

Connor looked back at LaCroix. "Carry on, and remember what I said about those firing solutions. Do you need additional support?"

"That won't be necessary, sir," LaCroix said.

Connor headed back to the command area and Reisman followed him.

"It's neither here nor there unless we can find them. Otherwise, we're going to keep picking away at the Vemus. They're not searching that hard for us given that they just keep heading toward Titan Space Station. Have you found a way to contact the *Banshee*?" Connor asked.

Reisman gave him a bored expression. "Of course. Just need the final word on the plan and the coordination involved."

"I'm thinking fire and run," Connor said.

"Major Cross won't like that. She likes to fight," Reisman said.

"She'll get her chance. Let's go over the message. Are you sure it won't be detected?" Connor asked.

"Oh, it'll be detected, but they won't be able to read it," Reisman said.

Connor gave him a look.

"Shouldn't be able to read it."

Connor nodded. "Alright, let's not give the enemy abilities we can't confirm they have."

CHAPTER EIGHTEEN

"MAJOR, we have an encrypted-channel, one-way communication from the *Vigilant*," Lieutenant Daniels said.

The bridge of the Destroyer *Banshee* became quiet. Major Savannah Cross looked up from her terminal.

"Send it to my screen," Savannah said.

They'd gone into stealth mode, or as stealthy as any ship of the wall could go. At least the *Banshee* was designed to loiter in enemy territory.

Savannah waved her XO over.

John Elder returned to the command area and looked at Savannah's screen.

"Message header looks authentic," John said.

"I concur," Savannah said and opened the message.

She read through her orders twice and allowed John to take a look.

"They want us to strike out and then retreat to Titan Space Station," John said.

"Evidently, General Gates would like to use us as a distraction and as bait. We're to get the enemy forces to commit their forces to the space station," Savannah said and sat back in her chair.

She hated those orders but agreed with them at the same time. The preliminary scans they'd managed to salvage from PRADIS showed a huge fleet of ships heading right toward New Earth.

Savannah opened a broadcast channel to her ship. "Crew of the *Banshee*, this is Major Cross. We've just received our orders from the *Vigilant*. Our enemy is called the Vemus. It's the only word that could be deciphered from recorded transmissions. Our orders are to strike at the Vemus's frontlines and draw their attack in toward Titan Space Station, at which time we are to report in to Colonel Douglass on Titan. Stand by for additional orders. We stay at Condition One. Cross out."

Savannah closed the broadcast comms channel. "Tactical, in a few minutes' time we're going to get targeting data from a scanner drone. We'll enable PRADIS for a short burst. Then you'll have a small window in which to formulate a firing solution," Savannah said.

"Ready, willing, and able, Major," Sergeant Brennan said.

"Helm, plot a course to Titan. Best speed," Savannah said.

"Yes, ma'am, best speed to Titan," the helmsman replied.

Savannah glanced at John Elder. "You'll want to strap yourself in."

"Thank you, ma'am," Captain Elder said and hastened to his seat.

Savannah kept her eyes on the main holoscreen, waiting for all hell to break loose.

"DRONE ACTIVATION IN ONE MINUTE, GENERAL," Sergeant Browning said.

"Acknowledged," Connor replied.

A timer appeared in the upper right corner of the main holo-screen. The onboard computer systems were about to get a heap of much-needed targeting data. Six rail-cannons reported "status ready." HADES IV missiles were loaded in the remaining tubes. Engineer Hatly had assured him that since they kept the reactors hot the engines could be quickly brought online. Connor didn't dare give the order before the scanner drone started broadcasting.

The timer dwindled down to zero and a connection status of "waiting for data" appeared on the main screen. Connor counted off in his mind. They were about to get a peek into the battlefield as it was in real time.

Vemus contacts began populating the tactical screen.

"You have thirty seconds, Lieutenant LaCroix," Connor said.

Connor put up another timer on screen. As the enemy contacts continued to show up on screen, he knew LaCroix was working up a firing solution.

"Fifteen seconds, Lieutenant," Connor said.

The tactical officer's fingers flew through the interface as he kept updating the targeting parameters with more Vemus ships.

"Ready for launch," Lieutenant LaCroix said as the timer reached zero.

"Fire!" Connor said.

HADES IV-B missiles shot from their tubes. No sooner had the order been given than another countdown timer appeared. LaCroix was already hard at work identifying additional targets for the next wave of missiles.

"Ops, you're going to bring PRADIS back online. Active scans," Connor said.

PRADIS came back online and the *Vigilant's* computer system fed the data from the scanner drone into it.

"Scanner drone has gone offline," Sergeant Browning reported.

That hadn't taken the Vemus long. Connor watched the PRADIS output and didn't know if it was an act of providence that had spared them from having any Vemus ships around them or if they were just lucky, but they were alone for the time being.

A second wave of HADES IV-Bs fired from their tubes.

"Helm, bring us about, toward the Vemus fleet," Connor said.

"Yes, sir, bringing us about," Sergeant Edwards replied.

"Sir, I'm showing HADES IV missiles have been launched from Titan Space Station," Sergeant Browning said.

"Acknowledged," Connor said, thankful Kasey hadn't wasted any time engaging the Vemus. "Tactical, account for the incoming HADES IVs from Titan into your targeting solutions."

"Yes, sir," LaCroix answered.

"General, one of the Vemus ships has broken away from the front and is on an intercept course for us," Reisman said.

"Ops, target that ship with the rail-cannon. It's big enough for us to hit it even at this distance," Connor said.

The rail-cannons were bolted into the superstructure of the ship. It was the only way they could be fired without tearing the ship apart.

"Colonel, any sign of the *Wyatt?*" Connor asked.

Reisman peered intently at his own holoscreen. He looked up at Connor. "Negative, sir."

"Understood. Helm, hold this position for twenty seconds and then plot a course toward Titan Space Station, best speed," Connor said.

Sergeant Edwards echoed his command. Connor watched as the Vemus battleship carrier drew steadily closer.

"Confirm hits with rail-cannon, sir," Sergeant Browning said.

"Good, keep pelting it. Tactical, what's our missile status?" Connor asked.

"All our birds are in the air, sir," LaCroix said.

They'd gone through their HADES IVs already? Connor glanced at the main holoscreen. There were still so many enemy ships. They had to get out of there before they were caught in the crossfire of their own weapons.

"Sir, I'm detecting a faint comms channel from the *Wyatt*," Sergeant Boers said.

"Can you lock onto their signal?" Connor asked.

"Yes, sir. Ship has been identified," Sergeant Boers said.

Connor looked back at the main screen. On the other side of the Vemus line, drawing steadily toward Titan Space Station, was a signal from the *Wyatt*. "Helm, plot a course to that signal, best speed. Tactical, make use of the Hornets as we go but keep twenty percent in reserve," Connor said.

This mission could go to hell at any moment. The Vemus ships were scrambling to find them. Connor had no illusions that this was a battle he could win. He was just determined to take down as many of the enemy as he could.

"Enemy missiles detected! Danger close! Brace for impact!" Reisman shouted.

Connor checked his seat straps to be sure they were securely fastened. It had been only a matter of time before the Vemus fired back at them. Now it was a matter of how long their luck would hold.

Connor felt a violent shudder spread across the bridge and then his body jerked hard against his restraints. He watched helplessly as Sergeant Browning crashed into his workstation panel and then slumped over in his chair. Connor gritted his teeth and held on. As the ship stabilized, Sergeant Boers and several others went over to help Sergeant Browning.

A massive overload registered on Connor's terminal. He opened a comlink to Engineering. "Damage report," Connor said.

"Sir, we lost two of our main drive pods. The system is completely overloaded. Main engine power down to twenty-five percent," Engineer Hatly replied.

Connor's mouth went dry. "What about the other two drive pods?"

"One is fully operational and we're attempting to reroute power to the other one. Pods three and four are completely gone, sir," Engineer Hatly said.

"Understood. Get me that other drive pod ASAP," Connor said.

He cut the connection to Engineering and looked over at the Ops station. Sergeant Browning was awake and back in his chair.

"Ops, I need a damage report," Connor said.

"Looks like they concentrated fire on our stern engines. Missile tubes six through fifteen are offline," Sergeant Browning said.

"Understood," Connor replied and looked at Reisman. "They're trying to disable us, and they knew where to hit us."

"Agreed. I think it must be what they did to the *Wyatt*," Reisman said.

Connor looked at the PRADIS readout. The ship that had the com signal from the *Wyatt* had disappeared.

"Comms, are we still receiving a signal from the *Wyatt*?" Connor asked.

Sergeant Boers worked with a frantic frown. "Negative, sir.

They're no longer broadcasting any signal," Boers said with a shaky voice.

The *Wyatt* was gone. Two hundred CDF souls aboard.

"Sir, I'm showing waves of HADES IV missiles making their final approach. We need to get out of here to achieve minimum safe distance," Lieutenant LaCroix said.

"He's right, sir. With the *Wyatt* gone, we should head back toward Titan Space Station," Reisman said.

Connor clenched his teeth. They were still just inside the Vemus front lines, and the enemy fleet hadn't increased their speed. "Helm, plot a course for Titan Space Station. Best speed. Execute as soon as you have it."

"Yes, sir," Sergeant Edwards said.

Connor ran the numbers on his terminal. With only one drive pod, even at best speed they only stood a slim chance of clearing the detonations of the HADES IV missiles.

"Come on, Hatly, get me that other drive pod," Connor said softly.

Reisman heard him and gave a grim nod. They needed that engine or they were going to die.

"Sir, I'm showing drive pod two is now active!" Sergeant Edwards said.

"Punch it!" Connor said.

The *Vigilant* lurched forward as the magneto-plasma drive pods sucked in power from their remaining reactors. Connor felt a shudder under his feet and he watched the plot as the *Vigilant* slowly moved ahead of the Vemus fleet.

CHAPTER NINETEEN

NOAH HAD REMAINED in the command center and continued to assist Caleb at the tactical workstation. He glanced at the time on one of the main tactical holoscreens that were tracking the missiles they'd launched at the enemy fleet. When Noah first joined the CDF, he'd assumed that missile deployments were effectively straightforward affairs. Nothing could be further from the truth. Even with the increased accuracy he'd been able to achieve for the HADES IV-Bs, they still had to reach their relative positions. Colonel Douglass hadn't gone for the simple and direct approach, which would have been to fire all the missiles in their arsenal. Each wave of missiles had an effective targeting location and they flew at different speeds in order to hit the enemy fleets all at once. There was a delicate balance of timing and precision that Noah had come to appreciate.

He glanced at the PRADIS screen, and none of the enemy fleet had broken formation.

"Colonel, I'm showing a CDF responder coming just ahead

of the enemy fleet's front line. It's the *Vigilant*," Caleb Thorne said.

Noah's eyes widened in excitement. They hadn't heard from the *Vigilant* since the attack first began.

"Sir, I have a comms channel from the *Vigilant*. It's General Gates," Lieutenant Foster said.

"Put them through," Colonel Douglass said. The comms channel registered as active. "I was beginning to think you were going to miss the party."

"We had a few shake-ups of our own. The *Wyatt* is gone. I sent the *Banshee* to you, but we've taken significant damage and I don't know if she made it," Connor said.

"Major Cross has checked in and I told her to stay close to the station. She'll get to see some more action before this day is done," Colonel Douglass said.

Noah's brows drew upward and he looked over at the colonel. Surely all the HADES IV missiles armed with their nuclear warheads would be enough to severely damage the approaching fleet?

"What's the status of the *Vigilant*?" Colonel Douglass said.

"The Vemus started to return fire on us. They targeted our engines and we're down to only two main engine pods left. Our analysis is that they were just trying to disable the ship so they could take us alive. One of the last broadcasts from the *Wyatt* was that they were repelling boarders. There's a good chance they're going to try the same thing on the space station," Connor said.

"Understood. We'll be ready," Colonel Douglass said.

There was a long moment of garbled static before the channel was cleared by the comms AI that automatically aligned communications signals for optimum performance.

"How long do we have, Kasey?" Connor asked.

Noah frowned at the somberness of the tone. He'd rarely heard Connor break protocol on an official CDF channel before. He looked over at Colonel Douglass and saw that the former Ghost's mouth formed a thin grim line.

"Not long," Colonel Douglass said, his voice sounding thick.

"I thought so. Our PRADIS array has taken some damage, so not all the scanner fields are working anymore," Connor said.

Colonel Douglass muted the comms channel so Connor wouldn't hear him. "Tactical, will the *Vigilant* reach minimum safe distance?"

"Hold a moment, we're picking up something on our sensors," Connor said.

Within moments, multiple contacts showed on PRADIS.

Colonel Douglass took the comms channel off mute. "We see them."

Captain Thorne worked through the blast radius from the HADES IV missile envelope whose detonation timing was closing in on the *Vigilant*. "It's going to be real close, sir."

Colonel Douglass nodded. "General, you're almost at a minimum safe distance. You're still in this. The noose is closing in standard V deployment."

"Understood. The new contacts are moving much faster than anything else we've seen so far. They're smaller vessels. Can't do the analysis here, but I suspect they're some form of Talon 5 assault crafts," Connor said.

Noah brought up a search on his terminal. Titan's computer systems held a data repository of all known NA Alliance navy vessels in existence when the *Ark* left Earth's solar system. He entered Talon 5 into the search field and his mouth went dry. Talon assault crafts were specifically designed to puncture a hole through bulkheads and deliver troops onto enemy vessels. They were also designed for speed and were highly maneuverable.

Soldiers were strapped into place and administered a special cocktail to help them withstand forces that were beyond the inertia dampeners' ability to compensate.

"Ops, I need you to confirm that," Colonel Douglass said.

"Yes, sir. We're tracking," Sergeant Moors said.

"We'll attack them from the rear, but you're going to need to unleash the fury and initiate Jade protocol," Connor said.

Noah glanced at Colonel Douglass. He'd never heard of Jade protocol and had no idea what that meant.

"Understood, General. I'll be in contact," Colonel Douglass said.

"Good luck, Titan," Connor said.

Noah watched as Colonel Douglass went over to his terminal.

"Colonel, the Talon 5s will be here within thirty minutes," Sergeant Moors said.

Colonel Douglass broke focus on his terminal session and glanced up. "Understood. Go to Condition One. Imminent attack on the station. Defense protocols authorized."

Noah heard the operations officer send a broadcast throughout the station. A new notification appeared on Noah's terminal with orders for him to report to the main hangar. He glanced at Colonel Douglass and noticed that several CDF personnel began leaving the Command Center. Other CDF personnel sprinted in to fill the vacant posts. Noah closed his terminal session, stood up, and went over to Colonel Douglass.

"Colonel, is this accurate?" Noah asked and flipped the screen of his PDA toward the Colonel.

Colonel Douglass stood up. "Donnelly, take over. I'll only be a few minutes."

Lieutenant Colonel Donnelly went to the command chair.

Colonel Douglass looked at Noah. "Walk with me, Noah."

Noah frowned. The colonel addressing him by his name rather than rank didn't make him feel at ease in the slightest, but he followed his commanding officer away from the Command Center. They went toward the lifts.

"Your orders are correct. You are to report to the main hangar and board the Frigate *Abacus*," Colonel Douglass said.

Noah's eyes widened. "I'm not sure I understand, sir."

Colonel Douglass glanced around to be sure they weren't overheard. "You're returning to New Earth."

"But why, sir? I can help you," Noah said.

He knew he was overstepping his boundaries by questioning his superior officer, but he didn't want to leave.

Colonel Douglass placed his hand on Noah's shoulder. "Listen to me. Jade protocol was put in place so we could ensure that key personnel would be transported back to New Earth in case this station fell into enemy hands. This is not a slight on your abilities. Quite the contrary. You're one of the good ones and essential for the defense of New Earth."

Noah swallowed hard. He didn't know what to say. He didn't want to leave. He wanted to stay and fight.

"Now, can I count on you to get to the frigate, or do I need to assign a security detail to take you there?" Colonel Douglass said.

Noah glared at the man. "Yes, sir."

Colonel Douglass gave him a firm squeeze on his shoulder and then headed back toward the Command Center.

"Colonel," Noah called out, and Douglass turned around. Noah stood up straight and snapped a salute. "Good luck, sir."

Colonel Douglass saluted in kind. "Good luck to us all."

As Noah ran toward the lifts, he brought up his PDA and looked for Kara's signal. Her personal locator showed that she was several levels up from the main hangar, in Engineering.

Noah went inside the elevator and selected the Engineering level. A group of soldiers ran toward the elevator as the doors started to shut and Noah thrust his hand out to stop them from closing.

The CDF soldiers piled inside, easily filling the space. One of the soldiers glanced at him. "Captain, you should be armed. The order was just given. Where are you heading?"

Noah hadn't heard the order. "Engineering. I'll stop at the nearest weapons locker."

"Phelps, give him a weapon."

The soldier named Phelps turned toward Noah and handed him an M11-Hornet. Noah took the SMG and thanked him.

"Are you familiar with that weapon, sir?" the sergeant asked.

"Yes, I've used one of these before," Noah answered. He'd kept up with his weapons training after his introduction to them when Connor had recruited him to Search and Rescue and then later to the Colonial Defense Force.

The elevator stopped and the CDF soldiers ran out. Noah hadn't even gotten the sergeant's name before the doors shut and the elevator resumed its descent to Engineering. As Noah checked the Hornet, the elevator came to a sudden halt. The lights flickered and Noah glanced at them in alarm. There was a muffled boom and he gasped. He went over to the doors and tried to pry them open, but they wouldn't budge. He opened the control panel and tried to override the door, cursing when it failed.

"Think, Noah!"

He glanced around and then looked up at the ceiling panel. He'd have to climb. He went to the side of the elevator and opened the service panel to metal rungs that led upward. Noah climbed up the ladder and reached the service hatch, which he unlocked and thrust upward. The hatch swung open and he climbed out of the elevator.

The long gray elevator shaft stretched out above him. The shaft shuddered as if something massive had slammed into the space station, and the elevator car jerked downward. Noah stumbled toward the wall. He was stuck between floors. Emergency lighting shined on the yellow rungs of a ladder built into the shaft. Noah ran over and began climbing. He reached the next floor and pulled on the emergency release for the door. The metal doors slid open and Noah yelled for help. He heard someone yelling, but they sounded as if they were far away. With one firm hand on the ladder, Noah reached across and grabbed the edge. He let go of the ladder and shuffled across, using his hands to hold him. The elevator car was only ten feet beneath him, so he wouldn't die if he fell, but he didn't relish the thought. Noah pulled himself up and swung his foot to the side, climbing out the rest of the way and pushing himself to his feet.

"Alert! Vemus forces have entered the station."

Noah's mouth hung open. They were already here! That must have been the loud booming sound he'd heard—the sound of those Talon 5 assault ships slamming into the station. Noah glanced over at the emergency container fastened to the side of the wall. Those containers were spaced throughout all the floors of the station. He raced over and opened it, pulling out a rebreather mask and then grabbing a few more, which he stuffed into the sack that hung inside. He slung the sack over his shoulder and tied it off. Since there were ships dive-bombing the station, there could be a sudden loss of atmospheric pressure. The one thing Connor Gates had drilled into him was the value of being prepared so he could adapt to new situations as they unfolded.

Noah ran down the corridor, worming his way among people as they scrambled to get where they needed to be. He opened a comlink and tried to reach Kara. He was one level above where she was, but there was no answer. Noah came to the end of the corridor and turned right.

There was a squad of CDF soldiers heading toward him. Their commanding officer scanned Noah's PDA and frowned. "Sir, you're supposed to be at the main hangar bay. Jade protocol."

"I'm heading there right now," Noah said and tried to worm his way past.

The soldier stopped him. He glanced at the collar of her uniform. T. Reynolds was stenciled on the shoulder.

"Not going that way you're not," Sergeant Reynolds said.

Noah pressed his lips together. "I'm going to Engineering to make sure my friend gets to the hangar too."

Sergeant Reynolds frowned. "Is this friend also part of Jade protocol?"

Noah had no idea if Kara was on this special list. "I think so," he said.

"Then they should already be making their way toward the main hangar. We'll escort you there," Sergeant Reynolds said.

The soldiers began ushering him back the way he'd come. "Stop!" Noah shouted. "I'm not going anywhere until I go to Engineering first, which is one floor below this one."

Sergeant Reynolds shook her head. "My orders are clear," she said.

"I'm giving you new orders then, Sergeant," Noah said. Technically he held the rank of captain in the CDF, but he'd never leveraged his rank before. "You can escort me to Engineering and then we can all go to the hangar."

Sergeant Reynolds' brows pulled together. "Yes, sir, but we can't go that way. The area at the end of the corridor has been depressurized."

"Okay, there's a maintenance shaft this way," Noah said.

He led the group of CDF soldiers back the way he'd come and stopped at the maintenance shaft.

Noah took a quick look down. "It's clear."

He moved to step inside the shaft, but Sergeant Reynolds stopped him. "Let one of my squad go first. Butch, you're up."

One of the CDF soldiers came forward and entered the maintenance shaft first. Another followed. Noah went next, and they quickly climbed down the shaft. Butch waved for him to come through and then told him to wait for the others.

Noah looked impatiently down the corridor. The Engineering tech lab was only a short distance away. He took a few tentative steps in that direction and tried to raise Kara on her comlink, then clenched his teeth together in frustration when she didn't answer. She was notorious for casting her comlink to the side when she buried herself in her work.

The rest of the CDF squad came down the shaft and they headed toward the Engineering lab. They heard sounds of weapons fire and Noah quickened his pace.

"Any security squads on deck J? Report," Sergeant Reynolds said on an open channel.

The light flickered overhead and Noah could hear the sounds of the station's defensive batteries firing into the approaching enemy fleet. They came to the end of the corridor and turned left. The entrance to the tech lab was a short distance away. A group of strange figures stood toward the far end of the corridor.

Noah frowned. Something appeared off about the shape of the figures. He brought up his M11-Hornet and aimed it. The end of the corridor was dark and he could only make out faint silhouettes.

"Sir, I get no transponders at the end of the hallway," Butch said.

The squad of CDF soldiers readied their weapons. There was

a loud screeching noise and a white energy bolt came toward them. Noah scrambled toward the wall and squeezed the trigger. Shots spat out of the M11-Hornet in rapid succession. Noah heard the other CDF soldiers fire their weapons. More white energy bolts came toward them, and one struck Butch in the chest. He crumpled down. The CDF squad kept firing their weapons and Noah saw the dark shapes at the end of the long corridor drop from view.

"Sir, Butch has been stunned," a soldier said.

"Pick him up," Sergeant Reynolds said.

Noah raced forward to the tech lab doors and banged his fists on them, then hastily entered his authorization code. The door opened. Kara Roberts sat at a workbench, frantically working at a terminal.

Noah shouted her name. "I've been trying to reach you."

Kara looked over as if surprised to see him. "What are you doing here?"

"I've come to get you. We need to get out of here. The station is under attack," Noah said.

"I know. I just need to finish this first," Kara said.

Noah ran over and tried to grab her arm. "We don't have time for this. They're on the station."

Kara evaded him and went back to her terminal. "I know. I've been picking up their transmissions."

Noah glanced at the bench and saw the transceiver. He opened one of the overhead cabinets, looking for the portable power supply. He found it and connected it to the transceiver.

"Come on, we've got to get to the hangar," Noah said and grabbed the transceiver.

"Alright, I'm coming," Kara said and reached out for a few other devices, stuffing them into her pockets.

They left the tech lab, and the CDF squad was waiting outside for them.

"Major Roberts, I have to get you out of here. Jade protocol is in effect," Sergeant Reynolds said.

Kara frowned, but before she could say anything, Noah said they were ready to go. They went back the way they'd come. Kara glanced around in surprise at the flickering lights and the sound of weapons fire. Sergeant Reynolds led them in a different direction.

"The maintenance shafts are this way," Noah said.

"I know but the quicker way to the hangar is this way," Sergeant Reynolds said.

Noah followed the CDF soldiers.

"Titan Station, this is Colonel Douglass. Vemus forces have entered the station and managed to get a foothold on the lower sections. Security forces have established a perimeter. I'm ordering a general evacuation of the base."

The message ended. Looks like they all needed a way off the station. Sergeant Reynolds quickened her pace and led them into a maintenance tunnel. Once inside, they ran up a ramp and came to the hangar entrance. Noah looked inside the hangar through the window in the door. There was no freighter. CDF personnel were racing toward the shuttles.

"We can't get out that way. They'll fill up the shuttles before we can get near them," Noah said.

Kara held up her PDA and opened a technical readout of the area they were in. "There are escape pods this way, near the end of the hangar."

"Good enough for me. Let's go," Sergeant Reynolds said.

Noah opened the door and heard shouts from the people storming the shuttles. Several shuttles lifted off and sped out of the hangar. They ran along an elevated walkway. The end of the hangar was over two hundred meters away and Noah was breathing heavily by the time they reached it. They entered a maintenance lift, which lowered them to the ground level. Kara ran to an escape pod and began entering her credentials. There was a series of explosions coming from across the hangar. Tall, dark shapes poured out of a smoking hole in the bulkhead. They moved so fast that they seemed to streak toward the mass of CDF personnel clamoring to get on the remaining shuttles.

Noah raised his SMG and fired at the dark shapes. Several of the CDF soldiers with him fired their weapons as well. A couple of the dark shapes went down and then rolled back onto their feet. Noah heard a loud snarling, and several of the Vemus fighters broke away, heading right for him.

Someone grabbed Noah from behind and shoved him into the escape pod. Kara was already inside. Sergeant Reynolds gestured for two of her squad to get inside.

"Not without you, sir," one soldier said.

Sergeant Reynolds looked at Noah and Kara. "We got this," she said.

Before Noah could protest, the sergeant slammed her fist on the controls for the escape pod. The doors hissed shut and the pod launched from the station. Noah cried out, but all he could see was a rapidly retreating view of the main hangar. Off to the side was a cigar-shaped ship that had crash-landed near the hangar. There was no way the small CDF squad could hold off that many.

Noah growled and slammed his fist against the reinforced door. He looked over at Kara, whose eyes were wide with terror. "Why didn't they come with us? They could have just come inside."

Kara glanced at him. "I knew the enemy was coming, but I had no idea. I didn't know."

An alert appeared on the central control panel. Kara opened the interface. "It's a broadcast," she said.

"Escape pods of the Titan Space Station. This is Captain Benson of the cargo ship *Chmiel*. I've included our coordinates in this message. We're not far from your position. Please input the coordinates into the pod's guidance systems and you should be able to reach us."

The message repeated. Noah watched as Kara updated the coordinates. He sat down next to her and strapped himself in. The pod's engines engaged, and Noah felt a small bit of force as the pod took them to the cargo carrier.

"Thank you for coming to get me," Kara said.

Noah was snapped out of his thoughts. "You weren't answering your comlink."

Kara glanced away guiltily. "I know. It's a terrible habit."

"What was so important that you ignored the fact that the station was under attack?" Noah asked.

"The transmissions are under a protocol we don't use. I was recording them so they could be deciphered. We'll need them," Kara said.

Noah looked away. He wanted to ask her why she'd been avoiding him but couldn't bring himself to do so. He kept seeing those dark shapes on the hangar deck. It was like they were made up of a swirling mass.

Kara opened the holo-interface of her PDA and went to work with the recorded signals. Noah looked at it and then joined her. If he couldn't be fighting the Vemus on the station, at least he could do this.

CHAPTER TWENTY

CONNOR SAT in the command chair on the bridge of the *Vigilant*. The visco-elastic used in the seat back and cushion contoured perfectly to his body, but there was no getting comfortable for any of them. Engineer Hatly had created a miracle in record time when he and his team managed to reroute power to the main drive pods, restoring their engine capability to half strength. They'd managed to stay ahead of the Vemus fleet for a short while until the enemy fleet as a whole seemed to wake up.

Even with the limited capability of PRADIS, they were able to see that the HADES IV-B missiles had extracted a heavy toll on the Vemus fleet. Kasey Douglass, Connor's longtime friend, had done his job well. The timed execution of the massive launch of their most powerful missiles, carrying multiple types of warheads, had partially decimated the enemy. They tore into the Vemus fleet, creating a powerful envelope that closed in on them from all sides, squeezing them together. It was a good plan, but it wasn't enough. There were simply too many Vemus ships, and their armored hulls had proven to be highly resistant to nuclear blasts in the vastness of space. Smaller ships hadn't had a chance, but the larger ones that were concentrated toward the middle of the Vemus fleet formations had managed to survive. They'd estimated that the Vemus fleet was down at least forty percent.

After the storm of HADES IVs had done their utmost to destroy the enemy fleet, their Talon 5 assault crafts sped toward Titan Space Station. There was no mistaking the enemy's intentions. The Vemus wanted to take Titan Space Station intact. Connor tried using the *Vigilant's* remaining mag-cannons to take out the Talon 5s as they flew by, but they were moving so fast and there were so many of them that they hardly made a dent in their numbers.

Connor shook his head. If the CDF had a hundred heavy cruisers of their own then perhaps they could have mounted a better defense. As it was, he'd lost a large chunk of his crew through damage to the *Vigilant* alone.

The main holoscreen showed bright flashes as Titan Space Station fought to keep the enemy at bay. The station's point defense systems, including auto-cannons and particle beams, tore into oncoming Vemus ships.

Connor's guts were twisted up in knots. He knew better than to order "all ahead" and help the CDF's first line of defense, but it was hard not to. The soldiers he'd trained were giving their all so the colony could survive, and he couldn't have been prouder.

He stopped himself from displaying any sign of weakness. He had to remain strong for his crew, but he felt a deep, roiling anger that, if left unchecked, would cause him to make more mistakes.

He should have fought harder for the secondary power station Titan needed. The space station even now was exceeding projected capabilities, and Connor attributed that to the CDF soldiers serving on it alongside Kasey Douglass. Connor thought about Governor Parish and the growing political movement that called into question the validity of an attack ever taking place. They'd had seven years to prepare for this, and there were thousands of lives on Titan Space Station that would pay the price. Connor kept thinking of all the things he could have done differently, given what he now knew —how he could have shifted priorities. It was a brutal rabbit hole to get sucked into, even if it was only in his mind, and Connor fought to pull himself out of it. He needed to stay focused.

He opened up the comms interface on his terminal. At least Titan Space Station still had their communications array working.

"*Vigilant*, this is Titan actual," Kasey Douglass said. His voice sounded strange and mildly distracted.

The former Ghost's face appeared on the screen and Connor stood up. The Command Center was a buzz of activity. Most of the CDF personnel Connor could see were armed. There was a shallow gash on the side of Kasey's head.

"Situation report," Connor said.

Kasey leveled his gaze at the camera. "I've ordered an evacuation of the station. Those of us who remain are fighting as long as we can."

Reisman came to stand at Connor's side.

Kasey saw him. "Hey there, you slippery bastard. You watch out for our CO."

"I will," Reisman said, his voice sounding thick.

Connor wanted to tell his friend to run, to get out of there, but the soldier in him knew it was impossible. He knew what Kasey was doing and would have done the same thing himself if he'd been in that position.

Kasey looked over at Connor. "At least it's not as bad as the Sandy Springs Op."

"But we got to walk away from that one," Connor said.

A sad smile appeared on Kasey's face. "I remember when Malarkey got stuck in the compactor. For a medic, he could curse with the best of them. I'll say hello when I see him."

Connor clenched his teeth together. "We both will."

"Going soft on me, General? I know you're not religious at all and don't believe in all that stuff. In fact, I believe you kept calling it superstitious nonsense," Kasey said.

"I changed my mind. I've seen the error of my ways. All is forgiven, right?" Connor said and felt the skin around his eyes tighten. "I wish I could be there with you."

Kasey glanced away from the camera and Connor heard shouting. "If we had ever developed a transporter, I would gladly teleport myself and my crew over to your ship. Regardless, we beamed the intelligence we gathered to COMCENT on New Earth."

A wave of bitterness stiffened Connor's muscles.

"It won't be long now. Vemus forces are fighting toward the bridge. They're vulnerable to our weapons, but they're more interested in capturing us than killing us. Several battleship carriers have continued onward. Do you think you can take care of those for me?" Kasey asked.

"We'll come up with something," Connor answered.

"Sir," Lieutenant LaCroix said, and Connor glanced over at him. "I'm detecting a thermal mass building at the station's main reactor core."

Connor looked back at Kasey and stood up straight. "I'll take it from here, Colonel. You've done more than anyone could have asked of you."

Kasey was about to reply when shouting erupted all around.

There were flashes of light. Connor heard the distinct sound of weapons fire before the comms channel was severed.

"Sir, the thermal mass is reaching critical levels. We need to make best speed possible to escape the blast," Lieutenant LaCroix said.

"Helm, get us out of here," Connor said bitterly.

The main holoscreen showed a massive swarm of Vemus ships surrounding the station, trading blows. Connor wondered why their forces were putting so much effort into capturing the station rather than destroying it and moving on to New Earth. The tactics they were using proved that they still fought an enemy they didn't fully understand. In some respects, the Vemus were extremely slow to respond, and in others, like Titan Space Station, they used an overwhelming show of force, as if their ships didn't matter. Connor frowned and felt like there was something he was missing.

"Ops, I want to know where those Vemus battleship carriers are—"

Connor stopped speaking. A bright flash came from Titan Space Station, and the feed to the main holoscreen cut out. The sensors were blinded. Connor balled his fists and glared at the empty feed, thinking about all those people who had just died.

"Get me their locations," Connor said, his voice sounding raspy and strained. "Wil, take the con."

He left the bridge and the two CDF soldiers assigned to be his security detail followed him.

Connor looked back. "I need a few minutes," he said and gestured to his ready room. The two soldiers stopped just outside the bridge.

Connor opened the door to his room and stepped inside, letting the door shut. The steady hum of the large aquarium cast a warm glow in the dim room.

"Lights," Connor said.

As the lighting in the room became brighter, Connor saw Sean lying on the floor. Connor gasped and ran over to him. He glanced down at Sean's hands and saw that they were bound together at the wrists.

"He's alive," a cold voice said from behind Connor.

Connor spun and was struck in the head by something hard. He instantly went sprawling face-first to the ground. Pain blossomed on the side of his head where he'd been struck. He moved his hands under his chest and pushed himself over. Standing in front of the aquarium, holding a hand-cannon on him, was Captain Alec Toro.

Toro locked the door.

Connor glanced at Sean and then up at the *Vigilant's* head of security.

"It was *you*," Connor said and started to rise.

"Stay down, General," Captain Toro warned.

Connor stayed on the floor and leaned back against the wall. He fingered the side of his head and felt a small trickle of blood. "So, what's your plan here? You kill me and then what?"

Toro's eyes became more intense. "I don't know. You screwed everything up."

"I screwed everything up? You poisoned Ian Howe. You were supposed to be his friend."

Toro charged forward and came to a stop. "I *am* his friend."

Connor glanced at the gun. "Oh, really? I'm sure he appreciated suffering from radiation poisoning right before he died. The doctor had him in a medically induced coma so he wouldn't feel the pain, so who knows if he had any last thoughts at all. That's what you did to your friend."

"It was supposed to be you. It should have been you, but you kept changing things. Always changing things. Testing. Constant drills. Updating your schedule. I thought I had you . . . I did have you," Toro said.

"What did you do to Sean?" Connor asked, wondering if the security detail had heard the commotion.

"He found me out. Traced the polonium to me. Here in this room, in fact," Toro said and gave a lazy gesture with his other hand.

"Here? Why would you come back here?"

"To take one more stab at you," Toro said.

Connor leaned against the wall and brought one leg up toward his chest while extending the other.

"We're being attacked by the Vemus and you still want to kill me. What the hell for?"

Toro shook his head. "I had everything thought out. I knew the way investigations were conducted. You were supposed to be at the mess hall after meeting with the engineer. And then Ian and Nathan were there. I tried to stop them, but it was too late. I knew Ian had ingested the poison and it was already too late," he said, glaring at Connor. "I thought I'd gotten you after that."

Connor frowned. He'd only spoken to Toro here in this room. "The coffee," he said, finally remembering. "You laced it with poison."

Toro nodded his beefy head. "Yup, and you took it onto the bridge with you. I thought for sure you would have reported to Dr. Allen, but you didn't."

Connor shuddered. He remembered losing his appetite and handing the coffee off to the soldier. No one else drank it either.

"Who ordered you to kill me?" Connor asked.

"How do you know I'm not working alone?" Toro asked. The head of security lowered his gun to his side, and his hand shook as it held the hand cannon.

"Because you're too damn stupid to have cooked this up for yourself," Connor said.

Toro's nostrils flared and he brought the hand-cannon up, pointing it at Connor's face.

Connor stared up at him grimly. "You're a coward," he sneered.

Toro cried out and lunged forward, his eyes narrowed menacingly.

Connor kicked out with his foot and caught Toro by surprise. The hand-cannon went off but missed him. Connor sprang to his feet and grabbed onto Toro. The head of security was so strong that Connor might as well have been wrestling a tree. He slammed his fist into Toro's head and tried to hold onto the wrist holding the gun, but his grip slipped. After several long seconds during which Toro didn't take the shot, Connor tore his eyes away from the hand-cannon. Sweat poured from Toro and his face was pale.

"You're dying. You've exposed yourself to too much polonium," Connor said.

Toro seemed to weaken right where he stood and then stumbled backward. He fell, landing near the unconscious Sean. Connor stepped toward Sean, but Toro pointed his gun at Sean's head.

"Haven't you caused enough death? We have an enemy that wants to kill us and we're here killing each other. It's over," Connor said.

"They weren't supposed to find us. The experts made such compelling arguments. Parish said it was impossible. No one was supposed to find us here," Toro said.

"Was it Parish? Is that who ordered you to kill me?" Connor asked.

He didn't glance at the door but he heard the two CDF

soldiers outside. Any second now, they were going to open that door. He had to keep Toro's attention on him or Sean would get shot.

"You changed things again. Instead of keeping the investigation quiet, you broadcast it to the whole damn ship. Everyone knew Colonel Howe had been murdered," Toro said.

The door to Connor's ready room burst open. Connor held up his hand. "Hold!"

The two soldiers glanced at him and then down at Alec Toro, who was pointing a gun at Sean's head.

Toro glanced at the soldiers, his eyes seeming to linger on their uniforms.

"Look at me," Connor said.

Toro swung his gaze toward Connor. "I know this kid is your friend. He's good. Really good. I can see why you keep him around. If I hadn't blindsided him, he would have caught me."

Toro pressed the hand cannon against Sean's head.

"You don't have to do this. It's over," Connor said.

"You're right; it *is* over. I'm dying. Either you or those soldiers are going to kill me—all because we wanted to believe a lie, that there was no invading force coming to the colony and that everyone we left behind on Earth was okay. None of this was supposed to happen," Toro said, and his lips pressed together.

"Don't. He's a good kid and deserves a chance to die fighting for something he believes in," Connor said.

Toro looked at him with red-rimmed eyes and winced in pain. "That's all *I* wanted," he said and then raised the hand-cannon to the side of his own head and squeezed the trigger. Blood and brain matter splattered onto the wall as Toro's dead body slumped into its final rest.

Connor went over to Sean and glanced up at one of the soldiers. "Get a medic in here, now!"

The other soldier went over to Toro's body.

"Get a decontamination team here. He had radiation poisoning and I can't be sure he doesn't have the substance on him," Connor said.

"Sir, you need to step away from him then," the CDF soldier said.

They cut the bonds that held Sean's wrists together and carried him over to the couch. A medic came and started to examine Sean. A few moments later he used smelling salts and Sean woke up.

Connor blew out a breath and rubbed his face. Toro had been right: he did care for Sean like a son—like the son he'd left behind on Earth who bore the same name. He wouldn't have been able to forgive himself if something had happened to Sean.

"Sir, are you alright?" the medic asked him.

"I'm fine," Connor said in a strained voice.

Sean looked over at Toro's body and then looked at Connor. "We found traces of polonium in his quarters and his locker. After I found traces of it on the bridge, I checked everywhere you'd been. It was on your desk, so I knew someone who'd met with you had to be the killer. He must have figured out that I was on his trail. I caught up with him here and he got me."

Connor nodded. "Don't beat yourself up about it. We should be hunting the Vemus, not each other."

Sean sat up but stayed on the couch. "Did he tell you who else was involved?"

"Not directly, but I have a strong suspicion," Connor said.

Sean frowned. "Who?"

"Let's say his orders came from the top, or at least someone close to Parish," Connor said.

Sean shook his head slowly. "What do we do now? We can't let them get away with this."

"Stanton Parish is the least of our concerns. We can worry about it if we make it back to the colony," Connor said.

"What about Titan Space Station?" Sean asked.

Connor's throat became thick. "It's gone."

Sean's eyes widened in shock.

"They called for an evacuation and then Colonel Douglass ordered the self-destruct," Connor said.

Sean swallowed hard. "Did it . . . stop them?"

"I don't know. I'm going back to the bridge. Want to join me?" Connor asked.

"Always, sir. You know that."

Connor did know that and was thankful Sean hadn't been killed, but how many more would he fail to save? He had to get back to the bridge. The self-destruction of Titan Space Station might have struck a crippling blow, but this battle was far from over. They had to activate the missile-defense platforms they had positioned throughout the star system. Perhaps they would be enough to weaken the remaining Vemus ships even further.

CHAPTER TWENTY-ONE

THE ESCAPE PODS carrying Noah and other survivors from Titan Space Station were actually part of the *Ark*, humanity's first interstellar ship that had ferried three hundred thousand men, women, and children out among the stars. Although anything but comfortable, the pods were equipped so that the people inside could survive for weeks.

Noah glanced at the holoscreen that showed them closing in on the *Chmiel*. The cargo carrier had become a lifeboat to hundreds of personnel aboard the life pods that were lucky enough to escape from Titan Space Station before the Vemus made that all but impossible. They'd used the pod's limited thrust capabilities to take them to the cargo ship, reserving just enough fuel so they could perform emergency maneuvers to slow down. Kara had reminded him of that little necessity when he'd suggested they reach the *Chmiel* as quickly as possible.

"The drone is almost here," Noah said.

Kara bobbed her blonde head once and remained focused on her personal holoscreen. Noah had disabled the distress beacon for their life pod. He wasn't sure whether the Vemus could track them, but he felt safer without the broadcast signal going out. The pod's short-range communications worked, so they could speak to other survivors, as well as Captain Benson of the *Chmiel*. The cargo carrier was equipped with a small army of drones that were designed to retrieve smaller asteroids but were now guiding the life pods into the main cargo bay. They would keep as many of the life pods as they could. One thing that had been drilled into the colonists of New Earth was the need to not waste anything that could be useful. In this case, the life pods themselves were made from high-grade materials. Noah had even done some calculations and determined that the cargo vessel should have just enough room to store them all.

Noah brought up the video feed on his own holoscreen. The *Chmiel* was a short distance away, and if there had been any windows on the pod, the only thing they'd have seen was the cargo carrier. There were several lines of circular objects heading toward the ship in steady succession. Although there were hundreds of escape pods, Noah knew that many CDF personnel had stayed behind to fight the Vemus.

He heard a clang as a drone made contact with their pod and propelled them toward the ship. Noah noticed that they were being guided to one of the shorter lines of pods.

He glanced at Kara, considering.

Kara noticed him looking at her. "What's the matter?" she asked and looked briefly at his holoscreen.

"Nothing. They're just lining us up, is all," Noah said.

"Oh, good. We're lucky Captain Benson decided to stick around," Kara said.

"It would have been a much longer trip home," Noah replied.

He felt foolish. Titan Space Station had been attacked.

They'd evacuated and here they were talking about how lucky they were. He was immensely grateful to be alive and ashamed all at the same time.

"Before all this happened, I was going to ask you something," Noah said.

Kara closed down her holoscreen and stretched her hands out in front of her before bringing them to rest in her lap. "About what?"

"I was reassigned back to New Earth, and I was going to ask if you wanted to come back with me," Noah said.

There, he'd finally said it.

Kara stiffened next to him. "I knew you were going to ask," she said quietly.

Noah's eyes widened. "You did? Is that why you've been avoiding me? Because you didn't want to come?"

Kara looked away from him and Noah felt a flush of embarrassment redden his face. He shouldn't have brought this up here in this cramped life pod. Of course she didn't want to come back with him. This thing between them was just a fling, something to pass the time during a particularly long rotation at the station.

"No," Kara said softly. "I was ashamed because I wanted to go with you. More than anything."

Noah looked at her. "You did? Then why did you avoid me?"

Kara swallowed hard. "Because I thought I'd be abandoning my post, shirking my duty. We were handpicked to be assigned to Titan Space Station because we were the best the Colonial Defense Force had to offer for defending the colony against the threat of invasion. I loved the work I was doing and the people I worked with. It was a close-knit community there. There's very little choice on the space station to be otherwise. Sure, we were way out on the edge of the star system, but we had each other. Then you showed up all those months ago. The legendary Noah

Barker, renowned engineer and integral part of the early colonial effort, a personal friend of General Gates."

Noah snorted. He knew he had a reputation but didn't think much of it. Certainly not among his peers. "Being Connor's friend isn't all it's cracked up to be. We often get the most dangerous assignments."

"It was General Gates and Colonel Douglass who approached me to be part of the CDF brigade serving on Titan. It was a tremendous honor even to be asked," Kara said.

Noah's eyebrows pulled together in understanding. "I didn't realize what I was asking you to give up. I'm sorry. We seemed to hit it off. We go together. Knowing the general, he wouldn't have viewed your request to return to New Earth with me as an abandonment of your post. The man may drive himself like a robot, but he understands people."

They were silent for a few moments and Noah heard Kara sigh.

"I would have said yes," Kara said, finally.

Noah smiled widely and he saw Kara doing the same. He took her hand in his and held it, and she gave his hand a gentle squeeze. Noah felt as if a great weight had shifted off of his shoulders, and a renewed determination swept over him. They had to get home. They had to find a way to thwart the Vemus invasion. For the first time since entering the life pod, he felt free despite everything that was going on around him. Then fear threatened to creep back into his thoughts. The Vemus. Why did they come? What did they want? How'd they even get here? But he didn't want to focus on that now and pushed those thoughts out of his mind so he could take this moment with Kara and remember it for however long his life would be.

A comlink opened to the pod. "Life pod 707, execute reverse thrust for final approach," the comms officer of the *Chmiel* said.

Noah looked at the life pod controls and hit the button to slow the pod down.

"Perfect. We'll have you aboard in just a few moments."

"Acknowledged, and thank you," Noah said.

The drone guided their pod to the cargo area, where they were handed off to the robotic loading arms. The arms brought the pod safely inside the cargo bay area. The pod was then shifted to the interior of the ship through a massive airlock. A few minutes later there was a knock on the hatch, and Noah pulled on the release.

"Welcome aboard the *Chmiel*. My name is Jim."

Noah gestured for Kara to go first and followed her out of the pod. Kara told Jim their names and ranks. Noah saw other pods being opened and their occupants coming out.

Jim's eyes widened. "Captain Benson has been waiting for both of you. Please, if you'll follow me to the bridge."

Noah glanced at Kara and then back at Jim. "Of course," he said.

Jim led them out of the cargo area and called out to the deck chief that he was taking them to the bridge. There were a lot of life pods that had made it already, and Noah thought about all those waiting to get on board. He wondered why the captain had seen fit to single out both of them.

"Do you know what this is about?" Noah asked.

Jim looked back at him. "I have no idea, but I have my instructions. We're scooping you guys up and then we're supposed to hightail it out of here as quickly as possible."

The *Chmiel* was a large ship, so it took them almost fifteen minutes to reach the bridge. As they entered the bridge, there was none of the formality Noah had gotten used to on the CDF military ships he'd been on.

Captain Benson was an older, dark-skinned man whose gray

hair and beard made him look like a sage. He glanced over at them with a deeply furrowed brow. "Major Roberts and Captain Barker?"

"Yes, sir," Noah said.

Officially, Benson wasn't part of the Colonial Defense Force, but the man was the captain of this ship and had just saved their lives.

Captain Benson eyed him for a moment. "I appreciate the sentiment, son, but though I'm captain of this ship I'm very much at the CDF's service. Regardless, I don't need someone to tell me the right thing to do."

"We appreciate it all the same, Captain," Noah said, and Kara nodded.

"I have orders for you, Captain Barker, and I need your expertise, Major," Captain Benson said.

"How can I help?" Kara said.

"We have to beat the enemy fleet back to New Earth. To do that I need better speed from the engines," Captain Benson said.

"Understood. I can help with that, but I must warn you that there's a significant risk of permanently damaging the engine pods," Kara said.

"I suspected as much," Captain Benson replied.

"I'll head down to Main Engineering and see what we're dealing with," Kara said.

"Look for Marcin. He keeps things running down there," Captain Benson said.

Noah watched Kara leave the bridge and turned back to the captain. "You have orders for me?"

Captain Benson nodded. "I have new encryption protocols you're to use to contact General Gates. You can use my comms station over there."

Noah went over, sat down at the comms station, and put on

the headset. Captain Benson enabled the new encryption protocols and then left him. Noah opened a comms channel and waited for it to connect. Once the link was established, Noah saw Connor's face appear on his screen. He was stone-faced, with a burning intensity in his eyes.

"Reporting in, sir. Escape pods are being loaded onto the *Chmiel* as we speak. Captain Benson had me brought to the bridge to contact you," Noah said.

"I'm glad you made it out of there. I have a job for you," Connor replied.

"I'll do whatever you need me to."

"I need you to update the targeting capabilities used on the defense platforms. After that, they must be fully engaged for danger close-fire configuration. Do you understand what I'm telling you to do?" Connor said.

Noah swallowed hard. Danger close-fire configuration would enable the defense platform to prioritize enemy ships regardless of whether there were friendlies in the area. "I do, sir," Noah said, knowing better than to waste time questioning Connor about his own orders.

"Good. We need to prevent as much of the Vemus fleet from getting to New Earth as we can. I've told Captain Benson he's to head back there using best speed," Connor said.

"Major Roberts is heading to Engineering to try and increase the speed once we get underway," Noah said.

"How long before you're underway?" Connor asked.

Noah had no idea. He glanced over toward Captain Benson and repeated the question.

"They're loading the escape pods now, but it could be another thirty minutes before they're all on board," Noah said.

Connor looked away from the screen for a moment. "Call Captain Benson over to you."

Captain Benson joined Noah at the comms station.

"Captain, the Vemus fleet is reeling from the destruction of Titan Space Station. I appreciate what you're doing, but there's a tough call to be made," Connor said.

Noah's insides went cold.

"I cannot abandon those pods, sir," Captain Benson replied.

"Keep loading as many as you can, but if you receive a signal from us that the Vemus forces are on the move, you're to cut and run. The top priority is for you to make it back to New Earth and for Noah to update the defense platforms. We've had no confirmation that COMCENT even knows the attack has begun. We believe this has to do with the Vemus, but we're not sure. Preparation is key, and the survival of the colony is at stake," Connor said.

Noah's mouth hung open as he watched Captain Benson struggle with what Connor had just told him. The cargo carrier captain walked away and began shouting orders.

Noah looked back at the screen. "He's gone, sir," he said.

"Sending over the updated parameters for targeting. This includes the PRADIS update in case active scans cannot detect the remaining Vemus fleet," Connor said.

A progress window appeared. "Data received, sir," Noah said.

"Noah, if Captain Benson won't leave, I need you to take control of the ship," Connor said.

"Sir, I have no idea how to fly a cargo carrier. How am I supposed to fly the ship?" Noah asked and glanced around to check if he'd been overheard.

"Calm down. I'm sending you my authorization codes that will give you master control of the *Chmiel's* systems. We checked, and Captain Benson already has a course plotted back to New Earth. All you need to do is execute it. Can I count on you?"

Noah frowned. "What if he overrides it?"

Connor leveled a look at the screen and Noah felt as if he were training with Search and Rescue all those years ago. "Don't let him. This is more important."

The thought of leaving CDF personnel behind made his throat thick. He hated it and glared at the screen.

"Hate me if you need to, but everything is counting on it," Connor said.

"Sir, where are you?" Noah asked.

"Our time is just about up. We're going to try and slow down the enemy as much as we can and get them to chase us right into the kill zone of the defense platforms," Connor said.

At last Noah understood. This could be the last time he ever spoke to his friend, his mentor, and he didn't know what to say.

"Stay focused and get it done," Connor said.

The comms channel was severed, and Noah stared at the blank screen. He sucked in a deep breath and glanced over at Captain Benson. Had the captain heard what Connor told him about taking control of the ship? Noah hoped it wouldn't come to that. In fact, he silently pleaded that it wouldn't come to that.

He opened the data cache and checked the updated PRADIS configuration. He'd have to wait until they were much closer to the defense platforms before uploading the update. It was the only way to confirm that the updates had been accepted by the defense platforms' onboard targeting AI. If he sent the updates out now and they were rejected, the defense platforms' systems could fail to target anything. He'd been part of the team that worked on the original operating code for those defense platforms, so he had a good idea how fragile they could be. Noah started to think about contingency plans if the updates failed to install. The *Chmiel* was a civilian ship and wasn't capable of doing anything but sending transmissions and getting them where they needed to go. There was no cyber warfare suite loaded onto a secondary computer system that was capable of running targeting analyses, and this wasn't something Noah could perform on the fly.

A comms alert from the *Vigilant* appeared on his holoscreen. Noah looked up and saw the same alert appear on the main holoscreen. The Vemus were starting to regroup. Noah's gaze darted to Captain Benson.

The captain returned to the command chair and Noah watched as a video feed from the main cargo doors was brought up. There was still a long line of escape pods from Titan Space Station waiting to board the ship.

Captain Benson looked over at Noah with a pained expression. They had to leave, and they were going to leave people behind.

"Open a comlink to the main cargo area," Captain Benson said.

"Main cargo."

"Deck Officer, you're to close the cargo doors for immediate departure," Captain Benson said.

There was a moment of heavy silence. The bridge crew seemed to huddle at their workstations, hunched as if weathering a terrible storm.

"Captain, there are still a lot of life pods out there. We just need some more time—"

"We're out of time. Close those doors or everyone in the cargo bay will die," Captain Benson said and cut the comlink.

Noah watched as Captain Benson waited a few moments.

"Captain, cargo bay doors are closing," said the ops officer.

"Helm, max thrust for engines one and two. Take us back to New Earth," Captain Benson said.

Noah's eyes became tight—all those pods still outside, their second chance taken from them. He felt hollow inside, as if he wasn't worthy of being one of the people who got to leave while other CDF soldiers were being sacrificed.

"Noah Barker, you need to focus. We all have jobs to do," Captain Benson snapped.

Noah swung his gaze back to his holoscreen. Captain Benson was right. There was work to be done. Deep in Noah's mind he imagined the screams of the CDF personnel still out there in life pods that were being sentenced to death. He was coming to understand the hardened glint that sometimes showed itself in Connor's gaze and he hated it. This was an understanding he didn't want.

A strong hand gripped his shoulder, and Captain Benson leaned down. "Focus, Noah. Make their sacrifice worth something. It will be the only way you'll find peace in the days to come."

Noah wiped his eyes and threw himself at his task, directing his anger and frustration at doing his utmost to destroy their enemy. In that moment, Noah left a much younger version of himself behind, and he began to wonder if he would even recognize himself in the days to come—if they survived.

CHAPTER TWENTY-TWO

CONNOR CUT the comlink to the *Chmiel.* He felt bile creep up the back of his throat and forced it down, knowing there was nothing he could do. They had a shuttle on board the *Vigilant,* but there was no way it could make the trip from the outer star system to New Earth. The call had to be made. The remains of the Vemus fleet were regrouping, and the escape pods from Titan that hadn't made it onto the cargo carrier would be left behind.

"Sir, the *Chmiel* has started heading back to New Earth," Sergeant Browning said.

"Acknowledged," Connor answered.

Reisman glanced over at him. "Now it's up to Noah. He has to get that targeting package uploaded to the defense platforms to guarantee they'll be able to hit the Vemus ships."

The loss of Titan Space Station exposed a major hole in their defense strategy. The missile-defense platforms could operate autonomously only to a certain degree. Now that Titan Space Station was gone, the platform's targeting computers couldn't be updated without getting into close proximity, something Connor hadn't accounted for in his plans, and now he was mentally kicking himself for the lapse.

Connor looked at the *Chmiel's* location on the main holo-screen and noted the increasing velocity. There were still hundreds of escape pods from Titan and there was nothing he could do for them. The occupants on the pods might survive for a few weeks, at best. Ordinarily a few weeks would be more than enough time to mount a rescue mission, but with the Vemus fleet in proximity, Connor had little doubt that the escape pods would be picked up by them. He didn't know what they would do with the survivors, but it wouldn't be good.

"Sir, I have the two Vemus battleship carriers on the plot now," Sergeant Browning said.

Those were his targets. Somehow he had to soften them up so when they did reach the missile-defense platforms, they could finish the job and destroy them. The *Vigilant* had no more missiles. They had ammunition for their few remaining rail-cannons and grasers that could be used for close-range combat. Range was ever the issue in space warfare. He glanced at the area of the PRADIS output that showed where Titan Space Station had been. The *Vigilant's* systems were still trying to make sense of the data in order to put it into some type of output he could use. They didn't know how many of the Vemus fleet had been destroyed by the Titan Space Station self-destruct sequence, but Connor knew it hadn't been all of them.

"Helm, plot an intercept course for the two battleship carri-ers. Keep our approach slow. I want ample time to react if they change course," Connor said.

"Yes, General, laying in course now," Sergeant Edwards said.

Major Hayes came onto the bridge and walked over to the command area. He'd been working with the damaged areas of the ship. News of Alec Toro's assassination attempt had spread throughout the ship. Reisman had raised the question of whether Toro had been working alone. In the end, Connor didn't know, and given their list of objectives, it wasn't something he could worry about at the moment. If someone else was trying to kill him while they were fighting the Vemus, then so be it. Sean stood off to the side and listened in.

"By all accounts, Toro completely lost it at the end," Reisman said.

Connor nodded. "He was becoming desperate because he was dying. I'm not sure it really registered with him that his main reason for killing me was null and void now that the Vemus are here."

"He cracked under the pressure, and the whole thing could have been avoided if we'd looked for the signs earlier," Major Hayes said.

"Toro was the one who would have been reporting in on stuff like that. Regardless, we need to focus on the bigger enemy," Connor said

Major Hayes glanced at their two targets. "How do we destroy something that big?"

Reisman shrugged. "It's not a matter of whether we can; it's how we want to go about it."

"Well, missiles are out. No more HADES IVs. They'd destroy us well before we could destroy them if we used our remaining rail-cannons. That's even if we had enough ammunition to take the ships out," Connor said.

"What about the *Banshee*? That ship had a purely offensive armament," Major Hayes said.

"Whereabouts are unknown. What we need to do is get aboard those ships and take them out from the inside," Reisman said.

Major Hayes's eyes widened. "You can't be serious," he said.

"Oh, he's serious," Connor replied. "And he's right; that's exactly what we need to do. Given our current resources, the only way we're going to stop them is from the inside. They're in relatively close proximity to each other, so that could work to our advantage."

Reisman nodded. "I was thinking the same thing—two for one, or at least seriously damaging the second one."

"All we need are some tactical nukes and a team to take them aboard," Connor said.

Major Hayes frowned. "We don't have any tactical nukes. All of our nuclear warheads went out with our missiles."

Connor was about to answer when his comms officer spoke.

"Sir, I'm picking up a faint transmission. It's from the *Banshee*. It sounds like a status loop," Sergeant Boers said.

"Put it on speakers," Connor said.

"This is Major Savannah Cross of the Destroyer Banshee. The Vemus have severely damaged our engines. They're closing in on our ship. I've deployed all available weapons to the crew and we're preparing to make our final stand . . ."

"I'm sorry, General. The message becomes garbled after that. I'll try to clean it up," Sergeant Boers said.

"What's the timestamp for the message?" Connor asked.

Sergeant Boers checked her terminal. "Sixty minutes ago."

Connor arched an eyebrow and looked at Reisman. "Tactical, can you trace the source of the transmission?"

"I'll try to isolate the signal, sir," Lieutenant LaCroix said.

"I'm not following. What's significant about the time of the message?" Major Hayes said.

"The message was sent out at about the same time self-destruct protocols were initiated on Titan Space Station, which might have affected the Vemus ship stalking the *Banshee*," Connor said.

He watched the PRADIS output and waited.

"I have it, sir. It's a weak signal, but it appears to be coming from one of the battleship carriers. The AI is basing its trace on the highest probability because the signal is so faint," Lieutenant LaCroix said.

One of the battleship carriers became highlighted on PRADIS.

"I think we have our target, gentlemen," Connor said.

"You want to catch up to that ship and do what exactly?" Major Hayes asked.

"Determine if the *Banshee* is still intact, for one thing, and whether the crew is still alive. The primary mission is to take out that ship. The secondary objective is to attempt to rescue the crew that's been taken by the enemy. Since we don't have any tactical nukes, we might find some on the *Banshee*. Either way, we're going on that ship," Connor said.

Reisman arched a brow at Connor. "For the record, as your second in command I must advise against you being on the away mission."

Connor pressed his lips together. "Noted, for the record."

Major Hayes frowned. "Does that mean you'll send a team?"

"You bet I will, and I'm going to lead it," Connor replied.

"Sir, we need you," Major Hayes said.

"Don't bother," Reisman said. "You'll never talk him out of going."

Major Hayes frowned.

"We need to get some intelligence on what we're dealing with. The only way that's going to happen is if we get down and dirty on that ship. That means a heavily armed away team," Connor said.

Major Hayes turned toward Reisman. "Colonel, please, I can't be the only one with these objections."

"I agree with the objections, and at the same time it will be both of us on the away team," Reisman said.

Major Hayes's mouth hung open in surprise. "Why?"

"Because we're among the few who were actually part of the NA Alliance military. Those ships look different, but underneath, whatever the hell the Vemus have done to those ships, the underlying system is Alliance military. I still have the access protocols in my implants. The same for the colonel," Connor said.

"And you think that access will still work?" Major Hayes asked.

"Won't know until we get there. Certain access protocols are contained within the implants themselves. They only come online with the correct challenge protocol. I'm not even aware of what they are, but I know they're in there. If Wil and I had officially retired from active duty, our implants would have been removed, but since that didn't happen, it's a potential advantage that we can't afford to pass up," Connor said.

"I hadn't realized that," Major Hayes said.

"It's not common knowledge. Plus, if there's a chance we can rescue the crew of the *Banshee*, I'm going to take that chance. I think we've left enough of our people behind," Connor said, thinking about the *Wyatt* and all of the destroyer's crew, and now the CDF soldiers who'd served aboard Titan Space Station.

"What about the risk of being exposed to the virus that was mentioned in the last transmission from Earth? I know the combat suits can protect the wearer from biological contagions, but what about the crew of the *Banshee*?" Major Hayes asked.

Reisman glanced at Connor. "He's right, General."

Connor nodded. "I know he is. We'll need to bring a doctor with us who can help with the assessment. I'm sure Dr. Allen could make a recommendation."

"Okay, it's clear you've thought this out, so I won't get in the way. Is it safe to assume you were planning to leave me in command of the *Vigilant*?" Major Hayes asked.

"I am," Connor said.

"What do you need us to do while you're aboard the ship?"

"I'd initially thought of taking the shuttle and finding a place to sneak aboard, but I don't think that's a viable option now," Connor said.

"Why not?" Reisman asked.

"We need to catch up to them first and figure out what we're dealing with. We thought the *Wyatt* was attached to the outside of the ship, and there's really no reason to believe the *Banshee* isn't in the same position. The Vemus so far have sought to disable our ships and take them intact. They targeted our engines as well. There's still a lot of interference out there, but I'm willing to bet that those two ships have already sustained some damage. I say we approach them and try to dock with their ship," Connor said.

Reisman smiled. "Even better. If the *Banshee* is outside, we send a team onto the ship and split up, with one team going aboard the main battleship carrier."

Connor nodded. "I like that. This way, if one team can't find warheads in the *Banshee's* armory, we still have the other team that's going on the main ship ..." Connor's lips twisted into a frown. "To disable that ship, we'd need to cause the main reactor to fail. Overload would be better."

"Yeah, but a ship that big is bound to have more than one reactor powering it," Major Hayes said.

"Oh, it does for sure, and there are contingencies in place that prevent a chain reaction to the overload of a single reactor," Connor said.

"Okay, so what's the plan then?" Major Hayes asked.

"We're speculating and we have some good ideas, but until

we actually get on board that ship, a lot of what we come up with will remain hypothetical. We know what kind of ships they were, but they've clearly been modified and have survived a two-hundred-year journey to get here," Connor said.

"That alone presents a multitude of questions, but the foundation for the ship's design is the same. It's a warship, but it all goes back to the same action. We need to get inside that ship," Reisman said.

Connor looked at Major Hayes. "You'll monitor the mission from here. Hopefully, we'll bring back some extra passengers. Assuming we do, we'll need areas established as quarantine zones. We know next to nothing about this virus, so we need a completely isolated system for quarantine. I want you to work with Dr. Allen on that."

Major Hayes nodded and then looked at Connor grimly.

"If it comes to it, you need to blow the ship up before we reach New Earth. If Noah does his job, the missile-defense platforms will be targeting the main Vemus forces. After that I told him to get to New Earth to update the orbital defenses," Connor said.

"Do you think they'll reach New Earth?" Major Hayes asked.

Connor glanced at the PRADIS readout. There was still a substantial fighting force intact. It would be a close thing. "We can only do the best we can. Our single highest priority is to prevent the Vemus from reaching New Earth. If we fail that, we've lost everything."

Connor hated all the assumptions they were making. Taken as a whole, they were stacking up, but they had little choice. The Vemus obviously had hostile intentions and they still didn't have a clear understanding of what the Vemus actually were. Sometimes one had to go into the monster's lair to see how much of a monster they really were.

Connor looked over at Sean, who'd been listening quietly.

"My team is ready, General," Sean said.

"Good. Tell them to assemble on the main hangar deck," Connor said and then snorted. "She's never going to forgive me for this."

Sean smiled. "I think she'll understand in this case."

Major Hayes looked confused. "I'm not following."

"Captain Quinn's mother is none other than the legendary Ashley Quinn—a force to be reckoned with," Connor said.

Major Hayes shook his head with a tired smile. "I hadn't realized."

Connor glanced at Sean. "See, it's working. No more special treatment," he said and looked back at Major Hayes. "When Ashley found out that her son had joined me in Search and Rescue, she punched me in the stomach."

Sean laughed. "She never admitted that."

"How do you think she reacted when the Colonial Defense Force was formed?" Connor said.

"What did she do?" Major Hayes asked.

"Let's just say I'm glad I'm a quick healer," Connor said.

Sean shrugged. "She always said you reminded her of her younger brother."

It was a momentary reprieve from what they were about to face, and Connor appreciated it. They all did, but after a few seconds a somber silence settled over them.

"The Vemus forces have been reactionary for the most part. Not sure why, so I think as we approach, if we don't show any aggression, they might just let us get near enough to board the ship," Connor said.

"By no aggression, you mean . . .?" Major Hayes asked.

"I mean we don't scan them or have our weapons pointed at them. Let's just fly right up to them and see what they do.

Earlier, they took a shot at us because we were firing at them; otherwise, I'm not sure they would have bothered with us at all," Connor said.

"That's the part that bothers me," Reisman said.

"You're not the only one," Major Hayes agreed.

"It's worth a shot. We can get our weapons online and hope they don't hit us," Reisman said.

"A shot in the dark is better than no shot at all," Connor said.

He aimed to shine a bright light on the enemy. There were too many unanswered questions. Allegedly, these Vemus had defeated the combined military forces of Earth and had then come here with a large fighting force. Connor couldn't help but think there was so much more they needed to learn about their enemy. Gaining more intelligence was worth dying for if it yielded knowledge that gave them a fighting chance.

"Helm, plot a course for the Vemus battleship carrier. Best speed possible," Connor said.

CHAPTER TWENTY-THREE

IN THE HOURS THAT FOLLOWED, Connor grudgingly agreed that he wasn't to be on the first away team. He had to concede that Sean's cold logic left little to be argued with. Let Sean and his team secure the initial area, and when the all clear was given, the VIPs could come aboard. Reisman was amused to no end, and Major Hayes approved. So Connor remained on the bridge for the moment. Being outthought by his protégé should have made him proud. It didn't.

Reisman glanced at him. "Still reeling from the upset? It's always the quiet ones you need to watch out for."

"You'll be saluting him before long," Connor replied.

"Maybe. I was thinking of retiring after all this is done," Reisman replied.

Connor arched an eyebrow at him. "You'd go crazy inside a few months."

Reisman nodded. "Ordinarily yes, but I'm sure I can think of a better way to spend my time than being stuck on a warship for the rest of my life."

They were still on the bridge and were speaking quietly.

"I know better than to ask what *you'll* do," Reisman said.

Connor frowned. "You mean after we survive annihilation? I hadn't thought of it. I guess I'm too busy with the whole 'staying alive' part."

"Overrated. We all need reasons to fight, sir," Reisman said and walked over to speak with Major Hayes.

Connor wouldn't allow himself to think beyond the next few objectives. It helped him focus on what needed to be done. During his career, he'd noticed that some people liked to think about what they would do in the future and make plans. It was a coping mechanism—that he understood. A person needed to believe there was a light at the end of the tunnel even if, in truth, there was just more darkness waiting for them. When he was younger, Connor hardly ever thought about dying on any of the missions he was part of. Death was always present, but as a young man, he'd felt invincible. However, those were a much younger man's thoughts. Connor didn't feel invincible anymore. Far from it. Most recently he focused on what he could accomplish now and how that work could be carried on in the event that he did die. These past seven years he'd been so focused on protecting the colony that he'd never really thought about what he'd do if the danger passed. He'd always assumed he'd figure it out later, but seeing Lenora again a few weeks ago had him questioning whether that approach was best for him moving forward.

"Sir, I have the images from the high-res tactical array ready," Sergeant Browning said from the operations workstation.

Connor returned to the command chair. "Put it on the main holoscreen."

Using the high-res array, which was a system of high-powered optical imagers that weren't used during normal operations, was a calculated risk. Preferring not to push his luck,

Connor ordered that the high-res array be retracted after they were done.

The rough outer hull of the Vemus ship appeared on screen. There were large gashes in the exoskeleton that surrounded the Alliance Navy vessel. Connor zoomed in on one of the damaged areas.

"Can you augment the darker areas inside that damaged section?" Connor asked.

Sergeant Browning tapped a few commands and the designated area of the image was rendered, but there wasn't much clarity with the updated image.

"I don't think we can improve on what we've already got, sir," Sergeant Browning said.

Connor zoomed out from that section of the image and noticed a metallic protrusion that didn't match the rest of the ship. On the starboard lower half of the ship was the cigar-shaped, gleaming hull of the *Banshee*. The destroyer appeared to be tethered to the ship by the same living exoskeleton that was part of the hull.

Reisman sat down in the chair next to Connor. "The ship looks intact."

"Yes, and it looks like several maintenance hatches are still available," Connor said.

"I'm not sure landing directly on the hull of the Vemus ship is a good idea. It could grab hold of the *Vigilant* and not let go," Reisman advised.

"Agreed. We'll use our own emergency docking clamps and attach them to the *Banshee*. Then the team can go through one of the maintenance hatches, make our way through the ship, and take it from there," Connor said.

"Sir," Sergeant Boers said, "should I try hailing the *Banshee*?"

"No, let's maintain radio silence for now. Continue to monitor for any communications," Connor said.

"Yes, sir."

They made their final approach to the Vemus ship and there was no indication that there was anything amiss. He wondered why the ship was traveling well below an ordinary battleship carrier's capability. Ships of the wall weren't designed for speed, per se; they were designed to deliver and take significant damage. The bulk of the remaining Vemus fleet was behind them. They'd seen the fleet increase their velocity for the assault on Titan Space Station. Connor and Wil had run some comparison analyses against what they knew of NA Alliance ships' capabilities, and so far they had been comparable to what the Vemus ships had shown.

"Sergeant Edwards, take us in," Connor said.

"Yes, sir," Sergeant Edwards said.

Aaron Edwards was part of the primary bridge crew for the *Vigilant*. His performance scores for piloting the ship edged him over his alternate on the secondary bridge crew. Connor knew the *Vigilant* was in good hands.

A wave of tension-filled silence settled over the bridge, with most people's eyes glued to their own terminals or on the main holoscreen.

"Tactical, any change in the Vemus ship?" Connor asked.

"None, sir. It's like they don't care that we're here," Lieutenant LaCroix answered.

Reisman shrugged. "You know the saying about looking a gift horse in the mouth."

"Yeah, but I'd rather not get kicked by that same gift horse," Connor said.

What kind of invasion fleet would let an enemy ship just fly right up to it like they were doing? Connor watched the active plot on the main holoscreen showing their position relative to the battleship cruiser. They moved into position next to the *Banshee's* stern maintenance hatch. This would put them close to the primary ammunition depot.

Connor looked at Major Hayes. "Depending on what we find over there, we should consider adding additional teams to offload any ammunition we could use."

"The *Banshee's* computer system appears to be offline, but if we can get that up, we might be able to use the automated systems for munitions offloading," Major Hayes said.

Connor nodded. "We'll check the ship's systems once we get over there."

Connor stood up and Reisman did as well.

"Sir, we've matched velocity with the Vemus ship. Holding steady," Sergeant Edwards said.

"Ops, commence emergency docking procedure," Connor said.

"Emergency docking procedure being executed, sir," Sergeant Browning replied.

Connor looked at Major Hayes. "You have the con. Good luck, Major."

"I have the con. Good luck to you as well, General," Major Hayes replied.

Connor headed for the door, with Reisman and their CDF escort following. He opened a comlink to Sean. "We're all lined up. You're a go once we're docked."

"Acknowledged, sir. We'll do a quick sweep and give the okay for the second team," Sean replied.

Connor closed the comlink and frowned.

Reisman snorted. "Feels strange not to be the first ones through the door this time."

"I was thinking the same thing. Too bad more of the old

team wasn't here," Connor said, thinking of Samson and Hank, who were training CDF Infantry on New Earth.

"Could have used Woods or Tiegen on this," Reisman said.

"Would have been nice, but they're working on the orbital defense system we have around home," Connor said.

Reisman glanced at him with a bemused expression. "I think that's the first time I've ever heard you refer to the colony as home instead of Earth."

"I'm evolving," Connor said and quickened his pace.

They went to the main hangar, where their combat suits would be waiting. He used his implants to check the status of the Away Team. They were making their way across the emergency airlock tube that connected the two ships. There were two combat suits waiting for them.

Sergeant Hoffer waved them over. "Right this way, General and Colonel."

He couldn't see Hoffer's face because he was already in his combat suit, but the soldier's name appeared on Connor's internal heads-up display, as did the names of the other soldiers on the secondary team. His Nexstar combat suit was split down the middle, with the chest plate opened. Connor climbed inside and activated the suite. His implants registered with the Nexstar's computer systems. The power armor closed itself up and the suite status showed on his helmet's HUD. He was green across the board. Connor felt the familiar adrenaline burst from being in combat armor once again. These combat suits were modified series eights, designed for space combat. They carried enough oxygen to last them for days, and the onboard medical systems could administer treatment depending on the type of injuries. The Nexstars were as tough as they came. He picked up an AR-71 assault rifle with grenade launcher attachment, Connor's preferred weapon these days.

Connor and Reisman moved toward the front where Captain Lee waited. Saluting with a combat suit wasn't practical, so Captain Lee simply greeted Connor.

"Captain Quinn is at the maintenance hatch now," Captain Lee said.

Connor nodded, and his armored head bobbed up and down. Time to find out what the hell these Vemus really were.

CHAPTER TWENTY-FOUR

CONNOR WAITED near the emergency airlock. Within ten minutes of Sean's platoon entering the *Banshee*, he opened a comlink saying they were clear to come aboard. They walked across the emergency docking tube and Connor stepped inside the *Banshee* first.

"No contacts at all?" Connor asked Sean over a comlink.

"That's affirmative, sir. It's like the crew of the *Banshee* all left. There are no life signs on the ship," Sean said.

The interior of the ship was sparsely lit from the emergency lighting along the ceiling. Connor scanned for any active comms channels, but there were none.

"Sir, we just got to the bridge. The systems here appear to be on standby. According to the logs, the crew left the ship," Sean said.

"Does it say where they went?" Connor asked.

"It was a quick entry from Major Cross. She just says the ship isn't safe and that they went inside the enemy ship to try to secure another ship to escape with," Sean said.

"That doesn't sound right. Major Cross wouldn't endanger her entire crew on a whim. There has to be more to it than that," Reisman said.

"See if you can restore emergency systems," Connor told Sean. "Captain Lee, I want you to take half the team and see what can be salvaged from the ship. We need to know if there are any intact warheads we can use."

"On it, General," Captain Lee said and began issuing orders.

Connor and the rest of the platoon headed toward the bridge. The Destroyer-class vessels were much smaller than the heavy cruiser. The scans they had of the ship from the outside showed that it had been heavily damaged before the Vemus disabled it. Savannah Cross hadn't given the ship up without a fight.

More emergency lighting came on as they made it to the bridge. Sean had CDF troops stationed outside. Connor and Reisman went inside and found Sean standing at the tactical workstation, where he had a holoscreen active.

"They used the forward hatch to get aboard the Vemus ship, sir," Sean said.

Connor used his implants to access the *Banshee's* systems. He skimmed the logs quickly. "They did repel boarders, but they suffered severe casualties. I still would have expected a small group to have been left behind."

"Wouldn't want to draw that short straw," Reisman said.

Connor glanced at him. "Come again?"

"Think about it. You've lost a bunch of your crew fighting this enemy and then the few that remain have a choice. Stay holed up in here and make the enemy come to you or head out on their ship and make them chase you," Reisman said.

Sean brought his hand up to his ear. "Go ahead, Anders."

"Sir, we've found some of the living exoskeleton stuff near the hatch. It's on the walls too," Anders said.

"Let's go check it out. I doubt we'll find anything of further use here," Connor said.

They left the bridge and headed along the corridor to the forward port hatch, where they met a three-man team. Along the walls was a glistening, thick film of brown sludge.

"Wynn, report. What is this stuff?" Sean asked.

Sergeant Nick Wynn was the medic with a background in biology.

"Seems to be coming from the Vemus ship. It doesn't react to stimuli, but it will stick to whatever it comes in contact with, so I wouldn't touch it," Sergeant Wynn said.

Connor looked at the closed hatch and saw that the brown sludge was coming through the door, which wasn't airtight anymore. At least it hadn't reached the door controls.

"Open the hatch," Connor said.

Sergeant Wynn stepped back while two soldiers went over to the hatch. Connor looked at Wynn. "Did you collect samples?"

Wynn's eyes widened and he shook his head.

"We'll need some samples to study," Connor said.

"I'm sorry, sir. I have a sample kit. I'll start collecting some immediately," Sergeant Wynn said.

The CDF soldiers at the hatch stopped while Wynn went over to the wall. He opened a metallic container and withdrew a thin plastic rod with a small scoop on the tip. He dipped it into the brown sludge and deposited a dollop into the container. Sergeant Wynn closed everything up and gave them a nod.

"If you see something you think is important, let us know and we'll make sure you have an opportunity to check it out," Connor said.

"Understood, General," Sergeant Wynn said.

"Open the hatch," Sean ordered his men.

A soldier activated the manual release and checked that the team was ready. Four more CDF soldiers held their weapons in covering formation. If there was anything on the other side of that hatch, it would be dead before it knew what hit it. The soldier pulled the hatch open. There was a slight hiss and the atmosphere equalized with that of the Vemus ship.

Connor's combat suit scanned the air for any contaminants. His internal heads-up display showed the analyses of the atmosphere, all of which indicated a breathable atmosphere that was standard for a spacefaring vessel.

"My scanners are showing that the air is good," Reisman said.

"Same," Connor replied.

Beyond the hatch was a dimly lit corridor. Connor's helmet compensated for the low light so he could see clearly. The dark gray walls had a purplish tint to them, as if there was a small electric charge running through the material, and appeared to have been created from a similar substance to that which they'd observed on the outer hull.

They slowly entered the enemy ship. Connor kept waiting for some kind of alarm to sound, but there was nothing. He used the butt of his AR-71 to test the sturdiness of the corridor walls. They were hardened and, upon closer inspection, Connor saw that there were multiple layers, as if they'd been grown.

"There's a lot of humidity. Could be why the walls have that glistening sheen to them," Sean said.

They delved deeper into the ship and still didn't see anyone else. Connor checked for open comlinks again, but there weren't any. They came to an open area where multiple deck levels were exposed. It was only then that Connor saw exposed pieces of material that were definitely manmade. There were angled edges of the metallic alloy used in NA Alliance ships.

"There has to be some kind of crew aboard this ship. There's no way it could be flown otherwise," Reisman said.

"I think the mere fact that this ship is here is miracle enough," Connor said.

"What do you mean?" Reisman said.

Connor walked to the edge of the deck and gestured over at the far wall.

Reisman gasped.

The black-and-gold lettering had once gleamed a proud name that was familiar to any NA Alliance soldier. The lettering was so faded that there was only the vague impression of their shapes, but they were clear enough to read.

Sean came to Connor's side and peered at the far wall. "*Indianapolis*! The *Indianapolis*? The battleship carrier you were last on before being shanghaied onto the *Ark*?"

Connor glanced at Reisman, who for once was clearly at a loss for words. He glanced around, unable to believe that over two hundred years ago he'd stood upon the very decks of this ship—a Barracuda-class battleship carrier, the pinnacle warship in the NA Alliance Navy.

"I can't believe it," Connor said at last.

He used his neural implants to find an open network connection using an encrypted Alliance protocol. Connor's eyes widened when the ship's systems replied to his request.

"There's an active computer system here that responds to Alliance protocols," Connor said, looking at Reisman.

Reisman's eyebrows pulled together in concentration as he used his own implants. A moment later he nodded. "This is too frigging weird. How the hell is this ship even here? It's like some cruel joke."

"What do you mean?" Sean asked.

Reisman gestured to Connor and then back at himself. "We

were both on this ship. All the Ghosts were. This ship intercepted us after the Chronos Space Station was destroyed."

Connor kept looking around, trying to peer past the strange material that covered the walls. Knowing it was the *Indianapolis* gave him a strange feeling of déjà vu. Connor probed beyond the initial network connection, seeking to get the status of the ship's systems.

"I'm only seeing systems that are locked out. It's like there was a system-wide lockout," Connor said.

"If that's the case, how are you even able to access the system for it to tell you that everything is locked out?" Sean asked.

"Because our credentials must still be in the system somehow," Connor replied.

"How is this ship flying without computer systems? We saw it use weapons and navigation. Those systems have to be working," Reisman said.

Connor's thoughts kept racing with all the possibilities. "I know where we can find the answers."

Reisman nodded. "The core systems. I can try to bypass the lockout there."

"Do either of you know where it is?" Sean asked.

"Of course. It's near the bridge," Connor said at the same time Reisman said, "near Main Engineering."

Sean glanced at both of them. "Which one is it? By the bridge or Main Engineering?"

Connor glanced at Reisman, who gave him a challenging look. "They'd never put the system core by the bridge," Reisman said.

"You're wrong. The system core is by the primary bridge in the forward section near the middle decks, where it has the most protection," Connor said.

Reisman shook his head. "I'm not wrong. You're thinking of

the secondary bridge just behind midship near Main Engineering."

Connor frowned in thought, considering. Was he wrong? He'd only served aboard naval warships early in his career, which was required for any active combat soldier regardless of the military branch they served in.

Sean pressed his lips together. "Could there be more than one computing core?"

Reisman shook his head. "No, there was a primary computing core with the ability to isolate different systems in case the cyber warfare suite failed."

Sean glanced at Connor. "We need a decision here. I'd rather not divide our team to chase two leads."

"Sir, come on, this is me," Reisman said. "I was the operations and intelligence officer in our old platoon. It was my job to know how to take down systems so if the shit hit the fan you could say to me, 'Wil, I need this broken ASAP,' and I'd be able to do it."

Connor shook his head. "Not quite like that," said Connor, giving his friend a pointed look. "We're in the aft section or just beyond it, so midship is this way. We can check it out on the way."

"When we get there, you'll be saying how sorry you are for ever doubting me," Reisman said.

Connor grinned and then blew out a breath. Sean had six of his team take point while Connor and Reisman stayed in the middle. Connor kept thinking about Admiral Mitch Wilkinson, who, to the best of Connor's knowledge, had remained the flag officer of the battleship carrier *Indianapolis*. Wilkinson had been referred to by Dr. Stone in the summary message that was part of a major update to the original *Ark* mission.

What virus or parasitic life form does this? Connor wondered. He glanced at the hardened substance on the walls.

A comlink from the *Vigilant* registered on his internal heads-up display and Connor called for a stop.

"General," Major Hayes said, "the two battleship carriers have increased their velocity. The remaining Vemus fleet has also caught up with us. We've run the numbers and I'm sending a timer out to you to show how much time we have before we reach the defense platforms and New Earth's orbital defenses."

A countdown timer appeared on Connor's heads-up display and the others around him confirmed they were seeing the same thing.

"Understood. We have it now. Captain Lee is still on the *Banshee*, looking to salvage materials," Connor said.

"He's already contacted us and we're starting the offload. There were only two warheads left intact, so they're removing those and configuring a detonator for them. We've also done some analysis of the remaining Vemus fleet. We've noticed that many of the ships don't match up with the NA Alliance Navy or any navy. Lieutenant LaCroix believes the Vemus fleet is made up of multiple ships merging together somehow. We're not sure of the reason, but some of the ships have features of civilian ships, particularly freighters. Anything with a lot of mass," Major Hayes reported.

"Still no reaction to our presence here?" Connor asked.

"None that we can detect. We've run passive scans, which they don't seem to mind. In the event that they attack us, I have a comms buoy set to deploy to COMCENT," Major Hayes said.

"Understood. We're checking the computing core to see if we can learn more about the enemy," Connor said.

The comlink closed.

"Merging ships," Reisman said thoughtfully. "The only

reason I can think to do that is to address resource needs."

Connor nodded. "So that brown sludge is absorbing the *Banshee*, and if we stay here long enough, it will start absorbing the *Vigilant* as well."

"Into the belly of the beast, as it were," Reisman said.

Connor sent a quick message to Major Hayes to monitor the living exoskeleton material and not let it near the *Vigilant*. Then they quickened their pace as much as they could. They didn't have schematics of the interior of the ship, so they were reliant on the faded maps on the parts of the walls that weren't covered by foreign materials, as well as Connor's and Reisman's memories. Not the most reliable way to navigate through an enemy ship, but it was what they had to work with. They stayed near the center of the corridors and had to occasionally backtrack because the way forward was blocked by a crag-laden wall of the hardened brown sludge.

As they neared the Main Engineering section of the ship, the hardened material was restricted to a bulging mass along the middle of the wall instead of covering the walls and the ceiling. The mass was rounded, with glowing material moving inside it.

"The system core should be up ahead on the right," Reisman said.

The way forward widened by several meters and there were two massive rooms on either side.

Sean was in front of Connor. He looked over to the left. There were multiple large tubes of the exoskeleton material going into the room. The room itself was a vast network of the same material, as if a host of vines had taken over the area.

"What is this place?" Sean asked.

"That's supposed to be Main Engineering, which includes the main reactor that powers the ship," Connor said.

"And over to our right, just where I said it was," Reisman

said, smiling triumphantly.

"I can admit when I'm wrong, but there *is* a computing core near the main bridge," Connor said.

Reisman nodded. "The secondary one."

Connor looked over to the right. The computing core was largely intact. The workstations were grouped together before a vast array of high-end server farms that were the brains of the warship. Glowing green lights came from the data storage arrays as electrical arcs walked their way through the vast array in rapid succession, only to be lost from view.

Connor walked over to the main workstation. An amber holoscreen showed that a system-wide lockdown protocol had been initiated. He glanced at the date and time stamp for when the lockdown had happened.

"Look at that," Connor said. "The lockdown was initiated twenty years after we left."

"That's around the time the *Ark's* mission was updated," Reisman replied.

Connor watched as his friend sat down at the workstation. He brought up several submenus and initiated login attempts. After a few minutes of failing to initiate a bypass, a single screen appeared and Reisman snatched his hands away from the interface.

"What the hell is this!" Reisman shouted.

::*Col. Gates protocol. Input required.*::

Connor stared at the prompt, his mouth agape.

"This thing just asked for you by name with your old Alliance rank," Reisman said.

"Well, I did try to access it before," Connor replied.

One of the CDF soldiers keeping watch in the corridor called out for Sean.

Reisman stood up and gestured for Connor to sit in the

chair. Connor sat down and tried inputting his date of birth and military identification number. The prompt just reset back to the same challenge. He tried to think of other things that would satisfy the challenge, but nothing worked.

"How about the date you enlisted?" Reisman suggested.

Connor tried it and that didn't work. He narrowed his gaze and concentrated hard. Suddenly, a thought blazed like a beacon in his brain and he entered a specific date and time that would appear random to anyone else but him.

::*Input accepted. Initiating data dump. Please specify destination.*::

Connor glanced at Reisman questioningly.

"One second," Reisman said and opened the holo-interface on the arm of his combat suit. "I've opened a secure channel to the *Vigilant*," Reisman said and made a passing motion of the channel to Connor.

A new data storage connection appeared on Connor's internal heads-up display and he mounted it to the session.

::*Success. Dump in progress . . .* ::

Connor stood up.

"What was that date you entered?" Reisman asked.

"The date my father died. He was close friends with Admiral Wilkinson," Connor replied.

"Why is that date important to Wilkinson?"

"My father was KIA and saved Wilkinson's life," Connor said.

Reisman glanced at the holoscreen. "This could take a while," he said, noting the progress. He brought up another window and started checking a few things.

Connor glanced over at Sean and noticed him speaking with his men. He walked over to them. "What's going on?"

"We think we've found the *Banshee* crew," Sean said.

"Where?" Connor asked.

Sean frowned. "That's the thing. Sergeant Anders picked up a partial link detection when they scouted down the corridor going toward the bridge."

Connor glanced back at Reisman, who was busy working away at the workstation. "Let's leave three men to guard Wil's back and the rest of us will go check out the bridge," he said.

Reisman said he was going to try to learn all he could about the ship before they had to leave. The countdown timer for when they would enter the defense platform's missile range was steadily drawing downward.

They headed toward the secondary bridge. Connor kept thinking about the system access challenge meant for him. Admiral Wilkinson must have set all this up, but how? If they were losing a war with the Vemus, why would he choose to single Connor out from any number of people who might have come onto this ship? What if no one had ever come aboard? Would that data have been lost forever? It was quite a gamble. What had happened to Earth during the final stages of the war? Wilkinson was a brilliant strategist, so it wasn't unlike him to have many pans in the fire at once, working toward the same goal.

"Your friend was really counting on you to be here," Sean said.

"I was just thinking the same thing," Connor replied.

"Noah is always going on about how there are ways to code subroutines that only become active if certain conditions are met. Same thing could have happened here," Sean said.

Connor scanned for comlink traffic, but they were still flat-lined.

"How far ahead did Anders' group scout?" Connor asked. They were approaching the secondary bridge.

"It's just over here," Sergeant Anders said.

Connor pushed ahead with Sean at his side.

The bridge doors were shut. One of the CDF soldiers palmed the access panel, and after a few moments, the doors squeaked opened. The secondary bridge was designed to take over the operation of a warship in the event that the primary bridge became compromised during a conflict. The workstations and command area were largely intact but for the scorch marks that dotted some of the workstations. There were long, faded, dark stains on the floor and behind some of the workstations. The onboard sensors must have detected their presence because some of the less damaged workstations sparked to life.

Dust swirled through the partial lighting, giving the bridge a ghostly flare. Connor headed toward the command area.

"What do you think happened here?" Sergeant Anders asked.

"These are calcium deposits," Sergeant Wynn said while squatting down. "These were bodies. People died here."

Connor stood in front of the command chair. There were no dark splotches on it from a battle that must have been fought here over two hundred years ago—more than enough time for a body to decompose, assuming the Vemus maintained even a partial atmosphere throughout the ship. Connor sat in the command chair and activated the terminal. He used his implants to provide his Alliance credentials. A long list of failed system statuses scrolled through the screen as if the computer systems were relieved to finally offload their burden. Then a lone active alert appeared. Connor frowned and selected the alert, which highlighted the main hangar bay.

The main holoscreen flickered on. Part of the imager was damaged, so they could only see a small part of the screen. There were flashes of light but no sound. Connor peered at the screen and saw several people moving. They were wearing CDF uniforms.

CHAPTER TWENTY-FIVE

CONNOR SPRANG FROM THE CHAIR. "I know where the crew of the *Banshee* went. They're at the main hangar."

"They're fighting something. That could be why no one has detected our presence here," Sean said.

The imager died with a fizzle as the aged circuitry finally gave its last breath and the main holoscreen powered off.

"Come on, we're heading to the hangar," Connor said.

He opened up a comlink to Reisman. "How's the data dump going?"

"About halfway through," Reisman said.

"We've found the crew of the *Banshee*. They're fighting Vemus forces in the main hangar. We're heading there now," Connor said.

"Acknowledged. Captain Lee has just arrived with the modified warheads. They're going to deploy them in Main Engineering," Reisman said.

"How are they getting inside it?" Connor asked, remembering the overgrowth of hardened materials throughout the area.

"They brought plasma torches and are cutting that stuff away. I'll send an update once we're all set to go here," Reisman said.

"Understood," Connor said.

"One more thing," Reisman said. "I've been poking around the ship's systems. It's like the entire thing has been through a major overhaul. Nothing is where it should be as far as systems go. There's some kind of broadcast signal coming through the main communications array, but it's using a protocol I've never seen before."

"Is it active?" Connor asked.

"Yes," Reisman answered.

"Can you shut it down?"

"I'm not able to. The only thing I can tell is that there's an active connection—a pretty powerful one—but I'm not clear on where it's coming from," Reisman said.

"Keep working on it. Send what you have so far to Major Hayes. Perhaps the *Vigilant* can detect the signal as well," Connor said.

The comlink closed and Connor bit his lower lip in thought. If these signals were consistently present among the Vemus fleet, it might be something he could use against them.

As they closed in on the main hangar bay, Connor and the others heard weapons being fired. He scanned the comms network and was able to find Major Cross's signal. He didn't open a link yet, preferring to get a better sense of what he was dealing with. Connor looked back at Sean and held up two fingers, then made a circular motion.

Sean signaled to one of the CDF soldiers and he nodded. The soldier reached into the storage compartment of his Nexstar combat suit, pulled out two reconnaissance drones, and tossed them into the air.

Connor used his implants to access the drone feeds. They flew into the hangar and separated, making a general sweep of the area. There were smaller attack craft lined up on the far side of the hangar, and the crew of the *Banshee* was clustered around a combat shuttle. They were firing their weapons at a group of large dark figures that stalked their way toward them. White bolts were being fired at the remainder of the *Banshee* crew, who scrambled behind cover. Connor zoomed in on the Vemus forces. They were massive, with some of them easily twice as tall as he was. Their skin was a deep, dark purple that glistened in the light. Their rounded heads angled to a pointed snout. Lighter-toned oval shapes could have been eyes, but Connor wasn't sure. They had thick legs, with rippling muscles that ended in clawed feet. They staggered their approach and another group was working their way toward the *Banshee* crew's flank. Between the dark shapes and how they kept on the move, it was hard to get an accurate count, even with the help of his combat suit's computer systems.

A series of high-pitched whistles and clicks came from the Vemus forces. They moved fast and seemed to be able to move as quickly on two legs as they could when hunched over like a quadruped.

The crew of the *Banshee* was mixed, with some wearing combat armor while others wore a breather. Their hands and other parts of their bodies were exposed to the atmosphere. They fired their weapons in controlled bursts, halting the Vemus advance while conserving their ammunition.

Connor opened a comlink to Major Cross.

"General! They can detect active comlinks. Go to short-wave IR," Major Cross said.

Just after she spoke there was an uptick in the whistles and clicks coming from the Vemus forces. Connor immediately deactivated the comlink and did as she asked.

"What's your status, Major?" Connor asked.

"I saw the drones. As you can see, we're pinned down. Every time we try to move, they press the attack. We were trying to use one of these shuttles to get out of here," Major Cross said.

"Is the shuttle operational?" Connor asked.

He saw Sean gesturing to the CDF soldiers. They were moving into position just inside the main hangar behind a barricade to provide covering fire. The drone feeds cut out at the same time. They'd been shot down.

"Negative, sir. None of shuttles are operational. I guess sitting in the hangar for two hundred years depleted their power cells," Major Cross said.

"We can provide covering fire. Can you make it to us?" Connor asked and shot an IR laser, marking their location.

There was bellowing from the Vemus forces. Connor peered past the wall and saw several of the enemy scrambling toward them.

"Take them down!" Connor shouted.

The CDF soldiers unleashed the might of their weapons, cutting into the Vemus as they charged toward them. The *Banshee* crew fired their weapons at the Vemus force's exposed flank, and the colossal giants started to fall. Dark liquid burst from their bodies. Connor and the rest of the team fired their weapons, scattering the Vemus forces, who scrambled to cover, where they returned fire. A CDF soldier next to Connor took a white bolt to the chest. His armor absorbed the blow and the soldier knelt back into cover. In a short span of time, they'd cut the Vemus forces in half.

Connor opened a short-range IR channel to Major Cross. "Now's your chance. Come on."

"You don't understand. Those things aren't dead—"

A loud ringing tone sounded and Connor was forced to cut the connection.

"Why aren't they coming?" Sean asked.

Connor glanced over the wall, looking at the fallen Vemus. "She said they aren't dead."

Sean frowned and looked over the wall. His eyes widened. "Some of them are starting to move again!"

Connor fired his weapon at a rising Vemus, but the standard round for the AR-71 had little effect. He accessed his weapons systems and changed it to fire incendiary rounds. When the nano-robotic ammunition had changed over, Connor aimed his weapon and fired. Flashes of superheated rounds burst from the barrel, and he caught the Vemus soldier in the chest. The scorching rounds burned a massive hole in the creature's chest. The Vemus soldier didn't so much as cry out in pain as it flew back onto the ground. Connor took several more shots, cutting up the remains. The rest of the CDF soldiers nearby updated their nano-robotic ammunition for their weapons to incendiary rounds.

"Lay it on them," Connor said.

He opened a comlink to Major Cross. The Vemus already knew they were there, so there was little risk at this point. "This is your chance. We'll provide covering fire and you make your way toward us. That's an order, Major."

Connor fired a grenade into a cluster of Vemus forces, blowing them apart. The crew of the *Banshee* burst from cover and Connor and the others provided covering fire. The Vemus forces whipped up into a frenzy. They charged out after the fleeing crew, heedless of the weapons being fired at them. They snatched a few stragglers, taking the CDF crew down to the ground. They hovered over them, tearing off masks and helmets. The Vemus opened their wide mouths and spat thick black liquid onto the CDF soldiers' faces.

Connor aimed for a Vemus soldier's head and fired. He watched as a struggling *Banshee* crewmember's body went into convulsions, their entire face covered in blackish goo.

Fallen Vemus soldiers began to rise again.

"What the hell is it going to take to kill these things?" Sean said while firing his weapon.

The *Banshee* crew was being picked off by the emboldened Vemus forces. Connor fired several more grenades, figuring the explosive impacts would slow them down.

"Bringing down the hammer!" Sergeant Woods cried.

The heavy weapons soldier fired a tactical missile, and the hangar floor behind the fleeing *Banshee* crew was engulfed in flames.

As the fire diminished, Connor heard the strange, high-pitched whistle coming from the Vemus forces caught in the blast, and the call was taken up by the remaining Vemus that were beyond the blast zone. Several flaming figures crawled away, only to collapse and stop moving. The remaining *Banshee* crew sprinted toward them. There was only a fraction of them left. Several CDF soldiers kept firing their weapons at the Vemus forces. The ones on the far side of the hangar started to regroup. They barreled into the flames, heedless of the heat, and their long strides carried them across the hangar despite Connor's efforts to stop them.

Major Savannah Cross came around the wall. Connor could hear her gasping.

"How did you hold out for so long?" Connor asked.

"We had to keep changing the type of ammunition we were

using. Only when they're blown completely apart do they stay down," Major Cross said, gritting her teeth. "They don't ever stop. They just keep coming."

Connor heard shouting from down the line of soldiers. Sergeant Wynn was down. Blue bolts were arcing through his combat suit. The sergeant screamed, and nearby CDF soldiers tried to take his armor off. The power armor was unresponsive and Sean used the manual release to pop the chest cavity. Connor peered at Sergeant Wynn's blackened chest as the man writhed in pain. Wynn looked as if he were struggling to say something, and then the dying soldier let out a gurgling gasp.

More blue energy bolts fired toward them and one hit Sergeant Anders. The CDF soldier screamed as he went down.

"Take cover!" Connor shouted and dove behind a barrier.

The Vemus forces had changed their tactics. They had weapons that could disable their power armor and kill the person inside. They had to get out of there, quickly.

"Sergeant Woods, do you have anything to cover our escape?" Connor asked.

"You bet, sir. I have a portable MS-Hydra," Sergeant Woods said.

The MS-Hydra was a robotic mini-turret capable of firing millions of high-velocity darts a minute, devastating to an ordinary attack force. They would soon find out how effective it was against the Vemus.

"Take it to the end of the corridor and get ready. We'll buy you some time," Connor said.

Sergeant Woods called one of the other CDF soldiers over and they ran down the corridor.

The rest of them continued to fire on the Vemus. There was a mix of ammunition being used, from blistering incendiary rounds to armor-piercing rounds and small grenades. Connor ordered them to fall back, and the CDF soldiers began to quickly move into the corridor. The Vemus forces detected the decreased rate of weapons fire and began to press forward.

"Time to go, sir," Sean said.

Connor backed away from the wall, and they shuffled down the corridor, firing their weapons in controlled bursts as they went. Soon after, they turned around and ran as fast as they could.

Connor reached the end of the corridor where the MS-Hydra sat on a tripod of thick legs that were drilled into the ground. The Hydra mount was a metallic, rectangular box and inside were thousands of high-velocity darts capable of piercing armor and destroying flesh.

"The Hydra is ready," Sean said.

"Good. Enable the sensors to fire on the targets when they're within two meters," Connor said.

He glanced down the corridor at the hangar beyond. The dark, colossal shapes of the Vemus forces started gathering at the corridor entrance.

Connor went toward the front and began leading his team back the way they'd come. High-pitched whistles and clicks seemed to echo all along the corridor.

Connor opened a comlink to Reisman. "Wil, what's your status?"

Reisman grunted. "Ah, data upload is complete."

Reisman sounded as if he were straining with something. "What's wrong?" Connor asked.

"Captain Lee planted the bomb, but something happened to them inside Main Engineering. They've been cut off," Reisman said.

Connor urged the soldiers in front of him to move faster.

"Are you hurt?" Connor asked.

"No—uh, just get back here. Watch out for that brown sludge on the walls. It's creeping into the computing core," Reisman said.

The CDF soldiers ahead of him checked the corners and then cleared them to proceed. Connor was about to tell Reisman to get out of there when an ear-splitting shriek sounded from behind them. The MS-Hydra had fired its payload.

Connor and the others quickened their pace. They had to make it back to the *Vigilant* or they were all going to pay the price.

They reached the atrium where the name *Indianapolis* in all its faded glory adorned the wall. Vemus forces appeared on the decks across from them. Connor and the others took turns firing their weapons to hold them off. These forces were much shorter than what they'd encountered in the main hangar bay, and they tracked from the other decks like a pack of rabid wolves. Shooting at them only seemed to ignite their ferocity. The Vemus weapons fire was a mix between the white stunner bolts and the armor-disabling blue bolts. Connor and the others made it to the corridor that would take them out of the vast atrium. He took one last glance at the Vemus forces. Some were attempting to jump across the distance to the deck he stood on. Several dark-skinned bodies missed and plunged down.

The Vemus stopped and clustered across the way.

"General, we have to go," Sean called out to him.

Connor took a step back but couldn't tear his eyes away. The Vemus forces were huddled together in a mass, their bodies quivering. Finally, one of them emerged and leaped onto the railing of the upper deck, stretching its arms wide. Connecting the creature's wrist to its feet was a thick layer of leathery skin.

"General!" Sean called again.

Connor aimed his AR-71 as the Vemus soldier leaped from

the upper railings. The creature glided across the atrium, flying straight toward him. Connor fired his weapon, aiming for the creature's head, and then adjusted his aim and tore through the wings. More of the Vemus emerged from the mass that huddled together. They vaulted from the upper deck.

At last Connor turned around and ran, catching up with Sean.

"What did you see back there?" Sean asked.

"They changed forms," Connor said.

Sean glanced behind him for a moment while they ran. "Shape-shifting?"

"No . . . well. Not quite. Only partially. It's like they can rapidly adapt. I've never seen anything like it," Connor said.

The weapons the former *Banshee* crew carried were depleted of ammunition. CDF soldiers from Sean's platoon shared their spare ammunition, but it was tough going while they were on the run.

Connor glanced behind him. He could hear the Vemus, but they hadn't come down the corridor yet. The team ahead of them stopped outside the computing core. Connor saw a webbing of hardened vines that stretched across the ceiling from Main Engineering to the computing core. He looked over at the workstations where Reisman was working and gasped. Hanging from the ceiling to the floor was a wall of the brown sludge that had hardened into an exoskeleton.

"Connor?" Reisman called out, and his voice was coming from the other side of the pillar.

Connor took a step into the room. "I'm here," he said and circled around the workstations, careful not to get too close. Reisman's combat suit looked as if it were partially submerged into the exoskeleton. Connor could see his friend's face through his helmet. He took a step closer, but Sean held him back.

"Probably a good idea," Reisman said in a mild attempt at humor.

"What the hell happened?" Connor asked and glanced around. "There were some plasma cutters around here. Go find them."

Sean repeated the order.

"There's no time for that. It's inside my suit. I can feel it working its way up my legs," Reisman said, and his face crumpled in pain.

Connor glared at the other CDF soldiers. "Damn it! Where are those cutters?" He looked back at his friend. "We're gonna get you out of there."

Reisman shook his head and gave him a solemn look. "Not this time, sir. You have to listen to me."

Connor glared over at the CDF soldiers who were scrambling to find something that would help, but they couldn't find anything.

"Fine," Connor said and checked his AR-71.

Deep in the corridors, the high-pitched whistling sound of Vemus soldiers could be heard. Connor saw several CDF soldiers take up positions on either side of the corridor, keeping a watchful eye on the way they'd come.

Connor set his ammunition to high-heat incendiary and aimed his rifle.

"No, you can't!" Reisman cried.

Connor paused with his finger on the trigger. If he could just cut a line on the edges of the base, Reisman could get free. "This will work," Connor insisted.

"It won't work. It's in my suit," Reisman said.

"Sir, perhaps we should listen to him," Sean said.

Connor clenched his teeth. The sounds of the Vemus forces came steadily closer. He opened a link to Reisman's suit computer, which quickly provided the current status of the suit. The last line of code felt like a punch in the stomach.

::*CAUTION: Foreign contaminant present.*::

Connor eased his hand off the trigger and lowered his rifle. "Damn it, Wil."

Reisman winced in pain. "I know. I know. I really stepped in it this time—" He cut off, crying out in pain. "I can feel it crawling along inside me."

Connor took a step forward. He wanted to crack open the combat suit and pull his friend out.

"You have to leave me behind," Reisman said.

Sorrow closed Connor's throat and he gritted his teeth. The sounds of the Vemus forces were becoming louder. The CDF soldiers called out.

"Sir," Sean said.

Connor knew what he was going to say, and he hated him for it. Sean called out to him again.

"Take them back to the ship," Connor said, scowling.

"Not without you, sir," Sean replied.

"That's an order, Captain," Connor said.

"With all due respect, sir, if I have to knock you out and order my men to drag you, I *will* do it," Sean replied stubbornly.

Reisman laughed. It sounded harsh and laden with pain, and it tapered off into a fit of coughing. "You trained him too well."

Connor looked at Sean. "Order them to fall back. I'm right behind you."

Sean narrowed his gaze and then turned around and began ordering them to fall back to the ship.

"You have to do something for me," Reisman said.

Connor looked back at his friend. His face had become pasty white. The AR-71 Connor carried suddenly felt heavy in his arms.

"I'm still in their systems. There's a signal the Vemus use. I'm still tracing it," Reisman said.

"Never mind that," Connor said.

"It's important. I've linked our suits so the data that comes to mine will flow freely to yours. You have to get off this ship and ensure that I'm not dying for nothing. You hear me?" Reisman said.

Connor glanced at the CDF soldiers in the corridor. They were focused. They'd hold the area as long as they could, but it wouldn't be enough.

"Hey!" Reisman called out to him.

Connor looked back at him. "I can't leave like this. First Kasey and now you, Wil. I won't do it."

Reisman's eyes softened. "Yes, you will. These people don't stand a chance without you. It's our time, not yours. Save as many as you can."

An alarm appeared on Connor's heads-up display and he looked at Reisman.

"I'll hold out as long as I can. Remember that case of scotch we liberated from that senator's office? What was his name?" Reisman asked.

Connor frowned. "It was bourbon."

"You're going to argue with me now? You . . . What was his name?"

Connor's brows pulled together. "Senator Wellington."

A countdown appeared on Connor's HUD.

"You need to run. In a hundred and twenty seconds I'm going to blow this area to kingdom come," Reisman said.

Connor knew he was right. Wil had engaged the self-destruct protocol of his combat suite. It would easily take out this entire room.

"Run!" Reisman said.

Connor clenched his teeth and took one last look at his friend. Wil gave him a firm nod. Connor turned around and called for the CDF soldiers to retreat.

They ran down the corridor, away from the approaching Vemus forces. Connor glanced at the data connection to Reisman on his heads-up display. As long as it was active, his friend was still alive. As Connor ran he felt a weariness take him, making his feet feel weighed down. Part of him just wanted to stop. Stop fighting. Stop trying. A primal part of him seemed to take control and he wanted to strike out at his enemies, make one last stand right here in the corridor, but he knew it was foolish. He'd be struck down and then it would fall to someone else to lead the Colonial Defense Force against the Vemus.

Blue bolts struck the wall near him, and Connor scrambled out of the way. The Vemus had caught up with them. Connor spun around and returned fire, as did several of the CDF soldiers near him. A loud pop sounded and the corridor that had been filled with Vemus became engulfed in flames. The data connection to Reisman's combat suit severed and Connor knew his friend was dead.

Connor cried out a rage-filled scream. Sean grabbed him and pulled him around while urging the others to run. They made it back to the *Banshee,* and a comlink opened to him from Major Hayes.

"We're the last ones aboard. Do you have the detonation signal from Captain Lee?" Connor asked.

"We have it but have been unable to reach Captain Lee for some time now, sir," Major Hayes said.

They ran through the CDF destroyer. Emergency lighting was still on. Connor could still hear the Vemus following behind them. Some of them must have survived the blast or had been out of proximity.

There was a cluster of soldiers waiting to get through the emergency docking tube to the *Vigilant*. There was nothing they could do but wait for everyone else to get aboard.

"Major, once we're all aboard, we need to get out of here quickly," Connor said.

"Understood, General. We'll be ready," Major Hayes said.

Connor kept his weapon pointed back the way they'd come. The Vemus were likely on the *Banshee* by now. Sean didn't say anything as he came to stand by Connor's side and readied his own weapon.

They heard the Vemus, faint at first but quickly becoming louder.

"Here they come," Connor said grimly.

He and Sean drew steadily backward, closer to the emergency dock. Connor kept his gaze fixed on the darkened corridor, waiting, anticipating the enemy's approach.

"I have an idea," Sean said.

Connor kept his attention on the end of the narrow ship corridor. "What?"

The emergency lighting cut out, plunging the already dimly lit corridor into darkness. The heads-up display in his helmet had already compensated for the lack of lighting.

"I don't think they're afraid of the dark," Connor said.

"No, but if they can see in the dark, they can be blinded by the light," Sean said.

Connor gave a mental nod to Sean. The young man was a fighter. He'd fight with everything he had.

Several Vemus soldiers came into the corridor and Connor and Sean engaged their helmets' lights. Bright searchlights cut a swath through the darkness, blinding the Vemus soldiers. Then they opened fire on them, catching the Vemus completely by surprise, and their bodies started littering the corridor. Connor had no idea whether they'd done enough damage to put them down permanently or not.

Major Cross called out to them, and Connor and Sean beat a hasty retreat to the emergency docking tube. They went inside and Connor closed the airlock doors. As they headed toward the *Vigilant*, Connor saw several white energy bolts hit the door. They had to move. The docking tube was pressurized, and if the Vemus weapons pierced the walls, they'd be sucked out into space.

"Go. Go!" Connor shouted.

First Major Cross made it onto the *Vigilant* and then Sean. Connor grabbed the handle and pulled himself over the threshold. He turned around and saw Vemus soldiers stepping into the tube. Connor pushed the doors closed and disengaged the tube.

"Get us out of here!" Connor shouted.

The *Vigilant* engaged its maneuvering thrusters and lurched away from the ship. Connor watched through the airlock windows as the Vemus soldiers were sucked into the vacuum of space. Their dark bodies still moved, even in the frigid temperatures.

The *Vigilant* moved away from the former battleship cruiser *Indianapolis*. Connor seized the detonation signal with his implants and sent it to the waiting nukes aboard the ship.

Nothing happened.

Connor tried again but the ship was still there. He slammed his fist against the wall, then opened a comlink to the bridge.

"Major, send the detonation signal," Connor said.

"Sir, we've tried . . ." Major Hayes replied.

"They're blocking the signal. We can't get through the interference," Sean said.

Connor clenched his teeth and then a message appeared on his internal heads-up display.

::Vemus signal analysis complete.::

Connor frowned. This signal was the one Wil had found. The price he'd paid had better be worth it.

Major Hayes had sectioned off the ship so they could follow decontamination protocols. Connor made his way through the waiting line of CDF soldiers, who stepped aside so he could pass. His Nexstar combat suit would need to be checked for breaches and decontaminated. Then Connor would need to be checked. The surviving members of the *Banshee* crew without combat suits were cordoned off to isolation and observation since they posed the greatest risk, having been directly exposed to the Vemus ship.

"General," Major Cross called out behind him.

"Yes," Connor said.

"If it's alright with you, sir, I need to see to my people," Major Cross said.

"Of course," Connor replied. "And Savannah, you did everything you could for them. The fact that you're still here is a testament to what kind of commanding officer you are."

Major Cross's eyes became hard. "The only reason we're still alive is because you and your team came looking for us. The combat shuttles were our last-ditch effort. We even brought improvised nukes of our own, adapted from a HADES IV warhead. The soldiers carrying them were among the first to die."

"Major," Connor said sternly, "you kept your people alive. Making a run to the hangar was a good decision. I would have done the same thing if I'd been in your shoes. Remember that."

Savannah Cross lifted her steady gaze up toward his. "Yes, sir."

She turned around and headed toward her crew. Though she was wearing combat armor, Connor doubted she'd leave her crew to their fate. She'd wait until they were all cleared through decontamination protocols.

An image of Wil Reisman trapped in a Vemus exoskeleton came to mind and he felt an ache in his chest. First Kasey and now Wil. How many more of them were going to have to die? A flash of Lenora Bishop's blue eyes blazed through his thoughts. The last time they'd spoken she'd been furious with him. He wished he could change that. He wanted to hear the sound of her voice, even if she just yelled at him. He glanced around at all the soldiers waiting to be processed through decontamination, but all he saw were the missing faces. So few of them had made it back. There were hardly any wounded. The Vemus had tried to take them alive until they'd realized they fought CDF soldiers in combat armor. Then their tactics had changed, becoming deadlier.

"Sir, they need you on the bridge," Sean said.

Connor glanced over at the young captain. He'd done a job that far exceeded what was required of his rank. Connor would need to rectify that.

"We're not done yet," Connor said.

"No, we're not, sir. Not until all the Vemus have been stopped," Sean replied.

As they headed toward the front of the decontamination processing area, Connor looked at the CDF men and women who'd gone into the belly of the beast and survived to tell the tale. There was no loathing or betrayal in their gazes, which was what Connor felt he deserved despite all they'd learned about the enemy. The fact that so many had died weighed heavily on him, the responsibility resting firmly on his shoulders. Going onto that ship had been the right call, but it was one he'd have to learn to live with. How long would it be before he could stop seeing one of his closest friends give his all so they had a fighting chance? Wil, Kasey, and so many other CDF soldiers had died to protect the colony. Connor promised himself that their sacrifices wouldn't be for nothing. He'd keep going. He'd keep fighting because that was who he was. Quitting wasn't something he'd ever thought about in his entire military career. There had always been the mission. He was weary, but he needed to be strong for his fallen comrades, to fight so the colony on New Earth could survive. They were all that was left of humanity. A few hundred thousand souls were a mere flicker in comparison to the billions of people they'd left behind on Earth and the colonies throughout the solar system. Those billions must be dead, fallen to an enemy they were still trying to understand. Their recent skirmish was just a taste of what they'd face if the remains of the Vemus fleet reached New Earth, and Connor would do everything in his power to prevent that. No matter the cost, it was his duty. For a brief moment, he saw Lenora's beautiful face in his mind. He made another promise to himself knowing the odds were stacked against his keeping such a promise, but he had to make it.

Connor marched forward with determination. This battle was far from over.

CHAPTER TWENTY-SIX

THE HOLOSCREEN in front of him blurred, and Noah rubbed his eyes.

Stay focused and get it done.

Noah kept Connor's last words at the forefront of his mind when he noticed the slightest bit of tiredness threatening to distract him. He felt like his face had formed a permanent scowl from concentrating so hard. He glanced over at Kara. They sat together on the bridge of the *Chmiel* and had taken over the auxiliary workstation.

"Thirtieth time's the charm?" Noah asked and sighed.

"It only has to work once," Kara reminded him.

"Who knew reprogramming the targeting computer on the defense platforms would be so darn difficult," Noah said.

If there was a finickier computer system, Noah hadn't encountered it. He guessed this was the price he had to pay for precision, trying only to hit enemy targets instead of every ship in the vicinity. When they'd first tried to apply the update to the

targeting systems of the defense platforms, they failed so spectac-
ularly that the system became unresponsive. The frozen targeting
systems had nearly given him a panic attack until the system fail-
safes automatically rolled back the update. The update had been
intended to enable the targeting computer to alternate between
scanning for active ship signatures and ship wakes from fusion-
powered engines. Noah had become much more cautious since
then because he didn't want to single-handedly leave the colony
defenseless. If he didn't get the defense platforms fixed, they
would be nothing but useless piles of junk that would let the
Vemus just waltz right into the inner system of planets
unchallenged.

Noah glared at the screen. The uncooperative nature of the
defense platform systems still made them piles of junk, in his
opinion, but he was trying to squeeze every ounce of usefulness
out of them he could while he still had the chance. The navigation system of the missile-defense platforms was much more reliable. Since his initial update to the targeting systems had failed,
he'd had to move all the defense platforms farther into the
system. This gave him time to come up with a fix and hopefully
keep the platforms they'd already passed in range for when the
update eventually worked. If it didn't, they were in serious
trouble.

There were downsides to moving the missile-defense platforms, the primary one being that the maneuvering engines of
each platform were limited, and they had to be sure there was
enough fuel in reserve to allow them to stop. Even with those
considerations, the platforms weren't meant for extensive space
travel, so they moved frustratingly slowly.

Another downside was the fact that Noah wasn't authorized
to move the defense platforms. He authenticated to the defense

platforms' flight systems by using Connor's identification. He didn't have time to explain the situation to the people at COMCENT, who were still unable to reach the *Vigilant*, and then wait for their reply. Noah pressed his lips together. He didn't think Connor would mind, and he hoped the CDF general wasn't incorporating the missile-defense platforms into whatever he was doing. Noah's stomach twisted in knots and he glanced at the comms workstation. They'd sent several messages to New Earth, apprising COMCENT of the situation, but hadn't heard back from them yet. He had to tell them some-thing; otherwise, COMCENT could override his orders to move the defense platforms.

"What are you waiting for?" Kara asked.

"I'm just trying to think if there's anything we haven't thought about yet. The targeting system really doesn't like the updates to PRADIS. Its entire design is predicated on the fact that it can precisely identify a target before it engages. We're essentially telling the computer, 'Nah, that's okay, don't worry about it. A vague impression of engine thrust is as good as a precise location. Fire your weapons,'" Noah said.

They'd fallen into hundreds of pitfalls due to the security protocols designed into the targeting system that was doing its utmost to prevent what they'd been trying to do. If something went wrong, the useless piles of junk *could* determine that the *Chmiel* was the enemy and needed to be destroyed.

"We went over it with a fine-toothed comb. Everything is going to be fine," Kara said.

Noah frowned. "A fine-toothed what?"

Kara smiled. "It's an old saying."

Noah snorted. Kara's family had originally lived in what had been known as the mid-western United States before the country was dissolved when the North American Union was formed. Kara had explained that the area was still known as the Midwest, and Noah had come to learn that there was no shortage of sayings from that part of the world.

"You betcha," Noah said in an attempt to allay his angst by using the only Midwest saying he could remember. He reached his hand out to launch the updated version thirty-point-one and stopped. "If this works, will you promise to make those fried ravioli things you talked about?"

Kara speared her gaze at him. "Stop stalling and send it out already," she said.

Noah pressed the digitized button and the update started to upload to the defense platforms. He watched the screen intently, willing it to finally work.

Kara leaned over and placed her hand on his arm, giving him a slight squeeze.

"Captain Benson, I have a comlink from General Mallory," the comms officer said.

Captain Benson glanced over at Noah. "Put him through."

Noah watched as Captain Benson spoke quietly on the comlink.

"No, General Gates is not on this ship . . . Oh, he's right here. I'll connect you. One moment please, General," Captain Benson said and jutted his chin in Noah's direction.

Noah put on his headset and waited for the comlink to transfer over to him. "Hello, General."

"Cut the 'Hello, General' crap, Barker, and tell me what the hell is going on out there," General Franklin Mallory said, his voice sounding strained.

"The short version is that we've been attacked. Titan Space Station has been destroyed," Noah said.

"We know about Titan," General Mallory said in a calmer

voice. "We received a data burst from them, but none of our replies made it back to them. Then we got the self-destruction communication from the station. What I need to know from you is why you're redeploying the missile-defense platforms . . . and where is Connor?"

Noah glanced at his holoscreen and the update he'd coded was still being pushed to the missile-defense platforms. "Sir, this is going to require a bit of explaining, so please bear with me for a few minutes."

Noah told the CDF general everything he knew about the attack on Titan Space Station and that Jade protocol had been initiated by Connor. Noah went on to tell him about the escape pods they'd left behind, and his info dump to General Mallory became a sort of confession for him, as if he was finally able to unload the burden he'd been carrying. The last thing he mentioned was Connor's orders for him to update the targeting protocols of the defense platforms.

"What's the status of the update?" General Mallory asked.

"We just started pushing it out, so we're waiting on final confirmation that the defense platform systems have taken it," Noah replied.

"Acknowledged. Did Connor specify whether the updates should be applied to the orbital defenses?" General Mallory said.

"No, sir, he didn't. Are they online?"

"As soon as we got the first alert from Titan," General Mallory answered.

Noah blew out a breath. They'd been so isolated that it felt good to hear from someone else. "Sir, about the people we left behind . . ."

"We won't abandon them. Do you know the status of the Vemus fleet?" General Mallory asked.

"The *Chmiel* is only a cargo vessel, so it doesn't have

PRADIS. We were relying on the missile-defense platform detections for that information," Noah said.

"Understood," General Mallory said and then covered his microphone to speak with someone else.

"We know Connor first engaged the Vemus fleet and then Titan Space Station took out a lot of the ships, but we're not sure how many are left," Noah continued.

Kara grabbed his arm. "Look," she said, gesturing to the holoscreen.

Noah looked at the status of the holoscreen and felt the edges of his lips pulling upward. The thirtieth time *was* the charm!

"Sir, the defense platforms are reporting in. The update worked. The targeting systems are coming back online and we should have telemetry in a few minutes," Noah said.

Kara clutched his arm and he leaned in toward her.

"Copy that. Good work," General Mallory said.

"I had a lot of help," Noah said, his eyes beaming.

The missile-defense platforms began to check in with their targeting updates and the plot on his screen filled with enemy ship signatures. The smile drained from his face and he heard several members of the bridge crew gasp. Vemus ships were gaining on them, nipping at their heels.

"Noah," General Mallory said in a knowing voice.

"Sir, the Vemus are almost here. I need to authorize the defense platforms to engage."

"Not yet," General Mallory said sternly.

The PRADIS systems on the missile-defense platforms were still discovering Vemus ships.

"Sir, they're out there. We have to open fire," Noah said.

"Listen to me," General Mallory replied. "We have to wait, draw them farther inside the funnel."

Noah frowned, wondering why the CDF general would be

reasoning with him, and then his eyes widened in understanding. With Connor's credentials, he could order the defense platforms to engage any time he wanted. They were closer to the defense platform on the *Chmiel* than COMCENT was back on New Earth, which also meant an account lockout wouldn't work. Noah glanced at the screen. There were over three hundred Vemus ships heading toward them.

Noah placed his hand on the edge of the workstation. "What do you need me to do?"

"The defense platforms aren't enough to take out that many ships. We need to wait until they're within range of our orbital defenses," General Mallory said, clearly relieved that Noah wasn't going to take matters into his own hands.

"Sir, if the enemy determines the nature of the defense platforms, there's a risk of them being taken out before they can deliver their payload," Noah said.

"That's right, there is. And that's also why I need you to have Captain Benson slow his ship down," General Mallory said.

"Slow the ship down? Why?" Noah asked.

Captain Benson walked over to him and waited.

"Latency," General Mallory replied.

Once again, Noah's eyes widened in understanding. They were closer to the defense platforms and could start firing earlier than if those orders came from COMCENT.

"In this, every second counts," General Mallory said.

"I understand, sir," Noah replied and explained to Captain Benson why he needed to slow the ship down. The added bonus was that they would be bait to draw the Vemus where they wanted them to go.

Noah looked at the plot on the holoscreen and then shot to his feet. He turned toward the main holoscreen, which was much larger than the one at the workstation, and peered at the ships lining the edges.

"Sir, the *Vigilant* has just appeared on the plot," Noah said, his voice rising in excitement.

They were still alive, at least for the time being.

CHAPTER TWENTY-SEVEN

ONCE CLEARED THROUGH DECONTAMINATION, Connor headed for the *Vigilant's* primary bridge. Sean followed along, with several CDF soldiers as an escort. They entered the bridge and Connor caught himself looking for Reisman in the *Vigilant's* command chair. It was a habit that had formed during the weeks they'd been aboard the ship.

Wil is gone, Connor reminded himself.

"General," Major Hayes acknowledged.

Connor approached the command area. "Sitrep."

"The Vemus forces are regrouping and the former battleship carrier *Indianapolis* has moved away from our ship," Major Hayes said.

Connor looked at the main holoscreen and noticed their current position on the plot, then glanced back at Major Hayes. "What happened? We were at the head of the vanguard when we went aboard the *Indianapolis.*"

"That's correct. The remaining Vemus fleet caught up to us

and now we're right in the middle of what's left," Major Hayes said.

Connor turned toward the main holoscreen. "Tactical, any response from the Vemus ships?"

"Negative, General," Lieutenant LaCroix said.

"It's almost as if . . ." Connor's voice trailed off and he glanced at Sean.

"We're not enough of a threat for them to deal with," Sean said.

"We were before. What's changed?" Major Hayes asked.

"They've been slow to respond throughout this whole engagement. They're reliant on superior numbers to achieve their objective," Connor said.

The Vemus fleet had focused on Titan Space Station with an almost singular purpose and now they were heading directly toward New Earth. He looked for the *Indianapolis*. Why had they moved away from them? Did the Vemus know they'd planted bombs on board?

"Why haven't the defense platforms engaged them?" Connor asked.

Those platforms should have delivered their missile payloads to the enemy by now. Connor looked at the system counts for enemy ships and there were still hundreds left.

Too many, Connor thought.

"Sir, the defense platforms have been moved. We only just discovered this a few minutes before you arrived," Major Hayes said.

Connor pressed his lips together. Noah must have moved the defense platforms, which meant something had gone wrong with the update for the targeting computers. They couldn't access the platforms because it might draw the Vemus fleet's attention. He had to assume Noah was working on the problem and was nearing a solution. Noah hadn't disappointed him yet, and he knew the stakes. Connor studied the plot and the enemy ship positions. He needed to get them bunched together so that when the defense platforms did engage, they could do maximum damage.

"The *Chmiel* must still be in front of the vanguard. Tactical, highlight the orbital defense range around New Earth," Connor said.

A few moments later New Earth was highlighted in yellow and the orbital defense range was shown in a paler shade of orange.

"They're drawing them in before they open fire on them," Sean said.

Connor nodded. "Noah wouldn't know to do that on his own. He's not a strategist. He must be in contact with COMCENT. Are we able to contact them?"

"Negative, General. We still have limited communications capabilities while we're so close to the Vemus fleet," Sergeant Boers said.

Connor looked over at the comms officer, considering. Moving away from the Vemus fleet would be a waste of time and opportunity. "How long would it take you to input a new signal protocol for the comms array?"

"Shouldn't take that long. Send over what you have, sir," Sergeant Boers said.

Connor used his implants to send over the Vemus signal Reisman had found. He'd taken a quick look at the analysis and couldn't make sense of it. There were limits to what could be done within an internal heads-up display.

Major Hayes glanced at him questioningly.

"While Colonel Reisman was in the Vemus ship systems, he

found this protocol that he thought was linked to all their ships," Connor said.

"I was very sorry to hear about Wil. He was a good man," Major Hayes said.

Connor clenched his teeth for a moment and kept his gaze on the main holoscreen. He looked back at Hayes and nodded.

"General," Sergeant Boers said, looking worried. "I'm not sure what I can do with that signal. It's really complex."

"Excuse me, sir," Sean said. "Sela, can you put what you have on the main holoscreen?"

Sergeant Boers looked at Connor.

"Go ahead," Connor said.

An image of the signal spectrum appeared on the main holoscreen. Multicolored peaks and valleys represented the many layers of the signal. Connor rubbed the bottom of his chin.

"I've seen something like this before," Sean said.

"What do you think it is?" Connor asked.

Sean stepped closer to the large holoscreen. He took control of the image and swiped it to the side. Then he brought up another communications signal. The wave pattern was similar to the Vemus signal but much less complex.

"This is a signal we use for encrypted CDF communications, which is based on the NA Alliance military protocols," Sean said and then brought up another image and juxtaposed it with the CDF signal. The pitches in the second signal hardly peaked at all but were a constant stream.

"What's that other one?" Major Hayes asked.

"It's the command and control signal for drones," Sean said.

Connor's eyes widened, and Sean brought up the Vemus protocol. They weren't identical, but they were a close enough match to show they were at least similar.

"This is why they're seemingly slow to respond. What if most of the fleet is being controlled by one ship?" Connor said. "Can you upload the protocol to the comms array as is and see what we get?"

"Yes, sir," Sergeant Boers said.

No sooner had the comms officer uploaded the protocols than a high-pitched feedback loop sounded from all the comms speakers on the bridge. Connor brought his hands to his ears and winced at the sound.

Sergeant Boers tore off her headset and adjusted some of the settings. The sound stopped.

"I'm sorry, General. The signal is too strong to listen to. It's overwhelming some of our sensors," Sergeant Boers said.

"Can you put the Vemus signal on the main holoscreen?" Connor asked.

The signal power was off the charts, above and beyond anything the CDF was using. The power requirements for maintaining that kind of a signal must have been immense.

"We don't have the capacity to jam that kind of signal," Major Hayes said.

"We don't have to jam it," Sean said.

Connor shared a knowing glance with the young officer and gave him a nod. This was something they'd both picked up from Lenora.

"We just need to disrupt it," Sean said.

Major Hayes frowned and he looked at Connor. "I'm not following."

"We disrupt the signal by broadcasting one of our own," Connor said.

"We do that and whatever ships are within the vicinity of our signal will be cut off from wherever the broadcast is coming from," Sean said.

"Can we trace the signal?" Major Hayes asked.

Sergeant Boers shook her head. "No, sir, it's too strong. We'd have to move far away from the Vemus fleet."

"What good will disrupting the signal to a few of their ships do?" Major Hayes asked.

Connor watched the signal output on the main holoscreen and then turned back toward the major. "It will get them to follow us," Connor said.

Major Hayes nodded in understanding.

Connor went to the command chair and sat down. Major Hayes sat next to him in the XO's chair.

"Action stations. Set Condition One throughout the ship," Connor said.

His orders were repeated by Sergeant Browning, who sent a broadcast throughout the ship. All crews would be reporting to their combat posts, and bulkhead doors were closing and sealing in case of decompression.

"Helm, plot a course right through the middle of the Vemus fleet. Close quarters. When they start shooting at us, I want their ships as likely to be hit as we are. Then stand by," Connor said.

"Yes, sir, plotting course and standing by," Sergeant Edwards said.

The course appeared on the plot that showed on the main holoscreen. Connor engaged the straps on his chair and they came over his shoulders, securing him in place. He heard the same as the rest of the bridge crew strapped themselves in.

"General, Vemus ship on approach vector," Lieutenant LaCroix said.

"Looks like they finally noticed us," Connor said. "Comms, start broadcasting the Vemus signal, max capacity."

"Yes, sir, broadcasting now," Sergeant Boers said.

"Helm, you're a go," Connor said.

He felt a slight shudder through the bridge as their two remaining engines engaged and the *Vigilant* lurched forward.

"Tactical, stand by countermeasures and short-range weapons," Connor said.

"Yes, sir, standing by countermeasures and short-range weapons," Lieutenant LaCroix said.

Connor watched the plot. The tonnage of the Vemus ship heading toward them was similar to theirs, which led Connor to believe it was a heavy-cruiser class vessel.

"Helm, push our nose to starboard by three degrees and punch it," Connor said. "All ahead full."

"Ahead full, yes, sir," the helmsman reported.

The ship began to shake as the engines came to full power and the *Vigilant* surged forward.

"Enemy ship hasn't altered course," Lieutenant LaCroix said.

Connor watched the plot. They were closing in on the ship. "Tactical, tag that target as alpha until we pass it. I need a firing solution for our remaining rail-cannons on that ship."

"Yes, sir. Firing solution ready," Lieutenant LaCroix said.

"Ops, any change with the enemy ship?" Connor asked.

"No, sir. Same heading and speed, sir," Sergeant Browning said.

Connor was playing a hunch. He glanced at the countdown timer to intercept with the enemy ship. They were closing in.

"Fire, Lieutenant," Connor said.

The rail-cannons on top of the ship began firing at the Vemus ship in rapid succession. The rail-cannon was a crude weapon that had been kept in service to appease a certain nostalgia of a bygone age where two ships would slug it out.

"Confirm multiple hits, sir," Sergeant Browning reported.

The rail-cannons peppered the hull of the Vemus ship and then became silent as the two ships passed each other.

"Ops, monitor that ship and let me know when it alters course," Connor said.

"That would be our effective range for broadcasting the Vemus signal," Major Hayes said.

"Yes. Now the cat and mouse game begins," Connor replied.

The Vemus fleet continued on toward New Earth, and the *Vigilant* was firing on another ship in the fleet before the alpha finally changed course.

"Can we boost the broadcast signal?" Connor asked.

"We'd need to divert more power to the array, sir," Major Hayes said.

"Get someone from Engineering on it," Connor said.

Major Hayes went to his own comlink and started speaking to someone from Engineering.

"General, multiple Vemus ships are altering their courses. It's like they can't get a lock on where they want to go," Lieutenant LaCroix said.

Connor surveyed the plot with grim satisfaction. The Vemus ships on PRADIS appeared to be tracking toward multiple trajectories, none of which were where the *Vigilant* actually was.

"Sir, Engineering says they can route more power to the array but would need us to stop broadcasting in order to do it," Major Hayes said.

"For how long?" Connor asked.

"More power to the comms array requires higher-capacity cabling to the power assembly for the array. They can lay out everything they need beforehand and perform the switch in fifteen minutes," Major Hayes said.

Connor sighed. "Tell them to get started. Once everything's in place, I'll order the broadcast stopped."

They needed to find a way to survive for fifteen minutes while utterly exposed to the Vemus fleet. Connor glanced over at the plot. Their current heading had them crossing the Vemus fleet formation in tighter quarters, making steady progress toward the front. There was no easy way out of this. If they retreated to a safe distance, the Vemus fleet would regroup and quickly recover, but if they stayed and stopped disrupting the Vemus control signal, they ran the risk of being destroyed while they were trying to increase the broadcast range. The Vemus knew they were here even if they couldn't locate the *Vigilant* at this time.

There was no other way. Increasing the broadcast range of the Vemus signal was essential if they were going to protect New Earth.

"Sir, Engineering is ready for the cut over," Major Hayes said.

Connor looked at the plot and their current position. "Helm, try to keep us near the center of the enemy fleet formation."

He glanced around the bridge. They all knew that the odds of surviving what they were about to do were stacked against them. Even if they miraculously stayed alive for the fifteen minutes required to reroute more power to their comms array, they were well within range of the defense platforms. Either the Vemus ships or missiles from the CDF defense platforms would destroy them. They couldn't even abandon ship. Their escape pods weren't equipped to repel the harsh radiation from nuclear warheads and couldn't get far enough away to escape. Only by remaining on board the *Vigilant* did they stand the slightest chance of survival, but more importantly, they'd stand a much better chance of delivering a crippling blow to the enemy.

CHAPTER TWENTY-EIGHT

THE CARGO CARRIER had slowed its velocity to a crawl to allow the Vemus fleet to catch up to it. Noah watched the plot, which the frustratingly slow ship's computers had to update based on the data feeds sent back from the missile-defense platforms. There was probably at least a twenty-minute delay because the processing power of the *Chmiel's* computing systems was nowhere near that of an actual warship. On a ship like the *Vigilant*, the data feeding the plot would be processed in almost real time.

"I still can't figure out how he's doing it," Noah said, probably for the third time.

Kara stood next to him. "It's like they can't see him for some reason. General Gates likely found a way to throw off their sensors, but the range is limited."

The Vemus forces held their formation along the edges of their approach, but the ships toward the interior were breaking formation as they pursued the *Vigilant*—at least they had been as of twenty minutes ago.

Noah glanced at the timer for the next data refresh and sighed heavily.

Captain Benson came over and stood beside them. "General Mallory just informed me that the three orbital defense platforms have been moved into position."

"That took a while," Noah said.

"They reside at the Lagrange points so the distance they had to cover was pretty great," Captain Benson said with a shrug.

Noah shook his head. "Did you know they're only partially outfitted?"

Kara glanced at him sharply. "What do you mean?"

Noah bobbed his head up and down. "There's supposed to be a full complement of HADES IV missiles on those platforms. They have the anti-ship missile tubes but not the missiles. Resources were diverted elsewhere since we'd already completed the missile-defense platforms."

"Governor Parish?" Captain Benson asked.

"The one and only. So the orbital defense platforms have a couple of rail-cannons each and one plasma-cannon each," Noah said.

"What about the moon base where the shipyard is?" Captain Benson asked.

"There's a CDF battleship carrier being constructed using the remaining resources from the *Ark*, but it's nowhere near ready. Any defenses on New Earth's moon will be on the wrong side of the planet by the time we get near it," Noah said.

The timer on the main holoscreen dwindled down and the main plot started to update with new information. As the information refreshed, Noah's eyes widened at the snapshot from twenty minutes ago that finally appeared on their screens. He stepped closer. The Vemus ships seemed to be converging on a single point of contact with rigid clarity.

"Whatever they were doing isn't working anymore. You have to authorize the launch," Kara said.

The remains of the Vemus fleet were well within range of the missile-defense platforms. If he authorized them to fire now they could destroy the *Vigilant*. Connor's ship was in trouble.

"Even if we did fire on them now, it wouldn't mean they'd be in time to make a difference," Noah said.

Though Kara outranked him, he had operational authority over the defense platforms, so it was on him to execute the launch commands.

"You don't know that. All the calculations in the world can't tell you that. If you launch them now, at least they might have a fighting chance," Kara said.

Noah walked back over to his terminal. He felt like he was on autopilot, as if someone else were moving his body and he was just along for the ride. He brought up the command module for the missile-defense platforms and hesitated. His mouth went dry and he glanced up at the plot.

Captain Benson walked over to him. "Your friends are on that ship?" he asked gently.

Noah's throat became thick. "Yes," he answered, his voice sounding husky. "They're my family," he said, thinking of Connor and Sean. He had other friends in the colony, but from their earliest days together a powerful connection had been forged among all of them, even Dr. Bishop, who had looked after him like an older sister. How could he face Lenora if he did this?

"What would they do in your place?" Captain Benson asked. His deep voice was soothing, but there was an edge to it.

Noah pressed his lips together tightly. He knew exactly what they would do. They'd push the damn button. They'd hate themselves, but they would do it. Noah glared at his terminal and authorized the missile-defense platforms to finally engage the enemy. He closed his eyes for a moment and whispered a prayer, pleading that his friends . . . his family . . . would somehow survive what he'd done. A rush of adrenaline surged through his veins and a deep-seated anger stretched throughout his chest. He wanted to scream and shake his fists above him, but he knew neither of those things would help.

"It's done," Noah said.

Now, they'd wait.

"Multiple bogies inbound, sir," Lieutenant LaCroix said.

Connor cursed. "Helm, keep us in tight near that ship."

When they'd stopped broadcasting the Vemus signal, their ships had quickly regrouped and targeted the *Vigilant*.

The Vemus ships used a powerful particle-beam cannon that melted deeply through their hull. The *Vigilant* was belching atmosphere from hundreds of hull breaches. Their only saving grace was being able to stay nearby a Vemus ship that had suffered tremendous damage from friendly fire. They peppered the hull with shots from their remaining rail-cannons and narrowly avoided the harrowing particle beams from their main batteries. They couldn't stay anywhere long, and if an opportunity came for them to move to another Vemus ship, they took it.

Connor looked at the status of the comms array. It was still red. The area near the comms array had taken damage and there were engineering teams trying to fix it. They were well beyond the envelope for piloting a heavy cruiser. Sergeant Edwards' skills as a helmsman were one of the reasons they were still alive.

"Sir, I'm seeing missile launches on PRADIS," Lieutenant LaCroix said.

That was it; they were out of time. The missile-defense platforms had been engaged. They either stayed where they were and got destroyed or made a run for it and likely got torn apart by Vemus particle beams. Those weapons had been new when Connor was part of the NA Alliance military. There must have been developments in the years since the *Ark* left the Sol System.

He kept thinking about the beings they'd encountered on board the *Indianapolis*. Some were human-like but so much more. It was known that they were some type of virus or parasitic organism that came from Earth's oceans and was able to target multiple species of mammals. The scientists had tried to stop the virus from spreading and made it worse. They had records they'd downloaded from the *Indianapolis*, but they hadn't had time to analyze them. Connor had ordered the data stored on multiple comms drones that hadn't been launched yet.

"How long until the missiles reach us?" Connor asked.

Lieutenant LaCroix updated the information on the main holoscreen. Not much time. The defense platforms were in close proximity. Given the capabilities of the NA Alliance military, Connor thought the Vemus would have made use of other weapons of war. This fleet relied on sheer numbers and large weapons like the particle-cannon. They didn't use combat drones or short-range fighters, and Connor didn't understand why that was the case.

"Sir, the comms array is coming back online," Sergeant Boers said, her voice high with hope.

Connor swung his gaze to Major Hayes, who was already on a comlink with the engineering teams in the area.

"The system's charging. Full power will be available in sixty seconds," Major Hayes said.

Connor nodded. "Ops, confirm the range of the broadcast with the higher-yield energy available once we start boosting the signal."

Connor waited for the capacitors to finish charging. "Comms, begin broadcast."

The battered communications array on the *Vigilant* started pumping out the complex signal.

"Broadcast has started at known levels, increasing incrementally," Sergeant Boers said.

"Helm, take us away from their shadow and stand by for evasive maneuvers," Connor said.

"Taking us out, sir," Sergeant Edwards said.

The *Vigilant* moved away from the Vemus ship. Scans had indicated that it was a cruiser class, but there was evidence of smaller vessels that had been absorbed into the main hull.

"Vemus ships in the area are firing their weapons!" Lieutenant LaCroix said.

Connor felt a gasp catch in his throat.

"Sir, they're firing blindly," Sean said, frowning at the tactical screen.

"Put it on screen," Connor said.

Bright flashes of charged particles being fired in rapid succession appeared on screen as if there were a lightning storm in space. Sean was right; the Vemus were firing blindly, banking on the off chance they might hit them, which meant they'd updated their tactics.

"Comms, boost the signal to maximum," Connor said.

"Boosting signal to maximum, sir," Sergeant Boers said.

"Tactical, focus our high-res optics on the ships farthest away. I want to know if they start firing their weapons," Connor said.

Their current trajectory didn't put them in the path of the Vemus weapons, but that could change at any moment. Connor watched the range of their broadcast leap across the plot as the more powerful signal doubled its range.

"Confirm additional ships firing their weapons. They're hitting each other, sir," Lieutenant LaCroix said.

"Helm, plot a course back to New Earth, best speed, but wait to execute," Connor said.

"Yes, sir. Plotting course back to New Earth," Sergeant Edwards said.

Connor waited.

Major Hayes glanced over at him. "Firing blindly isn't going to cut it."

"No, it won't—" Connor began.

"Sir, Vemus ships within range of the broadcast are altering course," Lieutenant LaCroix said.

Connor frowned at the PRADIS output. The CDF missiles were closing in on them. If they were going to live, they had to move.

"They've realized they're getting cut off from each other and are trying to find us," Connor said.

There was a bright flash as one Vemus ship's particle beam cut into another. More of the same continued to appear on the screen. It was chaos.

"Helm, execute course, emergency!" Connor said.

The lighting on the bridge dimmed and Connor felt a shimmy move through the weakened hull of their ship. Their two remaining drive pods gleamed as they were brought to maximum capacity. The *Vigilant* lurched forward with the maneuvering thrusters firing at the behest of the navigation computers that kept the ship on course. The energy drain on their main reactor was enormous, and Connor ordered all available power to the engines and the comms array. They had to keep that signal up for as long as they could.

The *Vigilant* flew through a nightmarish maze of charged particle beams in the heart of the Vemus fleet. Connor watched the PRADIS screen, knowing that a maelstrom of HADES IV missiles was about to tear the Vemus fleet apart.

"Detonation detected, sir," Lieutenant LaCroix said.

Connor looked at the main holoscreen and saw that the first wave of HADES IV missiles was striking at the rearmost forces of the Vemus fleet. They would drive the Vemus forces forward into the orbital defense platforms that were stationed at the Lagrange points around the planet.

Klaxon alarms blared on the bridge as a particle beam lanced through the forward section of the ship. There was nothing he could do for the CDF soldiers serving there. Bulkhead doors would automatically shut and there were damage-control teams moving to the area. The casualty count kept rising. How many more of them would need to die in order to stop this enemy fleet?

A rough shimmy worked its way through the ship and Connor gritted his teeth. He didn't need LaCroix to confirm that they were now within the shockwaves of multiple HADES IV missiles that had delivered their warheads.

The optical sensors went offline and the holoscreen blanked out. They still had PRADIS, but for how long?

CHAPTER TWENTY-NINE

The *Chmiel* had passed the orbital defense platforms and Captain Benson had his ship on an approach to New Earth. It seemed strange to Noah to be offloading people from the ship when there was an attack force on its way to the planet. HADES IV missiles had been launched from the defense platforms and the monitoring systems running on those platforms reported updates for as long as they could. Once the warheads started to detonate, they lost their visibility into what was happening to the enemy and, more importantly, what the fate of the *Vigilant* was to be. In the lengthy time between updates, the snapshots showed the Vemus ships in the interior of the attack force going into complete disarray and the ships on the edge converging in a feeble attempt to restore order.

The chaotic mass of enemy ships moved closer to them.

"Orbital defense platforms have begun firing their weapons," Kara said.

"How do they even know what they're firing at?" Noah asked.

"They're using the rail-guns to paint the targets, then the plasma-cannon to finish the job," Kara said.

Shuttles were inbound from New Sierra and would be arriving soon. Offloading the CDF personnel from Titan Space Station would begin as soon as they arrived. Noah felt completely drained and useless. They'd succeeded in updating the targeting systems of the missile-defense platforms, but this constant waiting was wearing on his nerves. Even now, those missiles were tearing apart the remains of the Vemus fleet, but there was no way for them to know exactly how much damage they were inflicting on the enemy. Were the orbital defense platforms enough to finish the job?

Thirty minutes later the shuttles arrived. They still hadn't gotten usable data from the missile-defense platforms. Most of them were now offline, which wasn't a surprise given how much interference there was from all the detonations in the area.

"COMCENT has sent a request for you to be in the first group to return to the planet," Captain Benson said.

Noah's brows pulled together. Jade protocol—protect the best and the brightest. "I'm not going," he said harshly.

Kara looked at him in concern.

"I may not officially be in the Colonial Defense Force, but refusing direct orders isn't tolerated, as far as I know," Captain Benson said.

Noah clenched his teeth. "You've done as they asked and delivered the message. I'm not going anywhere, not until I know what happened to the *Vigilant*."

Captain Benson regarded him for a moment. "I understand, and I'll have them informed."

Noah looked away and focused on the main holoscreen. He didn't want to believe the *Vigilant* was gone. They must have survived but were unable to contact them.

Stay focused, Noah thought to himself.

Captain Benson had given them full access to the ship's systems, so he went over to his terminal and opened the communications interface for the *Chmiel*. He started scanning different broadcast signals, hoping for some sign that the *Vigilant* was still intact.

The *Chmiel* was a cargo ship and wasn't equipped with military-grade sensor arrays or high-res optics. They had standard avoidance protocols, which could identify if a ship was in the vicinity of a communications array. The data that fed the plot on the main holoscreen was hours old, so Noah removed the plot in favor of using the limited optics on the ship. They could see flashes of bright red from the orbital defense platforms, but the targets the onboard computers were firing at were too far away to see. He rubbed his eyes, giving them a momentary respite. He couldn't remember the last time he'd slept and he was sure he could use a shower.

He snorted as a thought came to mind. Kara glanced at him questioningly.

"I just thought of something. Don't know why it hasn't occurred to me before," Noah said.

He opened a comms channel to the orbital defense platforms and connected to their onboard computer systems. Since the *Chmiel* had the slowest data processing capabilities imaginable, Noah stopped what he was doing to consider how best to access the data he wanted.

"I got this. We just need to see what it's firing at," Kara said and took over the comms session. She quickly coded a query to pull only the targeting data from the system and then had it output to the plot they'd used before.

The software suite took the new data and added it to the plot.

"Thanks," Noah said tiredly.

They watched as ships emerged from the area where their last payload of HADES IV missiles had torn into the Vemus fleets. The targeting systems first scoured the area for something to shoot and then fired their weapons. If the *Vigilant* was there, it would have to broadcast its unique identifier so the orbital defense platforms wouldn't fire at it. They couldn't tell what the condition the few ships appearing on the plot were in, only that they were there.

A bright flash shone from the sub-holoscreen, followed by an explosion as one of the orbital defense platforms went offline. The weapons systems on the remaining two platforms targeted another blip on the plot. The ship was still far away. There was another bright flash that lanced across their video feeds.

Noah's screen began filling with errors as the orbital defense platforms' systems became unresponsive.

"That has to be a main weapon from a battleship carrier," Kara said.

Noah was about to reply when he noticed another ship appearing on the plot, but then it just as quickly disappeared. Noah leaned in, peering at the holoscreen.

"What did you see?" Kara asked.

"I thought I saw the *Vigilant*," Noah said.

The CDF ship signatures appeared as green on the plot so they could easily identify friendly ships. Noah glanced at the terminal session he had open to the orbital defense platforms. The data connection for one of them was still alive. He did a quick rundown of the critical systems.

"We have to help them," Noah said.

"What can we do? This isn't a warship," Captain Benson said.

"I know what I saw. The *Vigilant* is still out there, fighting," Noah said.

He turned back to his workstation, his eyes taking in all the holoscreens with renewed vigor. "The plasma-cannon from that platform is still online. It can still fire," Noah said.

He pulled up the targeting systems and they were online as well. Noah frowned, trying to think of why the weapon wasn't firing, and glanced at one of the error messages on the screen.

::*Turret field out of alignment.*::

Noah pointed to the error message and looked at Kara. "Do you know what this means? What turret field?"

Kara peered at the error. "It means the actual turret is damaged and the system can't point the weapon in the right direction."

Noah rubbed the top of his head and pulled his hair. "We have to get out there," he said, rising out of his chair.

Captain Benson shook his head. "There are thousands of lives on this ship. We can't just stop offloading people to the surface."

Several members of the *Chmiel's* bridge crew turned in their direction and glanced at both of them.

Noah clenched his teeth. He suspected the bridge crew would overwhelm him if the captain ordered it. Regardless, the cargo ship captain was right. "What about a shuttle? Something. You must have something you use to do visual inspections of the ship."

Captain Benson's mouth hung open, then he swallowed hard. "We do have a shuttle."

"Fine. I'm taking the shuttle. Where is it?" Noah asked and started walking toward the doors.

"Mid-ship hangar. I'll tell them you're coming down," Captain Benson said.

Noah fled the bridge and Kara followed him.

"You didn't think I was going to let you go off by yourself," Kara said.

Noah knew better than to ask her to stay behind. Truth be told, he'd need the help. He didn't know how to fix a turret, but he had to do something. He had to find a way to get that plasma-cannon to fire its weapons again.

They ran to the small mid-ship hangar. The shuttle was strictly used on maintenance runs for the ship. Noah had learned to fly years ago because Lenora Bishop had questionable flying skills, and he preferred softer landings.

They climbed aboard and headed for the cockpit. After a quick check of the flight systems, they flew the shuttle away from the cargo ship. Noah punched in the coordinates for the orbital defense platforms. The distance to the Lagrange point from New Earth wasn't that far. There hadn't been any more weapons fire from the battleship carrier. The Vemus must have thought the platforms were no longer a threat. While the shuttle was en route, he and Kara slipped into EVA suits. They didn't engage their helmets, which were collapsed into a tight compartment near the base of the necks.

There was a debris field from the remains of the other platforms, and Noah piloted the shuttle through it, heading toward one of the larger sections that was intact. The shuttle was highly maneuverable and they quickly wove their way through. Noah engaged the searchlights.

"The cannon looks intact," Kara said.

It appeared that the orbital defense platform had been sheared in half and the section that housed the rail-cannon was nowhere to be found. Noah circled around the large plasma-cannon. There was a damaged section that was blackened from when it had been hit, but the cannon itself looked intact. Most of the damage was restricted to the base of the cannon where the rollers were that swung it in the direction it was to fire.

Noah patched into the platform's systems. Power levels were

slowly falling, but there was enough to fire a few more shots. Now all they had to worry about was aiming the plasma-cannon, and he had no idea how they were going to do it.

CHAPTER THIRTY

CONNOR DIDN'T KNOW how the *Vigilant* was still holding together. It might have been their relatively central position when the HADES IV missiles had hit the remains of the Vemus fleet. Or perhaps it was the Vemus signal they'd been disrupting that prevented them from launching countermeasures or taking evasive maneuvers. What he *did* know was that the enemy ships had formed a temporary cocoon that protected them from destruction.

Connor glanced through his helmet at the others on the bridge. He'd ordered the surviving crew to go to life support. There were large sections near the central part of the ship where the interior atmosphere was intact, including the bridge, but places like the forward rail-gun batteries were completely exposed.

"Ops, what's the status of 01?" Connor asked.

They'd been having problems getting ammunition to their only remaining rail-cannon due to extensive damage to the ship. Engineering teams were connecting a workaround to take the ammunition from other rail-gun batteries that were damaged beyond repair.

"They're still working on it. A few minutes more, sir," Sergeant Browning said.

Connor glared at the blank PRADIS output. They were still flying blind. There was another Vemus battleship carrier that had been hidden away in the rear of the fleet, and there had been a handful of smaller vessels that survived the onslaught of HADES IVs, but they'd been picked off by the orbital defense platforms.

The PRADIS screen became active and showed a Barracuda-class battleship carrier nearby. It was heavily damaged and Connor narrowed his gaze at the onscreen designation. *Indianapolis.* The battleship carrier had fired its main particle-cannon, which had chewed through the orbital defense platforms in short order.

They tracked the battleship carrier visually since their sensor array was offline. The damage-assessment teams couldn't make it to where the sensors were housed and the armored hatches that protected the secondary sensor array had been damaged. If it weren't for the optical array, they'd be flying completely blind.

New Earth appeared as a bright blue orb in the distance, but the Vemus battleship carrier was much closer to them. The exoskeletal hull had been burnt away by the fusion warheads of the HADES IVs, and there were large sections of the original battle-steel hull once again exposed to space.

"Do I have to go down to the forward sections and load the damn gun myself? I need that weapon now!" Connor growled.

If they couldn't get the rail-cannon back online, Connor would order the remaining crew to abandon ship and he'd take out the engines of the battleship cruiser himself.

"Sir, they're really close," Sergeant Browning said.

Major Hayes had left the bridge to organize the engineering

crews. Connor knew the man was doing everything he could, but it just might not be enough. The Vemus appeared hell-bent on getting at least one of their ships to the planet that the last of humanity called home. But no trace of the Vemus could be allowed to reach New Earth, which might include the *Vigilant's* crew since some of them had been exposed.

Connor could barely discern where the orbital defense platforms had been. All that was left of them was debris. All their preparation for the past seven years had led to this. That enemy ship must be stopped.

Connor opened a comms channel to broadcast to the entire ship. "All hands—"

"Sir, rail-cannon is back online!" Sergeant Browning said.

Connor glanced at the operations officer and gave him a nod. "We're about to make our final attack run on the enemy. We're all that stands between them and our home. Should this attack run fail to disable that ship, I will sacrifice this ship in order to stop the enemy from reaching New Earth."

Connor closed the comms channel. "Tactical, one more firing solution. Concentrate fire behind the MPDs. Helm, keep us in position as long as you can."

Connor's orders were confirmed. He heard some of his officers muttering a prayer. The die was about to be cast, and sometimes one had to roll the hard six.

NOAH AND KARA left the shuttle, each of them carrying a plasma cutter. He thought that if he could remove some of the damaged sections, he could free the turret enough so they could align it for a shot, but they had to move fast. The plasma-cannon was the size of a large building. They quickly circled around the base and closed in on the damaged sections. Noah peered at the area and there were several large pieces of twisted metal jutting out from the base. They looked to have been pieces from another platform.

He'd been poised, ready to use the plasma cutters, but when he saw the extent of the damage, he glanced down helplessly at the tool. If he had a week and a crew of fifty, he might have been able to do something.

"This isn't going to work," Noah said.

Kara had been standing off to the side and had an access panel open. "Come over here."

Noah walked over to her, his mag-boots keeping him firmly attached to the metallic surface.

"What did you find?" Noah asked.

"Look here. There are still some thrusters active," Kara said.

Noah peered at the maintenance terminal and his eyes widened. "You're a genius! Come on. We need to get back to the shuttle," he said, a plan forming in his mind.

He'd been so focused on trying to fix the turret that he'd overlooked the main problem of just aiming the weapon. The orbital platforms were large space vehicles designed to be stabilized while the weapons were active. Stability came with the use of gravity fields, along with redundant power stations.

"I should have caught this," Noah said as they went through the hatch and back onto the shuttle.

"We both missed it. I didn't even think of it until we saw the extent of the damage," Kara replied.

Noah sat in the pilot's seat and engaged the shuttle's controls, easing away from the base of the plasma-cannon.

"I have thruster control online," Kara said.

Noah swung the shuttle around so they could see the approach of the enemy warship. There were several bright flashes of light and he felt his mouth go dry. Kara gasped. If that ship fired on them, they had no chance of getting away.

Noah squinted, trying to extract every bit of detail from the tele-view on the shuttle's heads-up display. There were more flashes of light, but it was gleaming sections of the battleship carrier as it tumbled toward them, out of control. The flashing was from the ship's magneto-drive pods, half of which were disabled.

Noah brought up the platform's control systems. "I'm ready to disable the gravity field."

"Go," Kara replied.

Noah disabled the field and Kara engaged the platform's thrusters. The plasma-cannon swung around and Noah began priming the shot. Kara frantically tried to control the platform's thrusters, but she couldn't keep it stable enough. Noah tried to engage the gravity field, but it wasn't responding. Without it, they'd only get a few shots because there was nothing to keep the cannon in place.

The massive ship came barreling toward them and Noah waited for the remains of the orbital defense platform to come around again.

"Hold on," Noah said.

Gritting his teeth, he waited for the plasma-cannon to align on the target at point-blank range. At the last possible second, he fired the weapon. The plasma-cannon unleashed molten fury in a hail of magnetic bolts with superheated centers. The bolts tore into the hull of the battleship carrier while Noah maximized the shuttle's engines. He angled away from the ship and sped away. As they cleared the ship, Noah saw that the plasma-cannon was still active, which meant it was still firing. He swung the nose of the shuttle around and could see the battleship carrier being ripped apart. The barrel of the plasma-cannon was lodged in the belly of the ship. Noah glanced over to the side and saw two streams of white bolts coming from a heavy cruiser. It was the *Vigilant!* Sections of the ship had been shorn away, but its remaining rail-cannon fired mercilessly on the enemy ship. He watched as the large behemoth expanded and then the exoskeleton split apart the fusion warheads, rending the ship to shreds.

"Noah, get us out of here or we'll be caught up in it!" Kara shouted.

Noah got on the controls and maximized the thrusters. The shuttle raced away and Noah saw the *Vigilant* try to do the same, but the shockwave sent the severely damaged CDF heavy cruiser tumbling. The gleam from the remaining drive pods went offline as the ship slowly rolled over on its axis. The shuttle's power systems shut down because the destruction of the battleship carrier sent out an electromagnetic pulse. Noah knew they'd come back online because the shutdown was part of the emergency response built into the system fail-safes for smaller spacecraft.

Noah glanced over at Kara. "Are you alright?"

Kara looked around. "I think so. The shuttle's intact."

The power systems came back online, along with their heads-up displays. A massive debris field stretched out before them, filled with huge sections of the Vemus ship. Telemetry of the field showed that they wouldn't be coming near the planet. New Earth was safe.

They'd lost track of the *Vigilant* when they lost power, and the shuttle's limited scanning capability couldn't distinguish the *Vigilant* from the space debris in the area. Noah sent out automated ship hails on all comms channels. After getting no response, he flew the shuttle into the field and began looking for the *Vigilant*.

"If they abandoned ship, we should at least be getting beacons from the escape pods," Kara said.

They caught up to the dead CDF ship a few minutes later. Noah tried opening a comms channel to the ship, but there was no response. The *Vigilant* looked more like a ship under construction than a vessel that had just come from a battle. Noah kept trying to get a response from anyone alive on the ship and felt a tinge of desperation creeping into his voice.

Finally, a comlink registered on the shuttle's heads-up display.

"We're here," Connor replied, his voice sounding strained. "We're still here. Did we destroy it?"

"It's good to hear your voice, sir. No Vemus ships in the area. We have a lock on you. We'll transmit your position back to COMCENT and get rescue operations going," Noah said.

"That sounds good. Better tell them to use quarantine protocols," Connor said.

Noah frowned and glanced at Kara. "I don't understand. Quarantine protocols for what?" he asked.

"It's a long story. Better patch in COMCENT if you can. We need emergency medical supplies as well. What's your location?" Connor asked.

"We're on a shuttle near the remains of the orbital defense platform," Noah said.

"So you're the ones who got off that final shot. Good work. You saved us all," Connor said.

"I had help," Noah replied and Kara spoke up.

"Thanks to you, too, Major," Connor said.

"COMCENT is ready . . ." Noah said.

CHAPTER THIRTY-ONE

A WEEK HAD PASSED since the attack. It had taken several days to get the survivors organized and make sure that there were no more ships in the Vemus fleet. The *Vigilant* was towed to the space docks near the lunar base. Unless they rebuilt the entire ship, Connor doubted it would fly again anytime soon, if ever. Given what they'd faced, he wasn't sure investing in a fleet was their best option at this time. Officially, he and the rest of the *Vigilant* and the *Banshee* crews were still under quarantine. He was supposed to stay at the hastily constructed quarantine sections of the lunar space docks where they'd been building their own battleship carrier, but Dr. Ashley Quinn had cleared him and a small task force to leave. Connor had asked her to keep his clearance under wraps for the time being. None of the crew that had been directly exposed to the Vemus ship's atmosphere showed any indication of infection, which was both a very good sign and a troubling one because they were no closer to understanding how humanity had fallen.

Once news of the attack had spread throughout the colony,

the populace celebrated the Colonial Defense Force. The attack they'd all feared had come and they'd survived. All their preparation and sacrifice had paid off. But Connor had trouble thinking of it as a victory. They'd survived only by the skin of their teeth. Their defenses were virtually gone, and he was haunted by thoughts of the soldiers they'd left behind.

The CDF had commandeered the *Chmiel* and were heading back out to where Titan Space Station had been, looking for CDF soldiers still alive in the escape pods. Connor wished that was the only reason the *Chmiel* had returned to that area of space. The cargo carrier was also tasked with setting up a high-powered sensor array taken off the battleship carrier they'd been building.

Only a few people knew Connor had returned to the planet and he aimed to keep it that way for now. He had Noah going through the data Reisman had taken from the *Indianapolis*, which was hitting the "mother lode," as Noah liked to put it, in terms of learning about their enemy. One of the first orders of business Connor initiated from quarantine was to reposition their deep-space sensor array. At the same time, he'd ordered salvage crews to extract the Vemus communication protocols from the *Vigilant's* comms systems.

"I think our bird has finally come home, sir," Sean said.

Connor waited in a darkened office in the governor's residence. They'd easily disabled the security forces stationed at the governor's home, and Stanton Parish was on his way home. There had been celebrations of their "victory" over the Vemus, and Governor Parish had no end of speeches to give commemorating the occasion. Connor had brought a team of special CDF forces with him that was led by the newly promoted Major Sean Quinn. He deserved the promotion and was smart enough to know there was a lot more work coming his way.

"Target has entered the premises," Sean said.

Connor leaned against the wall in the shadows. The governor's desk was on the far side of the room. Connor had been to this office often over the years when Tobias Quinn had been governor but not so much since Stanton Parish had been elected. Connor heard Stanton's voice outside the office doors and then they opened.

Parish walked into the office and the interior lighting slowly illuminated to a casual brilliance. He walked over to his bar and poured himself a glass of scotch. Connor heard the ice hit the glass and then cleared his throat.

Parish spun around, spilling some of his drink. "Who's there?"

Connor stepped from the shadowy confines of the dark corner. "Hello, Governor."

"General Gates. I'm surprised to see you here," Parish said, blanching.

Connor didn't answer right away. Instead, he slowly crossed the room.

"I thought you and I needed to have a private chat. Why don't you have a seat?" Connor said.

Parish glanced at the door.

"Don't worry, we won't be disturbed. My men have your security forces detained for the moment," Connor said and sat down.

Parish swallowed hard and walked over to sit at his desk. "When did you get out of quarantine?"

Connor narrowed his gaze for a moment. "You'd be better served to just listen for the moment while I put the cards out on the table. Wouldn't you agree?"

Parish drained his scotch and set the glass on his desk with shaking hands. There was no question in Connor's mind that the man was afraid of him, as he should be. He'd thought long and hard about being in Parish's presence again.

"You tried to kill me," Connor said.

Parish's eyes widened. "That's absurd. I would never do such a thing. You're a hero. You saved us from the Vemus—"

Connor slammed his fist on the desk and Parish jumped. "You don't get to call me a hero. Not now. Not ever. I may not have the evidence to prove what you tried to have done to me, but I know it was you who put the pieces in motion."

Parish began to protest and Connor leaped from his chair and launched himself across the desk. He grabbed Parish by his shirt and slammed the man against the wall. "Colonel Ian Howe died a horrible death because of you, because your man screwed up while following your orders. Do you have any idea how painful it is to die of radiation poisoning? The utter collapse of your entire body? Here, have a look," Connor growled.

He slammed Parish down onto his desk and held him in place. Connor used his implants and sent a video feed to the nearest wallscreen. A deathly pale man lay on a bed in the *Vigilant's* infirmary.

"Look at it," Connor said and grabbed Parish's head, making him look at the screen. "We kept Ian in a coma because he was in so much pain. We had fifteen more soldiers suffering from milder cases of radiation poisoning, including Major Nathan Hayes. With one fell swoop, your efforts to have me killed almost took out the senior officers serving on the *Vigilant* right before the Vemus attacked."

Parish gasped for breath. "I didn't know. You have to believe me. I didn't know that was going to happen. I'm sorry."

Connor stepped back from the governor and sneered. "You're sorry. The enemy we were warned about has come and you're playing a petty scheme?"

Parish pushed himself up and staggered back against the wall. "I was wrong. I didn't know how wrong I was."

"Who else was working with you?" Connor asked while unholstering his sidearm.

"No one else!" Parish cried. "I swear, it was just Toro. That's it; he was my contact."

Connor glanced at his sidearm as if considering whether or not he was going to shoot the governor. Then he holstered his weapon. "I'm not going to kill you. While it would be immensely satisfying to me, it would set us back. This war isn't over."

Parish blinked and he opened his mouth. "What do you mean it isn't over? You stopped the Vemus fleet. Nothing has been detected from our sensors."

Connor sucked in a breath and sighed. "This wasn't the main fleet. They were being controlled."

Parish's eyes widened. "Not the main fleet? Over a thousand ships came. How many more could there be?"

"We don't know. They sent a scout force to soften our defenses, learn what we're capable of. When they come at us again, they'll bring the full measure of their attack force," Connor said.

Parish was silent for a moment and licked his lips. "How do you know this?"

"We found their control signal. It was how we stopped them. We interfered with the signal, which sent their fleet into disarray. Otherwise, they would have gotten past all our defenses," Connor said.

"My God," Parish said and swallowed hard. "What do we do?"

Connor glared at the man. There were so few of them left that Connor knew they needed every able-bodied person if they were going to have a chance of survival.

"Why is it that men like you make your speeches and look at soldiers like me as a necessary evil, but when your life's in danger, you look to me to save it for you," Connor said with a sneer.

He took a few steps away, not trusting himself to be near the governor.

"I was wrong. Is that what you want to hear? I was wrong. Now tell me how we can survive what's coming," Parish said.

Connor shook his head. "That's just it. I don't know if we can survive."

Parish stepped around the desk. "You must have something in mind, some kind of plan. We wouldn't even be here if it weren't for you."

"Not me," Connor said. "Thousands of CDF soldiers gave their lives so you could talk about victories at public events."

Parish held his hands in front his chest in a placating gesture. "What do you want me to say? The public has a right to know. They need to celebrate those victories. It gives them hope."

"You're just making up for all the doubt you've sown for the past year you've been in office. I can't fight an enemy with my men conflicted about what they're fighting for," Connor said.

"All that is done now. You'll have whatever you need," Parish said.

Bile crept up Connor's throat. The governor stank of fear and was now trying to barter away everything he could to ensure his survival.

"I know I'll get whatever I need now. I may not be able to prove in a court of law that you tried to have me killed and worked to manipulate the Colonial Defense Force in such a way as to sow dissent among our ranks, but you represent a sickness, a cancer that needs to be removed," Connor said.

Parish stepped back. "You said you wouldn't kill me."

Connor nodded. "You're right; I'm not going to kill you. You'll always know where you stand with me. I have a question for you."

Parish pressed his lips together. "What?"

"How badly do you want to survive? Would you give anything so the colony can survive?" Connor asked.

"Yes, of course I would," Parish said.

"Are you sure? Because that's what it's going to take. Setting aside our differences and coming together is what I think is going to give us our best chance."

"You're one hundred percent right."

"I'm glad you think that way. So you won't have any objections to stepping down as governor then?" Connor asked.

Parish's face twisted into a confused frown. "What . . . stepping down? I'm not sure I understood you correctly."

"I think you understood me perfectly. You've spent the last year running the CDF around in circles, denying critical requests. I think the only way forward is for you to step down as governor of the colony," Connor said.

"Who would take my place? You?" Parish asked.

Connor's lips lifted into a smile that didn't reach his eyes. "Not me."

"Who then?"

"There's a fascinating bit under emergency powers in the articles of the colony from subsection thirty-six. It talks about an elected official who's called upon to deal with a situation he's not equipped to deal with," Connor said.

Parish looked away.

"This is your chance to atone. Step down and restore Tobias Quinn as governor of the colony. He understands the threat we face," Connor said.

Parish turned away and brought his hands to his hips, his

head hung low. "Alright, you win. I'll do it. I'll call a press conference in the morning and announce my resignation."

"There *will* be a press conference called tomorrow, but not by you," Connor said.

Parish turned back toward him in alarm.

"Governor Quinn, did you get that?" Connor asked while showing the comms channel he'd had active since Parish had entered the office. The wallscreen changed to show Tobias Quinn's face.

"Yes, I did," Tobias said and looked at Parish. "We have it on record, and I would strongly caution you against making the argument that you're abdicating the governor's seat under duress. We'll handle the formal transfer tomorrow, but effective immediately, the powers of the governor are transferred to me. Do you concur?"

Parish glanced at Connor for a moment. "Yes," he said in a tight voice.

"Good," Connor said. "I'll leave you to it."

"Thank you," Tobias said. "Franklin is waiting for you at CDF headquarters with a full staff."

Connor left the office. Tobias would handle the legality of what had just transpired and then they would all regroup in the morning. In the hall, CDF soldiers stood over the governor's security personnel, who were lined up against the wall.

Connor walked over to Sean. "Leave a team here to secure the residence and make sure Parish doesn't try anything. You and the rest of the team will be coming with me to CDF headquarters."

"Yes, sir," Sean said and issued orders to the men who were staying behind.

Sean caught up to Connor. "I'd say the hard part is over, but that would be a lie."

They headed to the troop carrier that was standing by. "You're right. The hard part is just beginning, but we have an idea of what to expect now."

They climbed aboard the troop carrier, which left the governor's residence. It was in these quiet moments that he felt the loss of his old friends and those from the colony. He still felt that Kasey and Wil were just a simple comlink away. He'd come to rely on them as trusted confidants. He wanted their counsel now more than ever as people looked to him to come up with a way to defend them against the Vemus.

The door to the cockpit opened and Connor heard the heavy thuds of combat boots trudging along. He glanced up and saw Juan Diaz staring down at him.

Diaz gave a playful punch to Sean's arm. "He's got that look again, that look that says the world is riding on his shoulders. Don't worry, General, we got your back. Always have. Always will."

Connor felt his face lift into his first genuine smile in a long time. "It's good to see you."

Diaz plopped down in the seat next to Connor. "I have to admit, I almost hoped we were wrong."

Connor nodded. "So did I," he said and sighed.

Diaz glanced over at him. "Focus, Connor, we've got a lot of work to do."

There is a small part of this book that is based on actual events. The event in question involves the collection of a lot of frogs, a five-gallon bucket, and the women's bathroom at an undisclosed campground. The incident unfolded pretty much as Wil Reisman describes for Connor. There wasn't a whole lot of thought that went into the actions of my ten-year-old self and the others who were there that night. If you're a member of the opposite sex who happens to be reading this, then the forty-something that is me apologizes but the ten-year-old cannot stop grinning. Boys will be boys.

THANK YOU FOR READING NEMESIS - FIRST COLONY - BOOK TWO.

If you loved this book, please consider leaving a **review.** Comments and reviews allow readers to discover authors, so if you want others to enjoy *Nemesis* as you have, please leave a short note.

The First Colony series continues with the 3rd book - **First Colony - Legacy**

ABOUT THE AUTHOR

Ken Lozito is the author of multiple science fiction and fantasy series. I've been reading both science fiction and fantasy for a long time. Books were my way to escape everyday life of a teenager to my current ripe old(?) age. What started out as a love of stories has turned into a full-blown passion for writing them. My ultimate intent for writing stories is to provide fun escapism for readers. I write stories that I would like to read and I hope you enjoy them as well.

If you have questions or comments about any of my works I would love to hear from you, even if its only to drop by to say hello at KenLozito.com

Thanks again for reading *First Colony - Nemesis.*

Don't be shy about emails, I love getting them, and try to respond to everyone.

Connect with me at the following:
www.kenlozito.com
ken@kenlozito.com

ALSO BY KEN LOZITO

First Colony Series

GENESIS

NEMESIS

LEGACY

Sanctuary

Ascension Series

Star Shroud

Star Divide

Star Alliance

Infinity's Edge

Rising Force

Ascension

Safanarion Order Series

Road to Shandara

Echoes of a Gloried Past

Amidst the Rising Shadows

Heir of Shandara

Broken Crown Trilogy

Haven of Shadows

Made in the USA
Monee, IL
14 April 2020